Praise for Megan Crane

"A long adrenaline rush punctuated by sweet and sexy interludes . . . Crane takes her appealing characters on a breakneck adventure around the world. A well-balanced mix of romance and suspense makes this a sure bet for series fans." —*Publishers Weekly* on *Special Ops Seduction*

"Megan Crane masterfully combines romance, suspense, and a dash of family drama in *Special Ops Seduction* . . . A strong sense of place, whether it's the wilds of Alaska or the vineyards of California, draws the reader deeper into this irresistible and emotional story." —*BookPage*

"Filled with mystery, suspense, and romance, *Special Ops Seduction* will have readers interested from the first page until the last." —*Harlequin Junkie*

"*Special Ops Seduction* is a compelling, perfectly balanced read. There is just the right touch of romance, action, camaraderie, and suspense." —*Fresh Fiction*

"Megan Crane's mix of tortured ex–special ops heroes, their dangerous missions, and the rugged Alaskan wilderness is a sexy, breathtaking ride!"
—*New York Times* bestselling author
Karen Rose, on *Seal's Honor*

Bold Fortune

A Fortunes of Lost Lake Novel

❧

M. M. CRANE

JOVE
New York

A JOVE BOOK
Published by Berkley
An imprint of Penguin Random House LLC
penguinrandomhouse.com

Copyright © 2021 by Megan Crane
Penguin Random House supports copyright. Copyright fuels creativity, encourages
diverse voices, promotes free speech, and creates a vibrant culture. Thank you for buying
an authorized edition of this book and for complying with copyright laws by not
reproducing, scanning, or distributing any part of it in any form without permission.
You are supporting writers and allowing Penguin Random House to continue to
publish books for every reader.

A JOVE BOOK, BERKLEY, and the BERKLEY & B colophon
are registered trademarks of Penguin Random House LLC.

ISBN: 9780593335376

First Edition: December 2021

Printed in the United States of America
1 3 5 7 9 10 8 6 4 2

Book design by George Towne

To Lisa and David Hendrix, with gratitude

One

❧

Violet Parrish, PhD, should have known that her long-distance, never-consummated romance with Stuart Abernathy-Thomason—also a PhD, though the sort who viewed any inadvertent failure to acknowledge his doctorate as a deliberate assault—was doomed.

Looking back, there had been signs of his inevitable betrayal from the start. The long distance itself, because surely it wasn't *that* difficult to fly from London to San Francisco, and yet the much-discussed flight had never occurred. *It's been such a busy year, hasn't it*, Stuart had always said mournfully. The failure to engage in even the faintest hint of any intimate acts over their computers, when Violet had read too many articles to count that had insisted that said acts were *how* couples maintained their relationships across distances. *I want you, not a screen*, Stuart had told her, and could never be budged.

The glaring fact that when she'd excitedly told him that she was coming to London to visit, after making certain he had a gap in his schedule, he'd initially been excited—then had come back the next day and told her that he'd been called away on those exact dates. *What bad luck!* he'd said in his plummy voice.

These were all signs Violet would very likely have continued to ignore had there not been the naked-webcam incident.

"I don't understand," her boss and mentor said to her now, peering across the length of his crowded desk at the Institute of San Francisco, a small nonprofit with an academic pedigree and lofty ideals. Irving Cornhauser, too many degrees to choose just one, was often confused for a man in his eighties. He was fifty. "What does a *web camera* have to do with our work here?"

"I don't think we should focus on that," Violet said. She remembered all too well the office-wide effort to teach Irving how to use social media. They'd concluded he didn't *want* to understand. She slid her glasses up her nose and braced herself. "The issue is the relationship with Dr. Abernathy-Thomason. *My* relationship with him. My *former* relationship, that is."

She should have felt heartbroken. Wasn't that the typical, expected response to catching one's significant other in an intimate embrace with another woman? Then again, maybe this *was* heartbreak. Having never been in a relationship before—by choice, as Violet liked to remind her mother, because she was an intellectual with other things on her mind—she had nothing to compare it to.

She had not expected it to feel like heartburn, acidic and anger-inducing. With a deep and growing sense of outrage that she was now forced into this position. Standing in Irving's office on the first working day of the new year, confessing things that could only embarrass them both.

"Your personal life is your business, Violet," Irving said in faintly censorious tones, as if Violet had pranced in here for a cozy giggle about boys. Having never done anything of the sort before, in all the years they'd worked together. "The less said about it, the better. Our role here at the Institute is to lend our considerable focus to small environmental matters that make big differences, and in so doing—"

Violet wanted to scream. But she refrained, because she was an academic, not an animal. "I know the mission. I helped write our mission statement, actually." But he knew that, of course. "I'm not making a confession because I want to go on a double date with you, Irving."

He blinked at her in astonishment. Her fault for making reference to the fact that he even had a partner. More personal details he did not care to share on the job. Irving liked to think of these walls as a place of philosophical and intellectual purity. The less reference to the fact that they were humans, complicated, and with lives of their own, the better.

A philosophy Violet had always heartily supported, and yet how the mighty had fallen—to a con man dressed up in a pretty accent. She was surpassingly ashamed of herself.

"The problem is that I discussed my research with Stuart," she said before Irving could reply, because she wanted to get this out. Stuart's betrayal and her stupidity had been burning her alive all throughout the Christmas break, when no one at work—especially Irving—answered calls or emails. She'd tried. "And worse, our paper based on that research for the spring conference. I thought it was a circle of trust and I was mistaken. Badly mistaken."

The acid inside her lit her up all over again as she relived the whole nightmare.

It had been Christmas Eve. She had been at her mother's place in Southern California, hiding away from too much Prosecco, a selection of white plastic Christmas trees, and the near-constant caterwauling of off-key carolers at the palm trees in her mother's beach-adjacent compound. She and Stuart had talked as planned, and she hadn't given much thought to the kinds of questions he always asked her. He was so supportive. He was so *interested*. Despite her mother's dire warnings about the lonely lives of sad girls who lived in their heads, he was *involved*.

Violet had found someone who not only supported her work, but understood it, as Stuart was part of a think tank dedicated to the same issues. She'd been congratulating herself on that score after the call had ended while enduring a series of frustrating questions from her mother's sixth husband, who appeared to think Violet taught elementary school students. No matter how many times she corrected him.

Then she'd escaped to the guest room and seen that her laptop was still open. Upon sitting down at the desk to close it, she'd seen that Stuart had not turned his camera off.

It had taken Violet longer than she cared to admit to understand that Stuart had not, in fact, been playing some kind of game with that woman. Right there in his lounge in his tiny flat in London that she knew so well, after a year of looking at it through this same screen.

Naked.

She'd cleaned her glasses with great care, but no. It was still happening when her lenses were clear.

Maybe it really was the heartbreak and the betrayal that made her stomach hurt so much, but on the flight back to San Francisco the day after Christmas—after a holiday packed full of recriminations (hers) and justifications (his), until he'd sneered at her and told her that he'd been using her all along—all she'd really been able to think about was how *insulting* this all was. And how embarrassing it was going to be to explain to her colleagues.

She'd met Stuart at a conference in Nice last summer.

They'd had one marvelous dinner, followed by a perfect kiss, before Violet had raced to catch her flight home. And their romance ever since had involved a great many letters—okay, emails, but she'd felt like a modern-day Austen heroine all the same—and the odd video chat when their schedules allowed.

Far fewer said chats than there probably should have been, she saw that now. And none of them naked. But Violet had been so proud that *at last* she was having the relationship of her dreams. Not the *shattered glasses against the wall, screaming bloody murder* nonsense she associated with her parents' bitter union—finished before she was born but reenacted during custody skirmishes throughout her childhood—and most of their many marriages since.

Her relationship with Stuart had been cerebral, not physical. Violet had been sure that the next time they saw each other in person, the physical would catch up. How could it not? Everyone knew that sexual attraction started in the brain.

Better than the belly, she thought now, while hers continued its protest.

"I'm afraid that I was wrong about Stuart," she made herself confess to Irving now, because she might have made a horrible mistake but she, unlike Stuart, was capable of facing her own actions. She straightened her shoulders. "Terribly, horribly wrong."

"Right. Er. Well." Irving now looked as if she'd slapped him. "I suppose we can't all be lucky in love."

"Irving." Violet was beginning to feel desperate. It was the dread, she thought. It had sat heavy on her this past week and had gotten worse as she'd prepared to come to work today—and that was before she'd seen the press release. "You don't understand. Stuart has taken our paper that we intended to unveil at the conference—or all its major points, anyway—and has presented it as his. His center sent out an announcement this morning with excerpts. He's claimed all of our theories on new technology avenues for brighter environmental solutions as his own."

This time, Irving understood her. She knew because he had a tell. She watched, with a strange mix of apprehension and relief, as her boss's bald head slowly and surely turned an alarming shade of red.

Like a shiny tomato of fury.

Finally.

Irving wasn't a yeller. He was a seether. He stared at her for a long moment while he grew ever redder, then turned his attention to the computer before him, banging on his keyboard as if it, too, had betrayed him.

But no. Only she had.

Violet's heart kicked at her, because she loved this place. Because they were such a small nonprofit, they functioned more like a research team—reminding her of her doctoral days. Her colleagues were more like friends and each paper they presented was a communal effort. Their most recent project—half a year of research and debate followed by half a year of drafting the kind of paper that had the potential to shift high-level thinking—had been about specific technologies that might or might not aid in certain proposed environmental protections in remaining wilderness areas, like the Alaskan interior. She wanted to beg Irving not to fire her. She wanted to offer him a host of rationalizations.

But she stayed where she was and she stayed quiet, because she hoped she was woman enough to accept whatever consequences came her way. She'd assured herself she was since Stuart had showed his true colors on Christmas Eve.

Still naked. So naked, in fact, that she'd kept getting distracted by the blinding whiteness of his narrow chest while she should have been laser-focused on his perfidy.

When she heard Irving's hiss of a breath, she knew

he'd found the headlines from the usual industry publications, all of them lauding Stuart for his innovative findings.

Her findings, damn him. Her colleagues' findings.

"This is a disaster," Irving whispered. His bald head was still getting redder, which wasn't a good sign. "Violet. This is a *disaster*."

She might have had a week to prepare, but she still wasn't ready.

"I wanted to be the one to tell you." She sounded stiffer and more wooden than she would have liked. But there was no helping it—it was that or crying, and she hadn't cried yet. She refused to cry *here*. It would be humiliating and also, it might kill Irving. She held out the sheet of paper she'd been holding since she'd walked in here. "I've prepared my letter of resignation."

"I don't want to accept it," Irving said, shaking his head. "You know I don't. I recruited you out of graduate school myself."

Which wasn't the same thing as not accepting it, she noted.

"I understand." Violet swallowed. "I prepared a statement. Explaining the situation to everyone here, so there can be no doubt that I'm taking complete responsibility for my lapse in judgment."

That was the part that really burned. Violet had always considered her judgment unimpeachable. She didn't like this discovery that she'd been wrong—that she'd apparently been human and fallible all along.

"Your taking responsibility is all well and good," Irving said, rubbing his hands over his face. "But there's the upcoming conference to think about. What do you propose we present now? What will we tell our donors? You know a huge part of our fund-raising is based on the reception our papers receive."

Violet felt a surge of temper, but she tamped it down. She'd always objected to the Institute's insistence on focusing on only one idea at a time. Surely, she would argue in meetings, their small size should allow for nimble navigation between many ideas. Not so much communal focus on one thing—though that was what had given the Institute its sterling reputation for intellectual approaches to modern environmental dilemmas. The application of those approaches—in places like universities and corporations or, better still, more broadly in the world insofar as that was measurable—was what excited their donors. Violet had always thought they therefore ought to present several papers each year, to better have more nuanced discussions in more directions. But she suspected that if she broached that theory again today, it would be seen as self-serving.

Worse, she honestly couldn't tell if it would be or not, since as of a week ago, she'd stopped trusting her judgment.

One more reason to detest Stuart.

"We're going to lose our funding," Irving moaned. But at least this was familiar ground. As the CEO of a nonprofit, he spent the bulk of his time concerned about funding. And his head was noticeably less red.

Violet was grateful that she'd had this week to plot. To do what she was paid to do here and think outside the box. To frantically research all the projects that had gotten away, either because there hadn't been enough in-house enthusiasm to make them *the* idea of the year or because they'd tried to get them off the ground in their initial debate stage, but had failed for one reason or another.

And she'd circled around and around again to the same place. To the big one.

The one dream project that could bring her back into the fold, not just having paid a debt for her sins, but as a rock star.

The very small nonprofit version of rock star, that was, but she would take her polite applause and strained smiles where she could, thank you.

She shoved her glasses into place and cleared her throat. Irving frowned at her.

"As a matter fact," she told him, "I have an idea."

Three days later, Violet found herself on an extended layover in the Anchorage, Alaska, airport.

Some people might consider having to suffer through a thirteen-hour layover a kind of penance, but she was choosing to see it as a celebration. Because she'd convinced Irving—and the rest of her colleagues, because, yes, she'd had to face that firing squad of mortification—that she could do this thing no one else in their field had managed to do.

Yet, she told herself.

Not that anyone at work really believed she was capable of the task she'd set herself, of course. She knew better than to believe they had that kind of confidence in her. It was far more likely they were sending her off into the literal dark of the Alaskan frontier in winter because they thought she might very well get eaten by a bear. An effective way for the Institute to wash its hands of her. She could see the solemn statement of genteel regret to the press now.

But bears or no bears, she was doing it. Violet was a thinker, not a doer, and she avoided outside things like the plague—but she was *doing this*.

She had no choice but to do this.

When it was finally time to catch her plane, one of three weekly flights to a tiny village in the Alaskan bush, it felt a lot like vindication.

The flight was rough—or the plane was small. Maybe

both. Her stomach, fragile since Christmas Eve, threatened a full-scale rebellion as they bounced around the clouds. Violet screwed her eyes shut and tried to think about anything else. Anything at all but the fact that she was *bouncing* in midair over the wild Alaskan tundra she had researched feverishly over the last few days while trekking back and forth between her apartment in the Marina District and REI in SoMa for the approximately nine thousand things she thought she would need to survive Alaska.

The trouble with the research she'd done was that she knew too well that she was currently flying over some of the most inhospitable terrain on the planet. Knowing that did not exactly help her stomach.

She thought instead about Irving and the way his tomato-headed fury had turned to disappointment, which was worse. She thought about the colleagues she had considered friends, many of whom had been unable to meet her gaze at their last meeting. Even her closest friend at the Institute, Kaye, had looked flushed with quiet condemnation when Violet had dropped off her enormous rabbit, Stanley, who Kaye had agreed to watch for the foreseeable future.

I'm going to fix this, she had declared to Kaye. A little bit fervently.

I wish you'd told me about Stuart, Kaye had replied softly, clutching Stanley to her chest as if using him as a rabbit barricade, her eyes wide and reproachful. *He has a reputation.*

I'm going to fix this, Violet had said again.

The cargo plane bounced again, hard.

She gripped the armrest, hard enough for her fingers to start cramping, and hoped she'd live long enough to even try fixing it. Something that seemed touch and go for a while there.

Later, happily alive and on icy, snowy, but solid ground, Violet huddled beneath all the blankets on offer in the hotel room she'd booked. And had been lucky to book, as there had been only two options for lodging here in this town of some three hundred souls that was nonetheless considered the regional center of the Upper Kuskokwim region. The area appeared on the map of Alaska as part of the vast swath of wilderness off to the west behind mighty Denali in the Alaska Range. The hardy town of McGrath hunkered down in a curve in the Kuskokwim River called an oxbow, which meant it was surrounded on three sides by water, all of it frozen solid at this time of year. She'd seen it as her plane had come in.

It was only her first stop, however. Tomorrow she needed to figure out more local transport options deeper into the interior toward her final destination in a part of the world that measured distance in air miles. Not only because the distances were vast, but because there were no roads.

She clutched her trusty, much-read guidebook to her chest, having marked many of the pages with stickies— cross-referenced with the other guidebooks that hadn't made the cut, but which she'd read through two days ago in the bookstore—so she could more quickly reference the important parts when she set off on this adventure.

Like the bear population here in McGrath. Brown bears, grizzly bears, black bears, bears in colors yet to be discovered—she was worried about them all.

But there were no bears in her cozy little hotel room, buffeted by the January winds outside. So instead, she found herself considering the no-less-overwhelming problem of Quinn Fortune. The grumpy, forbidding representative of a critical land trust and the reason she was trekking into the land of endless night and terrifying bears in the first place.

Quinn Fortune, whose response to the well-researched appeal she'd sent him the same day she'd made her confession to Irving was a very short email in return. Blunt, unfriendly, and to the point. He'd announced that he only did business over a beer at his favorite bar and if she wanted to discuss anything with him, he'd see her in the frozen wilderness he called home.

Only he'd used far fewer words.

Violet doubted very much that he expected her to take him up on that offer. But she, by God, was nothing if not prepared to defy expectations if it could get her out of this mess.

And that was how she found herself heading even deeper into the wilderness the next afternoon in an even smaller plane. Because, apparently, Alaskan bush pilots would fly anywhere in any weather, no matter how alarming the flight. The chatty pilot she'd met over breakfast at her hotel kept up a running commentary on the Kuskokwim River that wound around below them as well as the remote, mostly Native communities spread out along its banks, stretching some seven hundred miles from Mount Russell near Denali to the Bering Sea far to the west. Violet listened closely, making notations in the margins of her guidebook when appropriate. The pilot told her of past and present mines that brought settlers here from the Lower 48. He talked about the Upper Kuskokwim Athabascans, who tended to live Western these days while still hunting and fishing in the tradition of their ancestors. He offered many an opinion about the way city folks didn't really understand the reality of the people who lived out here.

Violet took her notes, nodded along because she suffered from that same lack of understanding, and kept her gaze out the window as much as possible.

Alaska was like a different planet.

Violet had gone to school on the East Coast and had thought she knew her way around a winter, but this was something else entirely. The scale of it was so different. Epic. The guidebook had told her so, and she'd prepared accordingly, but seeing it with her own eyes was astonishing.

There was more snow here than people, a humbling sort of thought.

It was dark again when her new friend landed in Hopeless, home to 103 residents, according to the internet. It seemed to be little more than a handful of hardy, utilitarian buildings clustered together against the howl of the wildness outside.

An actual howl, that was. A metaphor couldn't have rattled the plane as it bounced to a rough landing.

Or sliced straight through her outside the Hopeless General Store after her mercifully brief walk from the spot where her plane had taxied, her glasses fogged up the moment the air hit her.

Inside, the store was ramshackle and cozy at once. There were nonperishable groceries on a selection of shelves, with refrigerators and freezers lining the back wall. The air smelled of hamburgers and coffee, and her belly rumbled as if she hadn't eaten her weight in hash browns at breakfast back in McGrath.

"You look lost," came a deep voice.

She looked up and found a man watching her from behind the counter. At first she thought he had to be as ancient as he was large. But a closer look suggested he was merely magnificently bearded and much younger than she'd first imagined, with that slouchy hat and all the plaid.

"Am I in Hopeless?" Violet asked. He nodded. "Then no, I'm not lost. I'm trying to get to Lost Lake."

"Why?"

She reminded herself that she was out here in a place

where there were very few people. Maybe intrusive questions no one would ask in San Francisco were the norm here. Her fingers itched to make a note of that, but she restrained herself.

"I'm looking for Quinn Fortune," she told him.

The man studied her, not even remotely friendly. Which flew in the face of everything Violet had ever heard about small towns and their supposed charms, but maybe not everything could come with pie on demand and a cheery attitude. "He know you're coming? Because I figure even Quinn Fortune would come on down and meet an invited guest." And there was a not-so-subtle emphasis on the word *invited*.

Violet considered lying but thought better of it. "He does not know I'm coming, as a matter of fact. Though an argument could be made that maybe he should. He issued a challenge and I accepted it."

"Some challenge," the man drawled. "It's hard to get here. Especially from way on down in the Lower Forty-eight."

Violet didn't ask how he knew she wasn't from, say, Anchorage. As she thought about it, in fact, not a single person she'd encountered so far—the hotel owner, the bush pilot, this man—had asked her where she was from. For the first time, it occurred to her that their failure to ask wasn't because she fit beautifully into these harsh surroundings, despite having bought herself every single thing her guidebook had suggested. Quite the opposite.

She beamed at him as she adjusted her glasses. "I like a challenge."

And was taken back when, after a moment, the man's face broke into a broad smile.

"Rosemary!" he bellowed, which didn't make a lot of sense to Violet until a woman came out to join him at the counter. She looked like someone Violet might encounter on the streets of San Francisco, not way out here in the hinterland. Pierced and ethereal, her presence recast the man beside her.

Because she'd expected many things in the Alaskan wilderness, like bears. Lots and lots of bears, hence the bear spray in her pack. What she had not anticipated were hipsters.

"This lady came all this way to see Quinn Fortune," the man said. "On a dare."

Rosemary moved to the edge of the counter, jutting out a hip to lean against it, her gaze shrewd. "Do you know Quinn Fortune?"

"Only by reputation," Violet said. And a great many internet searches, but she kept that to herself.

"And you came anyway?" Rosemary asked. Which made the man beside her laugh.

Violet ignored the laughter. "I can see on the map that Lost Lake is some twenty miles away. I'm going to go out on a limb and guess there's not a taxi service around here. I'm hoping I can charter something to get me there? Or rent some snowshoes, maybe?"

The woman before her looked entirely too entertained. "I'm Rosemary Lincoln. This is my brother Abel. Don't you worry, we'll make sure you survive long enough to meet Quinn Fortune. Who doesn't know you're coming."

Violet looked back and forth between them. "That sounds ominous."

They laughed again. And as neither one of them looked inclined to share why, Violet didn't ask.

"I'm not usually a taxi," Rosemary confided. "But this I have to see for myself."

She disappeared back into the kitchen and when she re-emerged, was dressed for the cold. She murmured something to her brother, then led Violet outside into the dark night.

The dark night that had fallen at about 4:20 P.M.

Rosemary stowed Violet's pack on a sled connected to a snowmobile parked outside, then indicated that Violet should take the high passenger seat to the rear. She climbed on in front, and then took off.

The snowmobile's headlight gave only rushing, flickering impressions of the small frontier town that quickly gave way to nothing but snow and snow-drowned trees. The engine was loud, and the ride was not particularly smooth, and Violet found herself smiling wider and wider as they bumped along.

Because up above, the stars were their own wilderness in a night sky without the faintest trace of light pollution in any direction.

It was glorious.

Time lost all meaning. She would have sworn that there was no one else alive, anywhere. A stranger was taking her farther and farther away from anything that bore the slightest resemblance to civilization, but she couldn't work up any sense of alarm.

Violet couldn't stop smiling, even laughing a little to herself. Not when she'd lived her whole life so far without understanding that she could feel like this. Wild and free and filled with awe, hurtling forward through the endless dark without the faintest shred of fear.

This was what she'd always thought falling in love was supposed to feel like.

Though it certainly hadn't with Stuart.

When she saw the first light in the distance, she thought it was some kind of subarctic mirage. But as they roared closer, the lights only grew brighter. They were approaching the side of a hill, where it looked as if someone had stacked up a set of buildings like enormous children's blocks. She had the impression of a kind of big warehouse, red and wide, commanding the base of what seemed to be a haphazard pile of little red houses. There were other winter vehicles parked at all angles in front of it, enough to suggest they weren't at someone's home, but she couldn't imagine what kind of public establishment this was, twenty miles from what passed for a town.

Rosemary parked the snowmobile and when she turned off her engine, the silence seemed to rush in like a hard wind of its own. She swung off the snowmobile, then set about pulling Violet's bag from the sled in back.

Violet climbed off after her, took her pack, and looked around as she tried to slide the strap over the puffy shoulders of her brand-new parka. She gazed up at the hill, still not quite able to make sense of the jumble of red buildings.

"They call this Old Gold," Rosemary told her. "Once upon a time it was a gold mine. Trouble was, there wasn't much gold. Once the men who dug up the land moved on, the folks who stayed on here claimed it for themselves."

Violet patted her pocket where her guidebook waited, filled with careful maps. "The mine?"

"The mine, the land, and the mineral rights."

"Who lives here now?"

Rosemary headed toward a wide set of red and white doors that reminded Violet of barns. Or, more accurately, the pictures of barns she'd seen. "That depends on whether the youngest Fox grandchildren are here or in Fairbanks. But it's never more than twenty."

"Twenty," Violet repeated. She saw more people on the way out of her apartment building in San Francisco every morning. "Twenty people count as a town?"

"It takes twenty-five to be a proper municipality. This is a community." Rosemary nodded her head to the door before her. "And this building is called the Mine."

She pulled open one set of doors, crossed the small vestibule, then pushed through the next. Violet followed, dazzled by the sudden shock of heat and light. Her glasses fogged over, so she took them off and when she wiped them clear and popped them on again, she found herself standing in . . . an entire little town in one vast space, like a rustic, rural version of the Ferry Building back in San Francisco.

It was magical.

There weren't the farmers' markets and high-end food stalls of the Ferry Building here, but there appeared to be a variety of different shops and stalls packed into the big, open room. There were post office boxes to one side, a small grocery, a couple of shiny new ATVs parked near another set of doors, closed against the weather. In one corner she saw a woodstove and leather chairs and, if she wasn't mistaken, a tiny library. In another corner there were couches arranged around a large fireplace. There was a bar at one end and some distance down from it, a space that looked like a diner, complete with a few booths and another set of doors shut tight. Longer tables and comfortable, well-loved chairs were scattered here and there, and Violet was so taken with the bright lights and the airiness of the rambling space that it took her a moment to realize that there were . . . people.

Staring directly at her.

"I knew Abel would call up here," Rosemary muttered from beside her, but Violet barely heard her.

Because a figure detached itself from the bar at the far end and something in her hummed a little, because it was a man.

Only not just any man.

Her heart kicked at her, and she had the sudden sensation that she was back out there on that snowmobile, hurtling through the heedless dark.

He had to be at least six feet and he wore his height with a kind of careless ease that made Violet's poor, abused stomach flip over and over. He wore utility boots and the kind of heavy-duty all-weather trousers she could see with a quick glance that almost everyone else was wearing, too. He had on a knitted hat that didn't quite contain all of his unruly dark hair. But this man was also wearing a T-shirt, of all things, that strained to contain a shockingly well-carved chest and biceps that made her feel deeply, inarguably silly. On a cellular level.

But she promptly forgot all of that, because his face had to be one of the great wonders of the world.

He had cheekbones to die for. There was a hint of dark hair from beneath his hat, and his dark eyes gleamed enough that she suspected at once they weren't black at all, but something more fascinating, like navy. *Midnight*, whispered that silly part of her. He had a mouth that should have looked out of place on a man who exuded such rugged masculinity with every step, but didn't. Maybe because his jaw was unshaven and his lips, sensual though they might be, were pressed together in what looked a whole lot like irritation.

Full-on grumpiness, in fact.

Violet couldn't breathe and told herself it was a knock-on effect of the cold. That was why everything was tingling. It had to be why.

More amazing, her stomach had finally stopped hurting.

"I'm Quinn Fortune," he rumbled, but she already knew that. She'd guessed the minute she'd seen him. She'd *known* on that same cellular level. His voice was as rough and wild as the landscape outside, and it made her feel silly and warm straight through. What was happening to her? "I could have saved you a long, grueling trip. Whoever you are, whatever you want, I'm not interested."

Two

❧

If a unicorn had come prancing through the door of the Mine with a flowing mane made out of rainbows, Quinn Fortune could not have been more taken back.

He scowled at the apparition before him, trying to make the woman make some kind of sense, because until this moment he hadn't actually known that parkas and serious cold-weather gear came in that shade of pink.

A very, very *bright* shade of pink.

Abel Lincoln had roused him out of his cabin on the happily less trafficked far side of the lake, so Quinn had already been working on his temper by the time he'd made it across to the Mine. He didn't like surprises. He especially didn't like surprises that turned out to be visitors. He wasn't a big fan of Outsiders even when he was out there in the Lower 48, among them in their natural habitat while representing the interests of the people here in Lost Lake.

"I'm not here to sell you anything," the unicorn said in a sweet, musical sort of voice that matched her appearance to perfection.

She was too bright. It took the wind out of him, like a gut punch, and that made him scowl all the more.

"Though do you actually get salesmen up here? This far away from anything?" She sounded as if she was ruminating on the subject. As if she'd trekked all the way out to an old mining town that failed to appear on fully 80 percent of all the maps of the area to *muse* on things like solicitation rates.

Somehow he doubted it.

"Maybe we do and maybe we don't," Quinn heard himself reply, when he shouldn't have been pandering to . . . whatever this was. "Just because a person sets out for Lost Lake doesn't mean they'll make it. What with winter being approximately ten months of the year. And the bears."

Her glasses were halfway down her nose, one lens fogged up, making it easy to see when her brown eyes went wide.

"You have a lot of bears, don't you?" She looked around the Mine as if she thought that there might be bears secreted about the place. Maybe tucked in behind one of the craft stalls or hidden on the grocery shelves behind the packages of Top Ramen. "How many people do you know, personally, who've been eaten by a bear?"

"Not enough," he growled at her.

He figured that was probably unnecessarily hostile when her eyes got even wider. Too wide.

"Lady," Quinn said, in the sort of quelling tone he usually used to end debates, scare off scavengers, and generally bend his small part of the wilderness to his will, "what the hell are you doing here?"

She blinked. That was all. And still, as he stared down into what little of her face he could see between the hat pulled low on her head, the scarf wrapped tight around her neck, and the furry hood of her obnoxiously bright pink parka, Quinn got the distinct impression that he was watching her . . . switch gears.

He had the most unruly urge to reach over and push those glasses back up her nose.

It appalled him. He kept his hands to himself.

"Right," she said. To herself. "Of course you don't know who I am. I apologize. It was the snowmobile and the stars and then a whole town in one giant room . . . Anyway, I'm Violet Parrish, from the Institute of San Francisco. We emailed a few days ago."

"I don't think we did."

Quinn was fully aware that there were too many people watching this interchange. Abel, naturally, had notified the entire lakeside community that there was a visitor headed up from Hopeless. Not just heading to the Mine on a lark, which would have been curious enough, but looking for Quinn. And, he had noted, she was female.

More folks had roused themselves than they might have otherwise on a night like this, when settling in next to a warm stove in a cozy cabin felt like a physical requirement, not an indulgence. Mia Saskin, self-appointed grandmother to the whole community, had heated up a pot of her famous chili for the occasion. When he'd arrived, Quinn hadn't been particularly surprised to see that the folks who lived here on the hill in the old miners' houses had come on down to watch the show.

He'd been more surprised, and less than thrilled, to see others, like ex-marine Noah Granger, his brother Bowie's best friend, who lived even farther out into the bush on the far side of the lake than he did. Not to mention his younger sister, Piper, who had only smiled blandly at him when he'd glared at her.

What was downright shocking was that those two hadn't made some popcorn.

"We did email, actually," Violet Parrish was telling him, in the same bright pink tone. "I sent you a detailed proposal outlining not only how you could convert the land you hold in trust into a conservation easement that could offer protection to the land itself, but how you could make this old mine a historical—"

"Yeah. No." He shook his head at her. "You know how many people want to proposition me about what I can do here? I don't even read the proposals. I send out a standard response and that's that."

"I take it the standard response is the whole *only doing business over a beer* thing, and only having that beer in your favorite bar," Violet replied. He didn't understand her reaction. She didn't sound chastened or even particularly upset that her trip had been in vain. Instead, she sounded the same. Happy. Bright. She waved a hand, hidden away in a bulky glove, toward the bar that was, in fact, his favorite. And where, sure enough, he'd been enjoying a beer. "Is that the bar you mean?"

"I'm not having a beer with you. I don't like being ambushed."

"I'm not an expert on Alaskan travel," Violet said, leaning slightly closer to him as if imparting a deep secret. "But I'm betting, since it's not exactly the easiest thing in the world to get here, that you haven't been ambushed all that often. Have you?"

"One time a lady friend with *romantic ideas* came on out from Homer," his sister piped up. Quinn shot a dark look over his shoulder at her, but Piper only shrugged, grinning wide and clearly enjoying herself. Brat. "Though she only made it to Hopeless before she was disabused of the notion that showing up might convince Quinn to rethink their relationship."

The pink vision before him huffed out a little breath and then wrinkled her brow in Quinn's direction. "I don't want to date you. I'm sure you're very . . ." Violet waved her glove again and he had the absurd urge to catch it. Hold it. He didn't do that, either. "I mean, anyone can see that there's an abdominal situation."

"An abdominal situation?" Quinn caught himself before he examined his own torso.

Behind Violet, in the act of stripping off her bulky outer layers, his sister's best friend, Rosemary, cackled. "It is definitely an abdominal situation. That's undeniable."

Quinn scowled at her. He held her responsible for this . . . pink assault. Since she could just as easily not have brought Violet Parrish and her proposals up here.

Rosemary had been lollygagging near the door, no doubt to revel in the drama. But after kicking off her boots she went to sit down with Piper, a safe distance from Quinn's temper. Smart girl.

He returned his attention to the woman before him, still dressed like a raspberry and still gazing at him with an earnestness that made him . . . itchy. "Why are you talking about my abdomen?"

"I don't want to insult you," Violet assured him with what sounded like sincerity. "I'm here purely in the interest of scientific inquiry."

"Scientific inquiry. Really. Of what? My abdominal strength?"

And as he watched, Violet's gaze dropped down the length of his T-shirt.

It wasn't the first time Quinn had distracted a woman, and God willing, it wouldn't be the last. He wasn't unused to the phenomenon.

But there was something about the way Violet Parrish lifted her gaze back to his. There was something about her eyes. Brown, yes, but laced through with gold.

And Quinn had the blood of generations of miners running in his veins. He didn't have it in him not to crave all the gold he could find.

To his astonishment, and consternation, his sex took notice—when he couldn't even see the shape of this woman's body. All he knew about her was that he didn't want her here and that she was dressed far too garishly. She was swaddled in that pink parka with its fur-lined hood and wrapped up in a scarf that was a clashing shade of pink. Her hat looked as if someone had taken every possible variation of pink and magenta fabric on offer and mashed them together. Even her boots offended him, because sure, they were top-of-the-line and would keep her feet warm and dry, which was the bare minimum required out here. But they, too, were so girly it made his teeth hurt.

And also pink.

Quinn would have said he didn't think there could possibly be that much pink in the world. He had clearly been too long without a woman if a big fluffy ball of a pink parka was doing it for him.

"I don't know how we got on the topic of your abdominal region," she was saying, primly. "I don't usually lapse off into unrelated tangents. What I'd like to talk about with you, here at your favorite bar, is the environmental impact corporate gold mining would have on—"

Quinn could have been sitting in happy silence in his comfortable cabin. He did not need to be out tonight at all, and certainly not engaged in one of Alaska's favorite debates. In fact, if it was up to him, he would have happily declared all land, mineral rights, and environmental arguments off-limits to anyone who hadn't grown up here.

"I don't see a beer in your hand," he interrupted her. "And there's certainly not one in mine. You need to turn around and go back to wherever you came from. I'm going to guess that's not Alaska."

"I could be from Alaska. Just because I'm not from *here* doesn't mean I'm not from somewhere else in the state."

"Darlin'. Please."

Quinn looked over at the motley little crew, otherwise known as his friends and family, gathered around to witness this exchange. He supposed he couldn't blame them. Out this way, anything could pass for entertainment and usually did. A stranger turning up in the middle of winter like this was going to be talked about for years.

Especially a stranger who looked as ill-equipped for the unforgiving Alaskan bush as this one did.

"Anyway," Violet was saying cheerfully, "Rosemary was kind enough to drive me up here in the dark. I couldn't find my way back if my life depended on it."

"Your life does depend on it."

Violet should have taken that as a threat. She should have looked even slightly disconcerted, or asked him what he meant, or indicated in any way that she was aware that she wasn't welcome here. Instead, the gold in her gaze seemed to gleam brighter.

She studied him for a moment and there was a kind of intensity in her gaze that made him want to reach over and get his hands on her. Starting with those soft pink cheeks.

He shifted uncomfortably, not happy with himself.

"I've never actually met an honest-to-God mountain man before," she confessed. She sounded nothing short of delighted. "All grumpy hermit this and scowly that. It's *marvelous.*"

He heard laughter, and the strangest thing was that he wanted to laugh, too. But didn't. And Quinn couldn't understand why he found her so . . . charming. When as a general rule he was pretty notoriously immune to charm.

He was still fighting off the urge to join in the laughter as it suddenly seemed to occur to her that she was inside

now and could remove her layers the way Rosemary had.
She had to be sweltering, though if he was brutally honest,
Quinn was kind of hoping that the flush on her cheeks
wasn't only because it was so much warmer in here than
outside.

All Violet was doing, standing there dressed like a Care
Bear, was pulling off one glove, then the other. Both of
them were stiff, proclaiming their newness, and fighting
back as she tried to shove them into an outer pocket. She
reached up and pushed back her hood. Then she fought
with the zipper of her plumped-out coat, shrugging out of
it and then dropping it onto one of the benches in the entryway, instead of hanging it on the pegs that were there for
exactly this purpose.

But he didn't correct her, because he was strangely
caught by this . . . well. It wasn't really a striptease, was it?
It was some outer layers, that's all.

And still Quinn stayed right where he was.

She tore off her hat and placed it on the pile of pink
down. And when she straightened, the red suspenders
of the red and pink—always with the pink, so maybe he
should have celebrated the red—patterned snow pants
she was wearing seemed to call more attention to the Fair
Ilse pattern in cream and—yes—more pastel pink on the
wool sweater beneath. She was holding a dog-eared copy of
an Alaskan guidebook before her, but he was paying more
attention to the way her hair, brown and gold just like her
eyes, tumbled all around her shoulders with enough curl to
indicate it was a little bit untamable.

He could have done without the knowledge that her hair
smelled like apples.

"Do you mind if I take notes?" Violet was asking him.
She shoved her glasses up her nose, clearly an unconscious
gesture, and uncapped her pen with her teeth. Leaving him

powerless to do anything but stare at that pen cap poking out from her lips.

Good Lord, he needed to get laid.

"Why would you need to take notes?" he asked, sounding grumpier than he felt. Because he realized that engaging with her was giving in, somehow, to this bright pink assault on his solitude. On his hard-won peace of mind.

But even as he thought that, he did nothing to take command of the situation. He didn't toss her back out the door the way, story went, his own grandfather had once done with a banker type the old man didn't like the look of. He didn't remove himself.

Quinn was too busy staring at her mouth, like an overexcited adolescent. She put the cap on the back of her pen, also with her mouth.

And he needed to get a grip.

"I'm fascinated by microcommunities," she shared with him then, still in that sunny manner. "And even more fascinated that no matter where they crop up, you can so often find the same kind of stock characters, if you will, as if they're actually necessary to the formation of communities. Like the grumpy hermit."

"This is Alaska, darlin'. Everyone who lives here for more than a winter is a grumpy hermit. That's how we like it."

Violet looked up at him from whatever she was scribbling in her notebook. And a bolt of that same unreasonable, irrational lust shot through him, because her eyes were wide and unfocused and she looked far, far away.

And until now he'd known of only one particular way to put that expression on a woman's face.

"Thank you," she said. Then she smiled at him, and that was the worst yet. It made his chest tight, it was so wide and *vivid*. "I wouldn't have considered that."

She looked back down at her book and began scribbling. "Alaska, a state filled with hermits, typically grumpy," she muttered as she wrote.

Quinn was deeply glad that his younger brother Bowie wasn't here tonight. It was bad enough that Piper was. But he knew that his wiseass kid brother, eighteen months younger than him and dedicated not just to flying bush planes all over Alaska—the more dangerous the better—but to being the thorn in Quinn's side, would be having a field day with this. Since Quinn was never usually at a loss. Ever.

He folded his arms over his chest and tried to beam the full force of his displeasure at her. But Violet Parrish didn't seem to notice. It wasn't that she was unaffected, he thought. She really didn't seem to *register* that he was pissed.

"You wear too much pink," was what he said, when he thought he'd opened his mouth to order her to leave. In no uncertain terms.

He was aghast. She didn't even look up. "What is quote unquote *too much pink*?"

"It's too bright. You'll scare off the wildlife."

That was patently untrue, but he was betting she didn't know that.

She shut her pen in her guidebook, but she didn't put it away. Her eyes were big again. "I would call that a point in favor of wearing it head to toe. Maybe fifty points."

He shook his head. "Are you color-blind?"

Violet frowned at him as if he was the one who didn't make any sense. And the crazy thing was, Quinn was starting to wonder if maybe he didn't. "I like happy colors," she said, as if that should have been self-evident. "And pink is the happiest, obviously."

Then, to his astonishment, she simply . . . stepped around him and wandered farther into the Mine.

Clearly dismissing him.

A concept so novel he did . . . absolutely nothing. He watched her walk over to his sister and start up a conversation, as if she didn't much care that she wasn't welcome here.

He didn't like strangers here. Not even if they were dressed in pink on pink on pink, had soft cheeks and gold-mine eyes, and were sporting the kind of plump lips that could drive a man to distraction.

Had already driven him to distraction.

Quinn looked around this place his ancestors had helped build, feeling the same surge of pride and the same weight of duty he always did. Because his sister, who made simple, necessary tasks like canning preserves and growing vegetables an art form—and actually had a following on the internet thanks to her artsy photography of the survivalist lifestyle his family considered the proper way to live—might think it was funny to welcome with open arms a woman who would chase him down out here. But he knew better.

It was his job to protect the legacy of this place. To keep it unspoiled and out of the greedy hands of developers and corporate wolves while at the same time making certain that he always kept the interests of the community as a whole foremost in his mind.

This wasn't just a place to him, this renovated and re-imagined old mine and the rest of the tiny community scattered around Lost Lake. It was home.

More than that, it was who and what he was.

Quinn had left this craggy lake, packed with fish and thick with ice. He'd been to places where people couldn't believe anything like this community could exist. He'd been out in the world and knew how to navigate it instead of fear it, as he knew some folks here did, and with good reason.

He knew the difference between hiding and thriving.

He considered that knowledge a crucial part of his duty to the community he called home.

Quinn's great-grandfather had chased gold all over the western United States and up into the Yukon before making his way into what was then the Alaska Territory. The mine here had been a bust by corporate standards, but he'd helped mine the tiny vein that had brought this community together after the bigwigs left and figured it was as good a place to settle down as any. He'd gone to Juneau to find himself a wife, had brought her back to claim land on the far side of the lake, and Fortunes had been there ever since. Some had moved away, opting to live with more modern conveniences in Juneau, Fairbanks, or, in the case of one black-sheep uncle, Kansas.

But those who chose to stay did so because they loved it. Because they couldn't live without it. The land, the quiet. The work of surviving here. The connection to a wilderness that could and would kill them without a second thought.

And when the glory of the land and the profound weight of the quiet weren't enough, especially during the long winter months, there was this spot. The Mine. Where the off-beat loners who chose to live this way, scattered around Lost Lake, gathered when they wanted a little taste of community.

Quinn had spent a lot of time in this big, airy, one-room town. He liked the various decorations on the walls, ranging from license plates of vehicles—the ones the foolhardy tried to drive up this way and were forced to abandon to the ravages of nature—to paintings by some of the locals, to photographs and various items of sentimental value only the residents understood. Like the rusted old padlock that the so-called owner of this mine had left on the doors when he'd left for greener pastures and richer ores.

Folks here had made it a party when they'd cut it off and claimed what everyone felt was rightly theirs.

This rambling old building was as much a part of him—as much a home—as the cabin he'd grown up in and the one he'd built later, with his own hands, when he'd become a man. He could remember bunking down here on nights the weather was too rough to risk the icy ride across the lake.

One building after the next, the descendants of the miners who'd come here in search of a better future had rebuilt the little mining town that had never amounted to much in the way of gold. But, for the handful of families who made up the bulk of the community here at the head of the lake, it was home. It was theirs. What had once been the mine's biggest building had been transformed into a space that could serve them all.

These days, Mia Saskin played her role of everybody's busybody granny, whipping up meals at any time of the day or night and making sure anyone who stayed here overnight—to wait out a weather system or to time their trek out into the bush better—had what they needed. Most of the stalls and shops, including the bar, operated on running tabs and the honor system, though Silver Saskin had once charged an Alaska State Trooper seventy-five dollars for a shot of whiskey, then had thrown him out.

That was a story folks liked to tell and retell. Just like all the stories of all the people who lived here and came through here, from puffed-up adventure-company types who wanted access to the lake or had big plans to reopen the mine to the real hermits who never came in from the bush. Quinn liked walking in here and knowing everyone in the room. He liked the tapestry of time and community that held them all together across the bitter seasons that easily broke those who weren't prepared.

If he wanted storyless strangers and anonymous places, he knew where to find them. He wanted that kind of thing to stay where it belonged. Where he could visit it, reaffirm that it wasn't for him, then come home. Because he was the one charged with keeping the world out of Lost Lake.

He'd been formally chosen for this duty—this honor, his father liked to remind him, as the previous holder of the title—when he was sixteen. Quinn was the oldest in his generation, so without a compelling reason to jump over him, he had always been destined for this role in the community. He'd always known that it would fall to him to safeguard this place and these people. Bowie had always run wild, destined for nothing but trouble, until the marines had made him into a man. The other kids around the lake had been the same when they'd all been teenagers, more interested in either disappearing into the bush or causing a ruckus.

You have to know what you're protecting this place from, his father had told him when he'd complained. *Or all we'll be doing out here is hiding.*

And that was why, when he was old enough to assume control of the trust, he'd made it his business to understand the people who wanted to buy this land. He'd studied the gold industry extensively. He knew his mineral rights backward and forward. He'd traveled all over the Lower 48, so infernally crowded that it had been a mystery to him why anybody would choose to live there. But he'd gone so he could understand.

Because it was always better with the devil you knew.

And the more devils he knew, the better able he was to identify them.

Tonight the devil had turned up in pink.

He watched as Violet wandered all over the Mine, talking to the locals and weaving her way in and around the little shops and stalls, periodically stopping to jot things down in her book. And instead of formulating a plan to get rid of her, he was trying his best not to notice the way she moved. As if she'd never worn snow pants before and found them cumbersome, but instead of looking awkward, it only seemed to draw more attention to the way she was curved.

It was a little too easy to imagine those curves beneath his hands.

Maybe inevitably, she circled her way back around to him. There was the crisp-apple scent of her hair. That was trouble enough. But this time when she came to stand beside him he could smell wildflowers and honey, too, like a sweet, long summer night.

"Will you really not let me buy you that drink?" she asked.

This time, she sounded something like wistful. It wasn't an improvement on all that cheer.

Quinn glowered at her. "No. For two reasons. One, because you can't buy drinks here. You either pitch in and work to pay off your tab or you replenish the stock the next time you're in town. Two, and more important, because I don't want you to buy me a drink. I want you to leave."

Her nod was very solemn and he really didn't understand why it got to him. Maybe it was because she bore no resemblance whatsoever to the kind of salesmen he was used to dealing with. Those hearty, jovial, backslapping men, always so florid and overly familiar, who were forever bellying up to Quinn, spinning tales of gold prices, and acting like they were the best of friends.

They all left a bad taste in his mouth.

Violet made him want to get her taste in his mouth, which wasn't the same thing at all.

"I'm really sorry that I ambushed you," she said quietly, and no matter how he searched her expression, he couldn't see anything there but sincerity. Sincerity and a vein of gold. "I understand why you're so protective of this place. It's magical. I'd love to know if there's any possible way I could change your mind."

Quinn opened his mouth to tell her that he didn't change his mind. Ever. That he was a man who knew his own mind well, so changing it wasn't generally necessary. That she could bunk down here until Rosemary hauled her pretty butt back down to Hopeless, where she could do as she pleased. Stay there, head back somewhere warm, whatever. He didn't care what she did, and he fully intended to tell her so.

He opened his mouth to send her on her way, but he didn't.

Because he was the direct descendant of Wild West miners, yes. Ornery, stubborn, deeply practical yet wildly optimistic folks who had chased dreams of a better life into the jaws of the ferocious Alaskan interior, then had decided they might as well build a home in the wildest part and settle right in.

Making it here wasn't the same as making it in big, fancy cities where they might sing songs about the accomplishment. Making it out here meant you were as much a fool as anything else, but the wild was in you. And once it was in you, it made you a part of the glory of it. When you went and tried to settle in those other, civilized places, the wild in you ached like a missing limb.

He knew from personal experience.

And because of the wildness in his blood, and how it had gotten there, Quinn didn't have it in him not to reward hardheadedness. He could ignore an email. Just like he'd ignored any number of corporate wolves who'd tried to cozy up to him over the years. Every time he set foot in the contiguous United States they lined up with their greasy smiles and tried to convince him they were the ones who could separate him from the mineral rights the community held in trust out here.

Not one of them had ever trekked all the way out to the lake. Not one of them had ever demonstrated this much initiative—or foolhardiness—particularly not in the dead of winter.

Quinn couldn't bring himself to throw her out. He was a Fortune, and Fortunes favored the bold, as his grandmother had liked to say. With a cackle.

"I have no interest in having a beer with someone who doesn't understand what it's like here," he found himself telling Violet instead. "You want to talk about this land? Then you need to demonstrate to me that we're talking about the same land."

Her head tilted slightly to one side as she considered his words, her gaze steady on him. "Is there some confusion about what the land is?"

He unbent enough to grin a little. "You're the one who's confused, darlin'. I'll be honest. I don't think you'll make it two seconds on the other side of those doors."

Her eyes widened as she looked past him toward the doors. Quinn hoped she was thinking good and hard about the trip up here from Hopeless. All that cold. All that dark. And in his experience, city people never thought to look up at the stars that made it all worthwhile.

"Is that something I'm going to have to prove?" Violet asked.

But as if she was fascinated by the possibility, not afraid of it the way she should have been.

"You can stay here tonight," he told her, frowning because she should have been intimidated. If not by him then by the tundra out there. Either one could and would eat her alive. "Tomorrow, when it's light, I'll take you away from all this cozy civilization and see how you handle it. Then we'll see about that beer."

"And if I handle it like a natural?" she asked, her shoulders straightening like she welcomed a fight.

And Quinn felt sucker punched. She was confounding, and he shouldn't like how easily she could surprise him.

But he already knew how this would go.

"You won't," he told her. Pitilessly, because he knew. "You'll be begging to go back home in two days, tops. Fluffy pink professors and Alaska don't mix."

Three

❧

I'm prepared to stay for as long as it takes," Violet declared with what she certainly hoped sounded like all the confidence in the world.

None of which she felt. Which wasn't to say she *wasn't* competent enough to handle a little Alaskan nature, up close and personal. She liked her chances. She'd read all the things. But her experience of Alaska thus far suggested that there was a gap between what a person could read and what it actually felt like to face subzero temperatures and a sun that didn't rise until almost noon.

She had no intention of admitting that, however. Not when she had personal rights to wrong, a job to win back, and a skeptical quasi-hermit to convince that conservation was better than capitalism, *no big deal.*

And her first inkling that her mouth had written a check she might not want to cash came when Quinn Fortune's intense midnight eyes gleamed with a kind of amusement she suspected was entirely at her expense.

Not the first time, she told herself stoutly, holding said intense midnight gaze as steadily as possible. *Unlikely to be the last.*

"Sure you can, professor," he drawled.

And then he reached toward her.

Violet froze. Her entire body went tight, then flushed with a telltale heat that she desperately tried to convince herself was anything but what it was.

Anything at all—but she knew better.

Even when that flush turned into something more like embarrassment when it turned out that all he was doing was reaching past her to pull his coat off one of the pegs on the wall. To begin readying himself for the relentless cold outside.

She could feel that her cheeks were blazing red, giving her away completely. Worse, she was afraid he probably knew *exactly* why. He looked like the kind of man who would know, on some kind of primal level. But she'd already traveled all this way and had already revealed herself in all her red-cheeked glory. There was no point backing down now.

"As long as it takes," she said again. "I'm actually not afraid of your wilderness. Maybe you should be afraid of the possibility that I'll not only take your challenge, but crush it."

"Uh-oh, Quinn," came his sister's voice, heavy with delighted laughter. "I don't think the good professor got the memo that we're all supposed to treat your word as law around here. Whatever will you do?"

Violet wanted to look over at Piper and maybe even laugh along with her—but found she couldn't tear her gaze away from Quinn.

As if something was physically preventing her from it. And that only made her feel hotter. Like he was a fever.

Naturally, he seemed unaffected. He pulled his hat

down lower on his forehead, so all that she could see was the exquisite, dizzying symmetry of those cheekbones. And her belly fluttered when his mouth curved, however slightly.

"I guess we'll see," he rumbled.

Violet told herself that was a threat, but her body reacted as if he'd issued an invitation. The kind of invitation that made her remember all the times Stuart had brushed her off.

Not that she could really bring Stuart's reedy face to mind just now.

Quinn jutted his chin in the general direction of Violet, his sister, and the whole of the Mine. Then he threw open the heavy doors and disappeared into the night.

Violet's heart was hammering as if it was a normal January and she'd flung herself into one of those *running challenges* that did nothing but lead her straight back to cake the first time she attempted the supposed beginner level of a gentle jog around the block. She turned slowly to face the rest of the Mine, not sure what her reception was going to be now that Quinn had left.

The older woman who'd introduced herself as Grand Mia waved at her, in a steely sort of way. Violet moved toward her gratefully. And also because she didn't dare disobey.

She kept a smile on her face as she walked across the huge space that felt neither cavernous nor too crowded. It had the feel of a converted barn, homey and practical at once, and she was surprised at how welcoming it was. And at how much she wanted to sit down and stay awhile when she didn't know a soul.

Grand Mia was standing, arms crossed, over a table of three people Violet thought were more or less her own age. And all of whom shared the look of the older woman, she realized in the next moment. A nose here and there. A stubborn chin.

"You're going to need to eat," Grand Mia told her. "If you're planning to go up against Quinn Fortune."

"I'm not actually planning to go up *against* him," Violet hedged. "I'm more interested in going more . . . *with* him, I guess. Or getting him to go with me, really."

"Amen to that," said one of the women, with a belly laugh. The other two at the table turned to look at her. "What? He's hot."

"Everybody's family here," replied the woman next to her, almost certainly her sister if their noses were anything to go by. With a frown.

The man only shook his head.

"And yet," said the first woman blandly, "we really aren't."

Violet didn't understand sibling dynamics, having never experienced any. She didn't think her permanently warring parents counted. She wished that she'd gone and sat with Rosemary and Quinn's sister, Piper, because she'd already spoken to both of them. Instead, she looked back and forth between the sisters—currently involved in what looked like an intense, if silent, conversation—and the large man who looked about as rough-and-tumble as the winter night outside.

"Don't mind us," the first woman said sedately. "We don't see a lot of strangers up here this time of year. We don't know how to act."

"Speak for yourself," her brother—because he had to be her brother—muttered.

The woman patted the empty bench on her other side, indicating that Violet should sit. And Violet did, because she was on this ride, for better or worse. And happily, this part of the ride was not a bush plane being ping-ponged about between winter storms. This part of the ride came with a big bowl of chili plunked down in front of her by Grand Mia with a hunk of corn bread on the side with the butter already thoughtfully slathered on.

"If you're thinking my brother sounds surly, it's not you," the woman beside her said as Violet picked up her spoon. "He was born surly." She smiled broadly when her brother made an indelicate suggestion. "We're some of Grand Mia's actual grandchildren." She nodded at the woman on her other side. "This is my sister Silver. My surly brother is Paz."

"Who died and made you the hostess of the Mine?" Paz asked. In what could only be called a surly tone, to Violet's mind. Meaning this woman's observations were accurate.

"That's Paz, short for Topaz." She pointed at another man, not sitting at the table but over by the bar. "Our other brother, Jasper. And I'm Amie, short for Amethyst. Maybe you're sensing a theme."

"It infected the cousins, too," Silver said, pulling her corn bread apart with her fingers. "Ruby. Garnet. Nyx."

"Nyx being short for Onyx, and isn't he a jewel." Amie grinned. "Never let it be said that our people can't run with a theme. Our family is nothing if not committed to our mining heritage."

They all looked at Violet expectantly. It took her a moment to realize that the appropriate thing here wasn't to write notes in her guidebook about the naming practices of the Saskin family and what the broader implications of that might or might not be.

She set down her spoon carefully. "I wish I could tell you that I have sisters named Lavender and Indigo. I'm sad that I don't."

"It's okay," Amie said. "Not everyone has the thematic commitment we do. It's a gift, really."

"Try being a man named Topaz," her brother muttered.

And then the conversation turned to old stories, which meant Violet was no longer called upon to worry over her potential interactions with people who were talking to her like friends, not subjects. It was a relief. She could just sit and listen and, yes, make a note or two when a detail struck her as particularly interesting. She could have stayed up all night listening to people telling stories that were fairy tales to her, so far removed from her own world did life here seem. But the later it got, the more people peeled off. Until Rosemary came over, yawning, and showed Violet down the hall that led away from the warm, bright main area and into what she called the bunkhouse. A dormitory-style room with a number of beds arranged between wooden privacy screens. There was a bathroom on the far end with a pair of composting toilets, a wide sink with a surprising mirror rimmed in stained glass, and a shower stall that looked anything but intuitive.

Then she showed Violet a big, freestanding closet stocked with sleeping bags, blankets, and old, soft towels.

"All the comforts of home," Violet said happily, feeling warmed straight through with warm chili, lashings of butter, and good stories told well around a cozy fire.

Rosemary only shook her head. "Sleep well," she said.

Then she left Violet to sit on the little cot in her alcove, alone at last. Violet knew she should take the opportunity to write out all her impressions. She looked at her phone, but it showed emails she hadn't read from earlier that morning in the B and B and she had no service now. And the longer she sat on her cot, the more she was aware that the bunkhouse wasn't nearly as warm as the main room.

She unzipped her pack, extracted her toiletry pouch, and then marched down to the bathroom to avail herself of the facilities. On her way back she collected a sleeping bag and a blanket, spreading them out on the cot and then cracking open the foldable emergency blanket she'd brought with her. Then she crawled in and lay flat, hyperaware of every creak of her cot, each loud, rustling sound of her sleeping bag and emergency blanket, and the inescapable fact that she was lying there in an alcove, not an actual room with a door. Or a lock.

There was no way she would fall asleep like this. No possible way.

But when she jolted awake, she fumbled for her phone and discovered that it was morning. Late morning—which meant that not only had she actually slept here, and well, but the sun was due to rise soon.

Violet rolled out of her cot and dressed quickly, then padded out in her heavy wool socks to the main room of the Mine. The bright lights from the night before were dimmed, though she could see a few people over in the diner area. There was the smell of bacon and strong coffee in the air, and she wavered, but the urge to actually see where she was proved too great.

It took her a solid five minutes to struggle into all of her cold-weather clothes, and when she was finally appropriately suited up for the temperature written on a chalkboard next to the doors it felt like the dressing alone had been enough of an undertaking. But she pushed forward anyway, moving through the two sets of doors that led outside, trying to walk naturally in her bulky snow pants.

Outside, the sun was peeking up in the east, enough to send light spilling everywhere.

And when her breath caught, it wasn't from the cold.

Not that the temperature wasn't shockingly low, it was. But Violet hardly noticed.

Because everything before her sparkled, almost bright enough to blind her, and it was beautiful.

The old mining town sat up on a hill overlooking a long, craggy lake that stretched out farther than she could see, the low sun sending gold tumbling everywhere. The trees surrounding the lake and marching out in all directions were dusted white, catching the morning light. And the surface of the lake gleamed enough in the new daylight that it took Violet a moment to recognize that she was looking at ice—plowed ice near the slope where she stood and, farther out, ice still covered in snow and marked with what she assumed were snowmobile tracks. There was what looked like an ice rink—or maybe a hockey rink—not far from land. There were snow-covered docks frozen into the water and a building near the water's edge that looked to her untutored eye like some kind of boathouse.

It felt funny to imagine a summer here. Unfrozen water. Maybe even some warmth and assorted watercraft.

Today everything was covered in snow, making a landscape that was undeniably harsh look soft. Almost fluffy. Her own breath was loud beneath her hood, and she had to make an exaggerated turn to look in all directions.

The red buildings were bright and happy amid all the snow. Festive, even. There were strings of lights in all the windows of the houses clustered uphill of the Mine, and she wondered how many of the residents of the little houses she'd met last night. And what it was like to wake up and look out at a view like this. So unwelcoming and yet so stunning.

It was as if she'd woken up in a perfect little snow globe.

She wanted to jump to see if she could shake it up—but didn't. Because she was sure that if she tried it, she'd fall flat on her face. No doubt in full view of every single person she'd met here.

Violet walked away from the Mine, wanting to get more perspective on this tiny little community that had taken her in last night. She walked out to where the flat part of the hill started to slope down toward the water and stopped there, looking back. Then marveled at the central hub of this place where she'd declared she intended to stay until she could convince an alarmingly attractive and not exactly friendly man to have a beer with her.

She laughed out loud to herself, the noise of it startling her in all the cold, white quiet—but that only made her laugh harder.

Because the truth was, she didn't even like beer.

But she would drink it anyway if that was what it took.

She heard the buzzing first. Insistent and coming closer, and it took her a moment to place it.

A snowmobile. But not the one she'd ridden on last night. That one was still parked where Rosemary had left it. Violet wheeled around on the hillside, trying to see where it was coming from, and had turned all the way around in a circle before she realized the sound was rising up from the lake.

Something curled around inside of her, then hummed a bright, hot sort of tune as she watched another snowmobile zip across the ice, then climb its way up the incline from the water's edge to the old mine.

And she knew even before he swung off the snowmobile and turned his head in her direction that it was him.

Quinn.

Violet was sure that she could feel his intense midnight gaze through the cold and all the layers that covered both of them.

It was only then that she remembered, with an accompanying surge of heat low in her belly, the kinds of dreams she'd had about him last night.

His much-discussed abdomen had featured prominently.

Her mouth went dry and Violet took the opportunity to

remind herself that she was here to save her job, first and foremost, and should therefore behave like the professional intellectual she was. Not the silly fool who had let Stuart Abernathy-Thomason make an idiot out of her.

Though, in fairness, she supposed she couldn't really blame that on him. Not really. After all, she was the one who'd been dumb enough to listen to him and believe him when there had been so many red flags, it might as well have been a parade.

Violet did not intend to make that same mistake again. This time she would focus on what the Institute needed, not the foolish demands her treacherous heart wanted to make.

She marched over toward Quinn, her every step so loud in the snow that she felt like she was shouting by the time she stopped on the other side of the snowmobile. Maybe it was ridiculous to keep a recreational vehicle between them, but she couldn't be too careful when perfectly symmetrical cheekbones were lurking about to catch her unawares.

"When you said daylight, you meant it," she said, even though her voice felt almost like a desecration in all the stillness. She tried to sound even more cheerful to balance it out. "It will take me five minutes to get ready. Then you can do your worst."

Quinn pulled part of his face covering off, apparently just to prove that he was actually even more attractive than she'd imagined last night. The light caressed his face, making him gleam when he certainly didn't need any help in that department.

"Professor. Please. You couldn't handle my worst."

Violet didn't know what that meant. She didn't know why her body reacted as if the very notion of his worst was fever-inducing.

Just like she didn't know why his dark eyes gleamed, or why his mouth curved.

But she knew she had never wanted to know anything more.

Violet wasn't one to shy away from the things she didn't know. On the contrary. She dived right in, and that was why, when Quinn turned around and sauntered back into the Mine, she charged right in after him.

"It's polite to take off your boots, too," he told her as she shrugged out of her layers. He gazed down at her with those intense eyes. And his voice rumbled and made everything inside her seem to dance around a little drunkenly. "No one likes puddles of snow all over the floor."

Last night she'd been too dazzled by him and this rambling little town tucked away in the most unlikely of places. Today, she noticed pegs in the wall and all the boots stowed beneath the benches. She hung up her parka, stuffing her gloves and hat and scarf into the sleeves, then sat down so she could work her way out of her boots, fully conscious of the fact that Quinn did all of those things in a quarter of the time, and with admirable ease.

"Do you ever not go out because you don't want to pile on all these layers?" she asked him.

He shook his head at her as if she had confirmed all his worst fears. "No. If I didn't like the cold, I wouldn't live here."

Then he waited with an air of impatience while Violet placed her boots very carefully beneath the bench. She straightened and looked at him expectantly. He looked back.

And it was only because she couldn't imagine this man standing about *gazing* that she didn't let herself get too carried away with the fact that, actually, that was what they were doing. She could only hope that he couldn't hear the way her pulse was reacting.

"Let's look at your gear," he said after a while, as if she

should have read his mind. And it was an outrage that she hadn't. Like she was *doing something* to him.

"My gear?"

"I'm taking you out into the bush. The secret to the land, professor, is preparation."

Violet bristled. "I can assure you that I'm very well prepared." She turned to pull the guidebook from her parka's pocket. Then she brandished it at him. "I have read every page of this guidebook. And not only this guidebook. I cross-referenced it with every other guidebook on Alaska I could find and did a significant amount of online research as well, so that I could divine the perfect list—"

He sighed. Dramatically, in her opinion.

"I'm going to go out on a limb here and guess that a list in a book that you picked up . . . where? Los Angeles?"

Violet scowled at him. "San Francisco, thank you. I might be Californian but I'm not *soulless*."

"That remains to be seen." Quinn was wearing a long-sleeved, dark T-shirt today, which only drew more attention to his magnificent biceps. Violet wasn't sure she'd ever noticed the magnificence of a bicep before and it was clear that she'd been missing out. "I'm betting that what you consider adequate preparation in San Francisco is not going to impress me."

"I packed for the weather, not you," she retorted. "And I stand by my research in all things."

"We'll see." He jutted his chin toward the various shops, which Violet's investigations last night had showed her offered everything from pretty earrings to practical camping gear and back again. "We can fill in the gaps here if we need to."

Violet drew herself up to argue, but then stopped. Because why was she arguing, exactly? She knew absolutely nothing about the Alaskan bush. It might rankle that he was so sure that her preparation wasn't up to snuff, but what if he was right? Did she want to die of exposure? Or find herself a snack for the hungry bears who maybe weren't hibernating this winter the way she hoped they were?

She couldn't say either grisly end was appealing. So she smiled at him. "I'm happy to show you my gear."

But she didn't move.

He raised one of his dark brows and she felt feverish again. And still paralyzed, for some reason.

"Are you going to summon your gear with your mind?" Quinn asked slowly. Very slowly. The way people talked to those they found *dim-witted*, Violet realized. Which was . . . new, anyway. "Or are we going to go back into the bunkhouse and look at it?"

Now she felt flustered and *indignant*, but she was already turning and setting off across the floor. Because she didn't know how to explain that the very idea of this man crowding into her little sleeping area . . . affected her. There was a bed there. She'd slept in that bed. She'd opened up her pack and her personal items would be right there, in view—

Her pulse picked up, her breath was coming too quickly, and Violet understood in that moment that she would actually rather die—by Alaskan weather or grizzly bear—than let him know how overwhelming she found him.

Violet had never thought she was inhibited, despite Stuart's accusations on Christmas Eve. Her parents had never married and had broken up before she was born. She'd spent her life being shipped back and forth between the two of them. She'd never shared space with anyone. She'd had a single in her college dorm, and her intimacies during those years involved the rabbit holes she'd liked to hurl herself into, head on, in her studies. She couldn't imagine the casual undressing or other communal aspects of life with roommates, treating the shared space like a kind of locker room.

And that wasn't even getting into how charged it felt to think of a man in her space.

She had found it almost unbearably intimate to allow Stuart into her private living space, and that had been through a screen.

She still didn't consider herself *inhibited*, but she certainly didn't know how to control her breath or her heartbeat when she found herself standing next to her bed in her little alcove with Quinn Fortune crowded in with her.

He was entirely too *big*.

And she couldn't seem to think about anything at all but the fact that they were standing next to a bed.

Violet was sure that the strange heat she could feel washing all over her, inside and out, meant that she'd turned as red as Irving's head. But as horrifying as that was, she didn't see that there was anything she could do about the situation she found herself in but bluster on through it. She could deal with her unruly feelings later.

She lunged at her pack, wrestling it up and throwing it onto the little cot. Then there was nothing else to do but stand idly by, trying to look casual when she didn't feel either idle *or* casual, pressed there against the wall. With Quinn Fortune taking up all the space between her and the entry, so if she wanted to bolt for freedom, she wasn't sure that she'd be able to.

The strange heat seemed to gather in her belly, then pool lower down.

She braced herself, sure that it would all turn tawdry at any moment, but all Quinn did was squat down and then, very matter-of-factly, start going through her pack.

As advertised, she told herself sternly. *You ninny.*

"You have a lot of Ziploc bags," he observed after a moment. "I'm afraid to ask why."

"All the backpacking sites I went to claimed Ziploc bags were essential."

"So you don't even know why you have them. You just have them."

She did know. Of course she knew. "Ziploc bags can be used for organizational purposes, to keep wet clothes away from dry, to make sure muddy shoes don't ruin everything else, and I could go on and on."

"I thought, you being one of those do-gooder environmentalist types and all, that plastic wouldn't be your thing."

Violet stared at him, too appalled to remember that she was plastering herself against the wall. "They are recycled and reused and will be again when I'm finished with them. *Obviously.*"

She thought maybe he laughed, but he was looking down again. And she really did try her best not to concentrate on the fact that those big, tough hands were sorting through her clothes. Touching her clothes.

It was almost a relief when she saw he was lining up on the bed all three cans of bear spray she'd brought with her.

"Are you planning a little party with our local bear population?"

"How many deaths are the bears responsible for?" she asked, trying to sound suitably scientific and unemotional. Even though her voice went up an octave. Maybe two. "Just, for the sake of argument, this winter alone?"

He was definitely grinning now, if that gleam in his dark eyes was anything to go by. The crook in his mouth made her stomach feel fluttery, only adding to that heat building inside her.

"Only folks who deserve to get eaten, darlin'. It's a merit system."

That was not comforting, even if he was joking. She assured herself he was joking.

Then again, maybe it was better to think about bears than it was to contemplate the fact that Quinn Fortune had touched her underwear.

And okay, maybe when all was said and done, she really was a twelve-year-old girl at heart. She really didn't like that Stuart had accused her of that at Christmas. She didn't want him to be right about anything, ever.

Though she found, as Quinn deftly packed away her things and then tossed her pack over his shoulder, that it was hard to remember details about Stuart while she was staring up at the glory that was Quinn's shoulders. His torso. His attention-seeking biceps.

"Not bad," he said. Grudgingly, to her ear. "Maybe you're not as fluffy as you look."

Violet looked down at herself as if she expected to discover she'd sprouted an angora sweater while she hadn't been paying attention. But, as expected, found nothing remotely fluffy on her person. "Intellectuals are rarely fluffy, Quinn. There's too much thought involved and thought is weighty. Serious."

He only grunted a little. "You're too pink to be serious."

And she couldn't argue with him because Quinn was already walking away, his long legs eating up the floor, so she could do nothing but scurry along behind him. Her attempts to address the subject were ignored as he walked through the stalls in the big room, picking up a few things here and there and writing down what he'd taken on the pads or notebooks in each stall. Clearly left there for that purpose.

Then he headed back toward the door, dressed for the cold, and walked outside. Still carrying her pack and without a glance her way.

Leaving Violet to follow after him, still smarting from the idea that he found her unserious. She didn't care if Stuart thought she was inhibited and unfeminine, on a professional level. It might hurt personally, but that was an opinion. If he told all their colleagues that she was an intellectual lightweight, however, that could stick with her throughout her career.

Assuming she still had a career.

But as she wrapped herself up tight in her many layers of cold-weather gear, she knew that it wasn't Stuart or worries about her career that bothered her today.

Not really.

She wanted Quinn Fortune, the grunting mountain man, to take her seriously, pink or no pink.

Worse than that, she wanted him to *like* her.

It was the symmetry of those cheekbones. It was the entire abdominal situation that did not exactly improve with exposure.

That way lay madness. She knew that. Violet was here to have a beer and a talk with this man. To convince him to do something that was good for the land, sure, but was also something she could carry back to the Institute like a trophy.

It shouldn't matter if he liked her. Only that he listened to her.

This is no time to flutter about, worried about whether or not you're likable, she lectured herself. *This is a time to be impressive.*

And the good news was that he apparently thought she would surrender within hours. Anything that wasn't that instant surrender could only make her look good by comparison. She didn't have to turn into an outdoor winter sports guru, all she had to do was . . . not surrender.

Who needed skills when there was stubbornness?

So she strode outside, attempting to exude the boundless confidence she really wished she felt, straight off into the jaws of the bear-studded Alaskan wilderness.

Which Violet intended to survive if it was the last thing she ever did.

And she, by God, would be wearing as much pink as possible while she did it.

Four

❧

Checking her pack had not been his most brilliant move. Quinn could have done without the knowledge that her love of pink wasn't confined to outer layers, for example.

But he'd realized his error too late and now there was no unknowing the things he knew.

Even though the bulk of what she'd packed was practical—if unused, untried, and therefore not necessarily trustworthy in real conditions—it was also all unabashedly feminine.

Until today, Quinn would have said that the trappings of femininity didn't do much for him, in and of themselves. He was more into actual females than what they wore.

But now, as they zoomed across the frozen lake, all he could really think about was what sort of frilly, matched set of pink lacy things Professor Violet Parrish might be wearing beneath all the pink and red outer layers.

You need to get a grip, he told himself. *Now.*

He focused on the lake, the center of everybody's world out this way—humans and animals alike. In the winter, the ice was thick and everything felt closer and cozier because it was so easy to get from one end of the rambling, vaguely horseshoe-shaped lake to the other. In the summer there were boats for that, or longer routes by land on four-wheelers. The fishing was plentiful in any season, as the little ice fishing huts they passed attested.

Quinn knew every inch of it. He knew every single craggy inlet. He'd camped and hiked all around the lake more times than he could count. He knew where the fish liked to go depending on the season, the weather, the day. He was prepared to argue over where the best swimming holes were with anyone in the Mine at any given moment, and he knew the best places to watch the moose swim in the summer. Just like he knew the distinct pleasure of a bright summer night in a canoe, floating out in the middle of the lake, listening to the sound of the birds and the rush of the breeze as if winter would never come.

His family lived clustered around the farthest inlet, where the edge of the lake formed its final point before, eventually, the foothills of the Alaska Range began. His ancestors had built their spread where the water came in like an arrow, pointing the way. Over time, Fortunes who didn't want to stay in the family compound had spread out around it, forming a rough sort of triangle there at the farthest end of Lost Lake.

Quinn's cabin was on its own rocky inlet. He'd built it himself so that all he saw were woods and water. It was a short hike up a small hill to see smoke from his parents' house, or his sister's little hut across the way, or Bowie's spot down from Piper's, with its own landing strip for his planes. He knew his siblings would argue with him, but he thought he had the best vantage point around.

But he wasn't taking Violet to his cabin. Instead, he drove them into a narrow little inlet a few down from his.

Because he had plans for his professor, and they didn't include the comfort of his home.

He wasn't planning to make her comfortable at all.

Quinn pulled off the ice and advised her to hold on as he took the snowmobile up the fairly steep hill that waited for them.

At the top, the wind felt much colder, and that made everything better. A proper Alaskan welcome, as far as he was concerned. He turned off the snowmobile, climbed off, and then waited for Violet to follow.

"We have to hike the rest of the way," he told her gravely.

She peered at the steep slope of snow and ice, the trees bent back against both, and Quinn wished she wasn't wrapped up quite so securely in all her cold-weather gear. Not because he wished hypothermia on anyone but because he imagined he would have enjoyed whatever expression she wore then.

"Hike," she repeated, as if she wasn't familiar with the word.

And Quinn thought this was it. This was when he broke her.

But then, even in all those puffy pink layers, he saw her . . . bloom. There was no other way to describe it. Like her automatic response to adversity was to beam at it until it went away. She actually clapped her brightly gloved hands together, leaving Quinn no option but to scowl.

Not that she seemed to notice. "How fun! Though I should tell you, I've never hiked in snow before. I don't know if there are practical considerations I should take into account."

"The snow is hardpacked," he told her gruffly. But she only gazed back at him until he checked a sigh. "You can walk on it easily enough. If it was more powdery, you'd fall through the surface. That would be a little bit harder."

She nodded enthusiastically, patting at her coat pockets. For that guidebook, he figured, which was one more way she was too pink and too silly to make it out here. As he intended to prove. "I really should write that down. We don't get a lot of snow in the Bay Area and—"

"You can write it down later. Maybe not out here in the cold."

He didn't wait for her response. He headed toward the trail he'd made earlier that morning, questioning himself with every step.

Questioning himself, sure, but not altering his plans any.

Behind him, he heard the rustling of her snow pants and a small sound of effort he assumed was her swinging her pack onto her shoulders.

What he didn't hear were the complaints he'd anticipated.

He led her up the steep incline, taking her on the most loopy, circuitous, unnecessarily difficult route possible. A route he'd designed to show her how ill-suited she was to the elements, but if she was getting that message, she gave no sign.

And when he glanced behind him she looked, if anything, content to be marching along, scrabbling up an icy little ridge with a pack on.

If she'd complained, or even breathed too heavily, or made the faintest sound that could have been construed as an objection, he would have felt vindicated.

Instead, he just felt like a jerk.

And that was before they made it to the shack. It was clear today, with an arctic blue sky, but even that couldn't pretty up this place. Quinn stopped in the clearing so she could pull her glasses out, slip them on, and get a good, long look at it.

The tiny little shack, barely big enough for its one room,

looking dark and grim there in the clearing. And the outhouse—something he knew tended to horrify folks from more settled parts of the world—wasn't even visible from this angle.

"Welcome to your new home," he said in as close to a bright tone as he got.

"This is your home? Wow. It's so . . ."

He waited as her voice trailed off, something surging inside of him that he told himself was anticipation—that she would prove herself the irredeemable Outsider she was, allowing him to feel absolutely certain that he was doing the right thing here.

She sighed happily, clearly smiling wide behind her rose-colored balaclava. "It's so rustic. How *wonderful*. I'm amazed that a person can live so simply in a place that seems so overwhelming to me. I can't wait to see how you do it."

Her enthusiasm offended him. That was what he told himself. That was what that pressure in the center of his chest was.

"This isn't a theme park," he snapped at her. "This is subsistence Alaskan living at its finest. The Native Athabascans have been doing it in this region for thousands of years. Are you ready for this?"

"Does it matter if I'm ready?" she shot back. Then laughed before he was tempted to imagine that was a sign of temper on her part. "It seemed pretty clear to me that this was supposed to be a test. I should tell you right now, I'm *excellent* at tests."

"This isn't going to be a test of your reading comprehension. Or even anything multiple-choice that you can fake your way through. You can't *think* your way through the wilderness, Violet."

"I am a woman of action," she informed him loftily.

He stared at her. Puffy, bright pink, looking alarmingly fresh and unruffled. With, clearly, no sense of her own peril here.

"No. You're not."

She laughed again. "I would like to be a woman of action, anyway. I feel, strongly, that deep inside me lurks that kind of woman. Just *lying in wait* for the opportunity to *burst forth* into . . . well, you know. *Actiony things*."

Quinn couldn't have said why the sillier she was, the grumpier he got.

"Is that how you do things down there?" he asked. "With made-up phrases like *actiony things*?"

"If by *down there*, you mean in and around academia . . . Yes. Yes, you could argue that we do."

"Up here, nowhere near any ivory tower, there's more than enough work to go around. If that's the kind of action you mean, you're in luck."

And then he pushed open the door to the little shack and let her in, not because he was courteous. But so he could have the opportunity of watching her reaction.

The shack was the very same one his great-grandfather had erected back in the day, when he'd first scouted this side of the lake. And then, after he'd gone off to Juneau and found himself Quinn's great-grandmother, the two of them had come back here and made this their first home. They lived in it for two years while they built the cabin that Quinn's parents now lived in.

He liked to think of it as a family museum.

And he doubted very much that Violet had ever set foot in a one-room dry cabin before, much less one as bare-bones as this. There was an old woodstove in one corner, a kitchen with no running water, just five-gallon jugs of water—or in the case of this cabin today, frozen water—one wall hung with equipment necessary for life in the wild and on the other wall, the same pile of furs his great-grandparents had called a bed.

"I feel like I've stepped back in time," Violet said, peeling back that balaclava so he could see that she really was smiling. *Beaming.*

He did not smile in return. "You have."

She stood there a step or two inside, looking all around. "I can't help noticing there's no bathroom."

"No bathroom, no shower, no running water," he said, feeling more cheerful with every word. He unzipped his parka, then pointed out the huge basin stowed beneath the counter. "If you want to take a bath, we can gather some snow and heat it up near the stove. But it takes a while."

He decided not to tell her, yet, about the main drawback of life in a dry cabin. Folks preferred them in places like this because there were no pipes to freeze. But there were challenges—like always having to heat up water on the stove to do dishes. Or wash your hands. Or anything else. Every single time.

"That sounds luxurious," she was saying brightly, looking at the basin as if it were a magic cauldron. "A cozy bath by the fire? In a sweet little cabin far, far away from it all? It's like a spa retreat."

This was not the reaction she was supposed to be having.

"It's nothing like a spa retreat," he corrected her. "Spas don't generally have outhouses."

That gave her pause. Her eyes got big and solemn and she took a moment as she readjusted her glasses. "An actual outhouse?"

"It's about twenty feet back from the cabin."

"Outside, you mean. In the cold."

He felt a current of something a lot like satisfaction

move in him, dark and deep, and accepted that this was what he'd wanted all along. "It's practically spring out there today, professor. Only ten below. Global warming is a bitch."

She looked dubious. "How exactly does a person go to the bathroom in ten-below weather?"

Quinn felt his mouth kick up in one corner. "Quickly, Violet. Very quickly."

She stripped off her parka but left her hat on. "I will keep that in mind."

"Spoken like someone who has yet to experience the joys of a frigid privy seat at four A.M."

Violet only shrugged. "People do it, so it must be doable." Quinn didn't think she was really taking an Alaskan wintry jaunt to the outhouse seriously, but before he could comment on it, she was pointing at the old stove. "Should we start that fire?"

"You know how to start a fire?" He didn't do much to hide his disbelief.

"If you mean, can I pick up a selection of twigs in the middle of the woods and produce fire somehow? No." She moved over to the kitchen area of the cabin and picked up a small box from the countertop. "These look a lot like matches. I know how to light a match, Quinn."

And then, she set about proving it, which made him grit his teeth so tightly that he was surprised his jaw didn't shatter.

Once the stove was going, the little shack was faintly less frigid—but it would take a while for it to get anywhere near warm. He was glad he'd brought a couple of sleeping bags over this morning to make sure they didn't freeze—though, in keeping with this game he was playing, he didn't intend to share that with her yet.

He thought it might do a city girl some good to imagine herself sleeping on a pile of furs, like any other self-respecting Neanderthal.

Violet set her pack on the floor near the furs, then, without being asked, hung up her jacket and various other outer layers near the door. Quinn did the same. Then it was just the two of them, padding around the cabin in nothing but their base layers.

Meaning she was basically wearing nothing now but thick socks, leggings, and a sweater. Though she removed the sweater, too, after a while, revealing the pastel lavender long-sleeved T-shirt beneath.

Because when the pink got to be too much, she went with lavender, rose, and occasionally peach. Something he knew now, because he'd had his hands in her things. A critical misstep.

Violet appeared to be completely unaware of the tension he couldn't seem to stop feeling. Heedless in every way to the thickness of it, humming in the air between them like the slow heat from the woodstove.

He couldn't remember a single other time in his life that he'd made so little impression on a woman.

It would have been humbling if he hadn't had the suspicion that she wasn't so much immune to him as oblivious.

The unfortunate truth was that Quinn had spent a very long night thinking about Violet Parrish and those curves of hers. And now she was within arm's reach in this tiny little shack where they were practically tripping over each other every time they moved, without another person around for miles. He was a little too aware of her for comfort.

Another example of his not-so-brilliant planning.

But he'd been positive that a creature so pink and fluffy

would have been rocking in a corner by now, desperate for some indoor plumbing and an actual bed, far, far away from here.

He didn't like that Violet kept surprising him.

Or maybe the real issue was that he liked it too much.

Quinn had stayed here a hundred times or more, especially when he'd been building his own cabin.

But he'd never stayed here with anybody else.

Certainly not with somebody who smelled like summer and seemed engaged in every single detail he had to impart about dry cabin living, which wasn't unusual in Alaska. The lack of running water bled into every choice a person made, like when and how to clean, and what to eat—because meat meant you needed to clean immediately, while most veggie options meant you could wait. Not having a shower or water taps meant not only chores but personal grooming realities required reassessment.

It was Quinn's perhaps deeply Alaskan belief that everyone should spend a little time in a dry cabin to get a feel for what they really needed in life. If only to get up close and personal with the stars and the quiet in a way a person never could unless they had to head out to the outhouse in the dark and the cold. He often missed that when he was back in his actual cabin, with its generator and water tank. And he never liked to go too long without a night or two out here at the shack, to remind himself of all the reasons he was lucky to live here.

But that wasn't the point of this visit. This visit was to make an Outsider break and run back home.

"What do you do all day in a place like this?" she asked, sometime later. She was standing at the counter, cutting up potatoes and tossing them in the pot he'd set out. He was trying not to brood about how easily she was seeming to adapt—but then, she hadn't made it through a night yet. "No electricity, no water. Just the chores?"

"Depends on the season," he replied. "I hunt or fish. There's a garden to tend. Winter, though, is mostly about hunkering down when I'm home."

All true enough.

"It seems very stark," she commented, in that musing tone that he was pretty sure led to her scribbling in her book—and he didn't want to analyze why he really didn't want to be some kind of intellectual exercise for her. "No books and nothing to watch. I would have thought, with the nights as long as they are here, that there'd be *some* form of entertainment."

In his actual cabin, there was all that and more. But he only raised an eyebrow at her as he prepared the moose meat he'd brought over this morning in the expectation that this city girl would balk at the very idea of moose stew. She had not.

"I find my solitude entertaining, Violet." He sounded pious and grim to his own ears. Dour straight through. "I don't require a lot of distractions."

His sister would have laughed in his face, but Violet nodded. "I've never understood boredom, either. I've always been perfectly capable of entertaining myself."

Another indication that she wasn't who he'd thought she would be. Quinn accepted that with his usual grace. "Is that what you do at that institute? Entertain yourself with plans and proposals for other people's land and rights?"

And he couldn't tell if she was pretending not to notice that he kept poking at her, or if she actually was that oblivious. About everything. All she did was nod again, as if they were having a perfectly reasonable discussion.

"It's entertaining, to some degree," she replied. "But mostly it's rewarding. Very rewarding. I didn't grow up in the wilderness, but I was isolated all the same. I spent a lot of time in my head. The only difference now is that I get paid for it."

Quinn told himself not to ask. But he did anyway. "How did you grow up? Why were you isolated?"

She let out a laugh, but for all that it sounded merry, he could see the look in her eyes. And he was interested, despite himself. Why would such a bright and fluffy creature have armor and defense mechanisms like everyone else?

But in the next moment it occurred to him that the brightness and fluffiness *were* the armor. They were the defense.

He didn't like how that sat on him at all.

"My parents have a very acrimonious relationship," she said after a moment. She laughed again, but it wasn't real, either. "My father believes that my mother got pregnant to entrap him. My mother claims to be outraged by the accusation. They've been going round and round, with varying degrees of bitterness, since before I was born."

Quinn didn't say anything, adding his meat to the pot while Violet continued chopping up the potatoes. He reached up and found a can of beans on the shelf above, then added it to the rest.

"I was always being sent back and forth," Violet told him, her attention on her potatoes while her glasses slid, slowly and inexorably, down her nose. He couldn't look away. "My father was always in the same place in Texas, but I wouldn't say that it was ever really welcoming there. Mostly I had to keep out of the way of his new wives. My mother moved from place to place and husband to husband, which was a different sort of disorienting. Happily for all concerned, I'm the only child either one of them had. All I ever had was me." She put down the knife, shoved her glasses back into place, then smiled brilliantly at him. "Done. What about you? What are your parents like?"

Quinn took the pot and set it on the stove. He took his time cleaning off the counter and utensils with the water he'd already warmed, then went out to collect some snow so he could boil it later to do their dishes after they ate. But when he was done, she was still standing there at the counter, gazing at him expectantly.

He could have pretended he didn't recall the question. But he did.

"My parents get along fine," he said shortly.

What his parents were, to his mind, were two peas in a ridiculously stubborn pod, but he didn't tell her that. Mostly because he kind of . . . *wanted* to talk to her.

What was *that*?

Violet didn't actually laugh, though her eyes were brighter than before. "Very illuminating. Thank you."

"We could also not talk," he growled at her. "That's the main part of a wilderness experience, Violet. You have to be quiet to fully experience it."

He expected her to argue, but as he was learning, every expectation he had about Violet Parrish missed the mark. All she did was shrug, then take herself off to sit on the furs, rifle through her guidebook, and scribble in it. Notes upon notes.

Quinn wasn't used to company, that was for sure. When he spent time with a woman, he was usually engaged in slaking his hunger. When he craved company he hung out at the Mine, or with his family. But mostly he was alone.

And Violet was only a little thing, all curves and big gold-shot eyes, but she seemed to take up too much space.

All the space.

He was aware of every breath she drew in. Every time she shifted position. Even the scratch of her pen against the paper.

"I'll be honest," he said when he couldn't take it anymore. The smell of the stew they'd made was rich and heavy and yet the least tempting thing on offer tonight. "I expected you to crack on the hike. I thought you'd be half-way to Anchorage by now."

Violet didn't take offense to that, like a normal person. She only inclined her head, sitting cross-legged on the furs. "I told you," she said, sounding grand and serious at once. "I am a woman of great action just waiting to come out, Quinn."

And somehow, he didn't have the heart to point out that she wasn't actually taking any action. She was sitting, that was all, and maybe there was something wrong with him that just looking at her felt like a punch to the gut. A repeated punch to the gut.

He expected her to turn up her nose at actually eating moose, the way tourists to Alaska often did, but she didn't. She took her first spoonful gingerly and took her time with the tasting, but then ate the rest happily. Afterward, she washed the dishes, and he tossed the dirty water out.

Then there were only the cozy confines of the shack in the lantern light.

Quinn had no one to blame for that but himself.

She kept up the reading and scribbling. He sharpened his knives with an old whetstone someone—possibly him—had left in the kitchen. When Violet yawned some while later, he set his jaw and pulled out the sleeping bags, then watched as she spread hers out on the furs.

"Are you going to sleep over here?" she asked when he stayed where he was, in one of the shack's two hand-carved wooden chairs next to a small, sturdy table.

He shook his head, deeply regretting that he hadn't thought to at least bring a freaking book to read. Anything to divert his attention from her—but he'd been too busy trying to lean in hard to the pioneer-lifestyle thing. "I'm fine here."

"That's silly. The furs look much more comfortable."

She didn't make some joke about protecting her virtue—or his. She didn't address the sexual tension at all.

Maybe she didn't feel any.

But he couldn't quite believe that. It was something about the way she looked away too quickly when their eyes met. It was the flush in her cheeks. It was the way she fumbled sometimes while messing with her glasses.

He had explained the outhouse rules to her over dinner, something he wouldn't have thought required that much explanation, but then, he already knew that no amount of information was *too much* for Violet. He watched how she sighed a little, then went and pulled on her boots and her parka and her other layers before picking up the flashlight from her pack.

"Not the flashlight," he said in a low voice from his chair. "Use your headlamp instead." And when she opened her mouth to question him on that he almost grinned. "You'll see why."

She muttered something as she dug around in her pack until she found her headlamp, strapping it on over her head. Then she fumbled with it, as good as announcing she'd never used it before. She eventually clicked it on, blinding him when she swung her head in his direction, then headed for the door. Slowly, as if she didn't really believe she had to go outside to take care of business.

"Around the back," he told her. "Directly behind the shack. You can't miss it. If you need anything, yell. I'll hear you."

"Assuming I haven't already been eaten by a bear, sure."

"You're obsessed with bears, Violet. It's a little weird."

"What I don't understand is how anyone could be anything but obsessed with bears," she retorted. "That's what's weird, *Quinn*."

But when all he did was grin a little, she huffed out a sound and then went out.

And Quinn might have been playing games with her, but he also knew that the Alaskan wilderness was nothing to mess around with. So he went over to the shack's little window on the back and watched her light as it bobbed along, so he could make sure she was headed in the right direction and not off to die of exposure in the woods. He heard the creaky sound of the outhouse door and knew she'd made it.

Still, he stayed where he was until she emerged again and headed back toward the shack. He moved from the window to take his seat again, expecting her to walk through the door in the next moment.

Yet she didn't come. And he was on his feet, prepared to go out and find her, when the door finally opened again.

"Did you get lost?" he asked, scowling.

But her headlamp was already switched off and her face was filled with wonder.

"I saw it," she said in a reverent whisper. "The sky. I saw something green and I turned off my headlamp and there it was. Dancing all over the sky."

"The aurora," Quinn said, and smiled despite himself. "Makes an outhouse run worth it, doesn't it?"

"It makes everything worth it," she replied, and he heard so much in her voice then. Passion. Excitement. A kind of hunger that seemed to reverberate all the way through him.

She set about tearing off her outer layers, then went right back to her book for some more scribbling.

Still with that awed look on her face and really, he hadn't prepared for this. By this point, he'd expected tears and demands.

Not all that joy and wonder that she'd seen the northern lights.

When she was done writing, she crawled into the sleeping bag and pulled one of the furs over her. She set her glasses on her pack, very carefully, and then lay there.

He knew she wasn't asleep. He could hear the way she was breathing.

"For the record, if this was my cabin, I certainly wouldn't sleep in a chair. These furs are ridiculously cozy."

"They're my furs. I know how cozy they are."

"Fine," she said with a sigh. "Suit yourself."

For a while, he did. He would have liked it if she'd tossed and turned a bit, but she didn't. As far as he could tell, Violet dropped right off to sleep without so much as a stray thought to intrude upon her sweet pink dreams. And maybe he could have pretended she wasn't there, but she started making sounds.

The most ridiculous sounds he thought he'd ever heard. Tiny little snores that made his ribs ache. Not long after that he found himself rationalizing that of the two of them, he was the one who needed his sleep. Since he was the one who had to make sure she lived through this, so she could go away.

He rolled out his sleeping bag and climbed inside, leaving a significant amount of space on the furs between him and the guest he'd expected to have hitched her way downriver by now. A few hours of sleep would be fine, he told himself. He'd figure out how to break that impenetrable cheerfulness of hers in the morning.

But all the rationalizations in the world didn't help him later. When he woke up to find that Violet had twisted around in her sleep and, though still in her own sleeping bag, was snuggled up against his side.

Still making those noises that should have been annoying, but were actually something a lot more like adorable.

A word he'd never used to describe a woman in his life.

But in the case of the soft, snoring woman at his side, pink and warm and impossible, only that word fit.

So he didn't move her off him. Quinn stayed where he was, staring at the ceiling of this old shack in the grip of the long, dark night, wondering why he'd ever imagined this was a good idea.

Five

❧

Violet spent the next couple of days indulging every *Little House on the Prairie* fantasy she'd ever had as a girl. Without actually churning butter or enjoying too-hot pig tails as a treat, sure—but the idea that she, too, was immersed in a pioneer lifestyle the way she'd dreamed when she was a girl made up for such minor disappointments.

She found that with no clocks and only lantern light when it was dark, she slept deeper and better. *Or maybe,* something in her piped up every time she thought that, *what you really like is sleeping in a pile of furs with Quinn Fortune while the wind prowls around outside and the woodstove pops and crackles all night long . . .*

Thinking such things was the quickest way she knew to warm herself up, no matter how cold it was outside. Because thinking about their nights together—not *together* together, but still—made her feverish all over again. And something alarmingly close to *giggly.*

Because she would wake up from the deepest sleep of

her life in the middle of the night, mostly because she needed to go to the bathroom. But no way was she getting up, finding layers and headlamps, and trudging out into the cold unless she was truly desperate. Which usually meant that she would wake up, note that the appropriate level of desperation had not yet been achieved, and discover that once again the two of them were pressed together. Somehow. As if their bodies were drawn together while they slept.

It made her shiver, deep inside, to imagine being *drawn to him* on some kind of heretofore unknown *cellular level*.

And there were things that she hadn't known before. Things that it would never have occurred to her to imagine. Like the fact that a man's bicep, so hard and tough, could feel like the perfect pillow. How was that possible when she usually preferred the softest down? Or that a man could generate more heat than the woodstove across the cabin. She kept thinking that surely she ought to be cold, sleeping on a floor in the middle of the untouched Alaskan wilderness, but she never was. Quite the opposite, in fact. Because the furs kept the heat trapped in and the sleeping bag was clearly made for below-zero conditions, but Quinn was her secret weapon.

He *blazed*. She often found herself kicking off her covers because she didn't need them.

Violet had always wondered how people slept together. Not how they had sex. She lived in a world of widespread internet access, so she knew about sex, thank you, even if she hadn't actually experienced it herself. There were examples of it everywhere. Endless accounts of what it felt like, too, so she thought she had a hazy approximation of what the actual deed must be like.

But *sleeping together* had always confused her. How did

two bodies manage to find comfortable ways to rest while touching? She flailed about while she dreamed, so she'd always thought that everyone else must, too, and no one seemed to talk enough about flailing. Everyone acted as if it was just as easy to sleep with someone else as it was to sleep alone, which she'd always thought was one of those smug agreements coupled-off people made to convince others their solitude was lacking somehow.

No one could have been more surprised than Violet to discover that, it turned out, sleeping next to Quinn was actually better than sleeping alone.

She did not record her thoughts on that topic in the blank pages of her guidebook. She kept that little nugget to herself.

On the first day, the sun came out in late morning and she charged outside to see where it was she was living for the week. She stood outside in the sharp, bright cold, astonished the same way she was every time at the *kick* of the air around her.

"Move around a little," Quinn advised her, following behind her at a far more leisurely pace. "Get your blood going."

That sounded reasonable, so Violet hiked around the shack until she felt less like her lungs were too frozen to operate. She made her way down to the icy edge of the water, then back up again. Then she climbed to the top of the little ridge so she could see down the length of the lake until it curved out of sight, and there was something about how beautiful it was, how beautifully stark and still, that made her feel like crying.

And not because she was sad.

It was that stillness that was the most arresting at first. Quinn made very little noise for such a big man, even when she thought he ought to have been making as much of a racket crunching through the snow as she did. He stood there beside her as she looked out over the lake, and she couldn't even hear him breathe.

There was only a quiet so intense it seemed to make its own kind of noise inside her.

By the second day, she thought that she'd gotten the hang of this dry cabin thing. There was an elegance to it, really. A pleasant simplicity. It made her very conscious of her choices, in a way that made it all too clear that for a person who spent a significant amount of her time worrying about how to save the planet, she spent very little time streamlining her own life. She would have said that she had a deep commitment to living green, but what did that really mean in a big city? Here in the cabin, water was precious and she became deeply aware of how and when and why she might have used it back home. Because choosing to use water here took forethought and preparation.

It meant that the coffee Quinn made in the morning tasted twice as precious because it couldn't be produced at the touch of a button. It also meant that she thought twice about doing anything that might normally end in washing something—a mug, her plate, her hands.

That second night, while looking for an extra dish towel, she found a chess set instead, nestled into a drawer with a deck of cards and a small cribbage board. And she didn't chide him for pretending he didn't have entertainment here, though she wanted to.

"Let me guess," she said drily as she set the chessboard down on the small table where he was still sharpening knives. She wasn't sure she wanted to ask him why he needed his blades *quite* so sharp. "You wanted me to sit here in silence and contemplate the error of my ways."

"Most Outsiders can't take the silence," was all he said, those midnight eyes gleaming as he lounged there, deadly weapons in his big, tough hands. Making her feel fluttery, for reasons she opted not to analyze too closely. "Sends them screaming back to all that noise and hustle."

"I like the quiet." She tried to look sphinxlike and powerful, a woman of inscrutable action who *chose* to be still, but worried that really, she looked like she was grimacing. Possibly in pain. "I thrive in silence."

"How would you know?" He sounded lazy, when she had the distinct impression that there was nothing lazy about this man. Inside or out. "There's nothing quiet about a city."

Violet opened her mouth to argue the point but closed it again, thinking of the stillness when she'd stood on that ridge. There hadn't been much of a breeze. The world around her had been white with brown beneath it, the sky in shades of gold and peach and blue as the sun had barely bothered to check in. And yes, she liked the quiet in her little apartment in San Francisco, but it was a layered quiet. Always the sound of traffic in the distance, her neighbor walking around above her, the hum of so many lives.

On that ridge it was like the silence was weighted. It pressed down into her, marking her. Her own breath was the only sound she could hear for miles. Her own heart was the only rhythm.

She had found it beautiful, but Violet hadn't dared say that. She'd known that he would scoff at her, or think she was only saying the things she thought he wanted to hear, and it had been too beautiful for that.

But when they'd turned back toward the cabin, she had found herself thinking of the word *pristine* in a whole new way.

With layers of quiet and an endless expanse of untouched snow.

Now at the small table, she still didn't feel the need to open herself up to his criticism. She wanted to hold the quiet inside and keep it to herself.

"I'll have you know that I was the president of the chess club in high school," Violet announced as she set up the board, ignoring his knife collection. She did not tell him that she was also the entirety of the chess club when she was in high school. That little detail was between her and the extracurricular activities section of her college applications, which had required some finessing for a person who preferred studies to socializing.

"Scary," Quinn replied, not looking scared.

And then he proceeded to beat her three times in a row. Easily. When she won the fourth game—and only barely— he laughed. Then went to give the night's stew a good stir.

Violet sat there in the buttery lantern light and watched him. Her heart was kicking at her, hard, and it took her a moment to understand why.

Stuart and she had played online chess and he hadn't liked it when she'd won. He'd turned cold and passive-aggressive every time. Another red flag she'd ignored, but then, she'd thought that was what all men were like. Given that her only real example of men was her father, who not only refused to accept that he was capable of losing anything, but had elevated his spitefulness to an art form.

Case in point: his insistence on each and every day his custody agreement with Violet's mother allowed. Not because he wanted any kind of relationship with his daughter. He didn't. But because he wanted to make things as difficult for his ex-lover as possible, as payback for, as he called it, *setting her trap.* Something he ranted about every time he was unable to avoid having a conversation with his only daughter. That and his vasectomy.

Violet had always assumed that this sort of behavior was a consequence of testosterone poisoning.

"You don't seem too bothered by losing," she observed, because if she was poisoned by anything, it was an inability

to ever just let things lie. She had accepted that about herself long ago.

*Though maybe don't prod the person you're stranded in
a remote cabin with,* an inner voice suggested drily. *Because that's really not very smart.*

Quinn didn't turn around from the stove. "Of course it
bothered me. Who likes losing?"

"You seemed to take it pretty well."

"Nobody likes a poor loser, Violet. Besides, you get
used to losing chess games around here. My mother is un-
defeated."

Violet had to sit with that, because he hadn't sounded
surly about his mother's chess prowess. Or sulky in any
way. He just stated it like it was a fact.

Maybe, that same voice suggested, *the problem is that
the men you've known before now were babies.*

Quinn Fortune was not a baby.

Violet was clear on that.

Any lingering doubts she might have had on that score—
and it was more that she thought she *should* have doubts
than that she could name any—disappeared on the third
day, when he went outside and chopped some of the wood
stacked high beneath an overhang. He stripped off a layer or
two as he went, and then all the rest after he brought the
wood inside, until Violet couldn't tell if there was actually
steam coming off him . . . or if that was just her.

Because his abdominal situation, it turned out, was even
more spectacular up close.

Meaning that no, Quinn was no baby.

Later that night, they stood outside for as long as they
could stand it in the dark while up above, the aurora
danced in the sky once more.

Haunting. Magical.

Inside the shack again, they both shrugged out of their cold-weather clothes quietly enough. But the cabin seemed smaller. As if the aurora had come inside with them and had claimed all the space.

"Quinn . . ." Violet whispered. "I . . ."

Suddenly he was too close to her. They were standing right next to the door, where her boots were already leaving puddles. Her knees felt weak.

She'd always thought that was a silly, made-up thing, too. Why would a person's knees cease to function for emotional reasons? But she actually slumped back against the wall to hold herself up, because she wasn't sure her legs were up to it.

Violet had been trying her best to pretend she didn't notice how beautiful he was, out here where he was the only view. And the best view. Those dark, dark blue eyes. The jaw he hadn't shaved in days that seemed to affect her more each day she spent with him. Everything about his tall, rangy body and his scent and his heat.

Quinn looked dangerous tonight. Elemental. No different from the aurora outside, a mystery far greater than the Alaskan night, the stars.

Every morning Violet would wake up first, but she would pretend to be asleep while Quinn heated up a pot full of snow on the stove. He used some of it to make coffee, which was lovely. But he also used some of it to wash himself, stripping down into only his boxer briefs, and ruining her life that simply.

Over and over again, she lay there in the furs and quietly burned alive.

Every morning over coffee she tried to pretend that she hadn't seen him. That she didn't know what it was like to watch soft, buttery lantern light dance over all of those hard muscles in his taut, ridged abdomen that was even better than it looked beneath his selection of T-shirts.

But tonight that was all she could think about.

That and the way he looked at her, somehow impatient and inviting at once.

"Quinn . . ." she whispered again, not even knowing what she was asking for.

She didn't know what she wanted. Only that she wanted something desperately.

And that he was the only man on earth who could give it to her.

Quinn's dark eyes dropped to her mouth and his own lips firmed. Violet held her breath—

But he stepped away. He turned his back, heading over toward the stove while she clung to the wall and wondered when her knees had turned to water.

"Better get some sleep," he said darkly. Over his shoulder. He didn't turn around to face her again.

But somehow, Violet didn't think it was a rebuke.

That night she would have said she didn't sleep at all. Because she kept herself awake, what-ifs dancing around and around in her head and always circling back to that moment, his mouth . . .

But at some point she must have fallen asleep, because she woke up again. Alone. No sculpted biceps to cushion her head. No glorious example of masculinity bathing himself in the glow of a lantern.

She reached her hand out to find her glasses and smashed them onto her face, then dug her phone out of the exterior pocket of her bag. There had been no hint of service since McGrath, which meant the phone's only function was as a clock.

It was a little after nine. How did she plan to convince Quinn to listen to her proposals if she was too busy proving that she was lazy—which would obviously also prove that she was as useless as he thought she was?

Not a woman of action, but a woman of naps.

Hardly the image she was going for.

She could smell coffee, though. And when she shuffled over to the kitchen area she saw the mug she usually used on the counter, filled up and still steaming. There was warm water in the pot on the stove and the cloth he used to wash hanging on the inside line.

But Quinn himself was nowhere to be found.

Violet assumed he was out there doing something arctic and manly. And she had no idea how she'd missed the usual morning show.

She reminded herself that she was a woman of action. A *pioneer* woman, equal parts hardiness and practicality. She reminded herself of that all the way out to the outhouse and back, in the almost-daylight dark that was just as cold as nighttime, but notably lacking in magical auroras.

Back in the cabin, she had a little wash herself, but in more of a hurry than normal, since she didn't know when Quinn would return. Just because *he* was apparently wholly unselfconscious about stripping down in mixed company, she certainly was not. The very idea of him walking in now and seeing her in nothing but her soft sports bra and little boy shorts made her shiver.

Violet assured herself she was cold. And then, maybe to make that true, she washed her hair at last. It was not as effortless as an actual shower, or even the taps of a sink, but she used the old metal kettle and she got the job done.

As she waited for her hair to dry, she eyed the dry goods portion of the kitchen, trying to imagine what they'd throw together for dinner tonight. And in the meantime, not wanting to deal with any dishes that might require more water to clean, she toasted a piece of bread on the stove with the handheld wire grill, and ate her toast with some peanut butter spread on top.

When she heard the sound of heavy feet outside, crunching through the snow, she brightened. *Quinn*, she thought, with more pleasure than was smart.

But the next moment, she froze. Because one thing she knew about Quinn was that he didn't make noise.

Not like that.

And then only one word slashed through her mind.

Bears.

She dived across the cabin, going down hard on her knees in the sleeping area. She scrabbled through her pack in a wild panic until she had a canister of bear spray in her hand.

And as she crouched there, listening to the sound of something heavy approaching, Violet understood that her whole life had been leading to this moment.

She had come here with every intention of avoiding bears. *Probably* they were hibernating, but who knew if that held when the climate was changing all around them? Her research had been inconclusive on that point. So she'd come prepared.

They hadn't let her on the plane to Anchorage with the single canister she'd brought, so she'd bought more when she'd landed in Alaska. Both small-plane pilots had shrugged and stowed all three cans where they couldn't blow up or do any harm if they did.

Maybe she was overprepared.

But every dream she'd had that wasn't about Quinn had been a nightmare involving enormous furry predators with fangs.

Now the bears had come for her, and she was ready.

Her heart was pounding so hard it made her head feel like it was ringing. Her mind spun around and around as she tried to think what steps she should take. She wasn't sure that bear spray would help her much in the long run. Bears were not mosquitoes. Maybe the spray would blind the bear, but then she'd be stuck in a very small cabin with a blinded bear.

That did not sound ideal.

She was going to have to get past the bear, then escape outside without breathing in the pepper spray. That meant she had to get dressed in her cold-weather clothes, or she'd die either way.

For a moment, the relentlessness of this place seemed to press her down to the floor of the cabin, like a heavy boot.

"I am a woman of action," Violet muttered to herself.

She pulled off the safety on the bear spray and took a deep breath. Then she rolled up to her feet and started toward her boots and parka, but before she could make it there, the door was flung open wide.

Violet jumped back, brandishing the bear spray in one hand—

But in the split second before she pressed the button and likely fumigated herself along with the encroaching wild animal, she registered that the figure at the door was not bear-shaped.

On the contrary, it was a man.

Or so she assumed, from his height and the wideness of his shoulders, though he was dressed in foul-weather gear she didn't recognize. Meaning it certainly wasn't Quinn. The man came inside in a rush of cold and shut the door behind him.

Violet didn't lower her arm.

Because for the first time since she'd come out to this cabin with Quinn, how isolated she was here impressed itself upon her.

There was no one she could call for help. With her voice

or with any other device. There were no devices. There was nowhere to run. She had hiked all around the little clearing where the cabin sat, but there was nothing.

Nothing but snow and ice.

She felt, suddenly, as if the starkness that had so affected her outside had settled itself in her chest. And it felt a lot less beautiful.

But she kept her arm steady.

"Is that bear spray?" came an amused male voice.

Violet was less amused. "I don't know what it will do to a human, but I'm assuming it will be unpleasant."

The man didn't come any closer. But he didn't leave, either. "If you thought a bear was coming through the door, why wouldn't you use a gun?"

She opened her mouth to tell him that *of course* she didn't have a gun, but thought better of it. "I don't like to start with shooting. I like to work up to it."

"I couldn't believe it when they told me over at the Mine that some tree hugger from down in San Francisco had actually come all the way up here," the man continued, blissfully unconcerned with his own peril.

Violet lifted the canister higher, thinking maybe he'd forgotten she was aiming it directly at his face. "I've never hugged a tree in my life. Who does that? Have you ever tried to hug a tree? I suspect that there's a bark impediment. It sounds scratchy, at the very least."

"I can't say as I've fully considered the implications of bark and a good old tree hug," the man replied, all drawl and amusement.

Still apparently unconcerned that she could spray him at any moment.

He peeled off the various things covering his face, and she knew who he was. Not that she'd seen him before, because she hadn't. But Violet had certainly seen those cheek-

bones before. It didn't take Sherlock Holmes to figure out
that anyone who looked this much like Quinn without being him had to be a relation.

"You must be Bowie," she said. Because, under duress,
Quinn had actually told her one whole ice-fishing anecdote
about his family the day before. She had taken very little from
the story aside from his younger brother's name.

Unlike his brother, Bowie seemed to have no trouble
whatsoever grinning widely. "Guilty as charged. What are
you doing in the shack?"

Was that a trick question? "What do you mean?"

"It's a little rustic." But he didn't wait for her to respond.
He jutted his chin at her extended arm and the bear spray
she held, still grinning. "I like that you're not taking this at
face value."

Violet lowered her arm and couldn't for the life of her
determine why she felt something like . . . let down. Almost
as if she resented someone coming in and interrupting her
solitude here. *Not quite solitude,* she corrected herself.
*What you resent is someone interrupting your time with
Quinn.*

But everything that lay down that particular road was a
land mine.

"If you came to see your brother, he's out." She lifted her
hand again and sort of circled it, taking in the one-room
cabin with a swipe of the canister. "Obviously."

"You two are really staying here?" Bowie was still
standing by the door, but that didn't mean she wasn't fully
aware of it when his gaze swept over the sleeping area. Two
separate sleeping bags down there in the furs, sure, but they
were awfully close together.

When he looked back at her, his gaze was speculative.

And for the first time, it occurred to Violet that she was
a floozy.

An honest-to-God, inarguable floozy, because she was now embroiled in a *second* potential scandal involving sex.

Still no *actual* sex, sadly enough. But it seemed astonishing to her that she kept having these *perceived sex* situations. She was an unlikely femme fatale, but she'd been forced to grit her teeth and suffer through that hideous meeting with her colleagues in which innuendos had run like wildfire over the conference table. She'd spent most of that squalid hour debating what was worse—that they all thought she'd been *blinded by sex* and *fooled by her sad longings* or that she . . . hadn't, but Stuart had taken advantage of her anyway. Now she was thousands of miles north and her sleeping bag was scandalously close to Quinn's. His brother clearly thought she was using sex to sway Quinn. She might as well wear a scarlet letter.

Especially because if she had the slightest idea how to use sex to sway Quinn, or just to use it, she probably would have. The man was built like a marble statue, but happily not in a manner that could be coyly covered up with a fig leaf.

Violet realized the next moment that she was, in fact, wearing a scarlet letter—because she turned red. Bright enough that she could light up the cabin with it without having to worry about lighting the lantern.

Bowie's question was still kicking around in her head.

"Yes," she said, trying to sound virtuous and studious and whatever else she could think of that wasn't *floozy central*. "We are staying here."

His grin never faltered, but she saw the assessing way he looked at her. "Outsiders aren't usually so hard-core. I don't know whether to be impressed or afraid."

"I can handle it," she said, with perhaps more bravado

than necessary. "Not for that long, maybe. I'm not moving in. I just need to show your brother that I can handle some time in the bush, that's all."

"Oh, I heard."

He turned then, his grin widening again as he threw open the door.

Violet hadn't heard anyone approaching, so of course, Quinn was standing on the other side. He did not look at all pleased to see his brother. Or her. Or at all, but it was possible that was just him.

"What are you doing here?" Quinn asked Bowie.

He laughed. "I could ask you the same question."

"When did you get back?" Quinn asked as he shut the door and stamped the snow from his boots. He tugged his hat and face covering off, and the look he shot Violet didn't make sense. It shook her. If she didn't know better, she would have said he was . . . checking on her.

No one did that. Why would they? She was made of stern stuff and could think rings around anyone and everyone. Still, it made her knees get foolish again. And maybe her face went a little weird, too.

Whatever it was, Quinn saw it and frowned at his brother. "I thought you said you were going to be jumping around Southeast until the Iditarod."

"March is a long way away," Bowie said. "Then I heard a rumor that my big brother was entertaining a woman who wants to get her hands on our birthright."

"Not my hands," Violet said then, because it was one thing to have this man think she was a brazen temptress, prepared to *barter her body* for an easement. But it was unacceptable that he should think she would do something like that for *private gain*. "That would defeat the purpose. I don't think anyone's hands should be on it."

"This is not the time or the place." Quinn shook his head at Bowie, possibly flashing secret brotherly things while he did it. She couldn't tell. "And since when do you care about our birthright?"

Bowie laughed, but Violet wondered if he was quite as amused as he sounded. There was something about his expression that suggested otherwise. "I care a lot about it, big brother. I'm just not as uptight about it as some."

Violet looked back and forth between them. Because there was a little too much perfect male cheekbone architecture for any one woman to take. That was a problem. But a far bigger problem was that she didn't know how to analyze brotherly interactions. Men were a mystery to her at the best of times—like professional interactions or what she'd foolishly thought was a romance with Stuart. After all, there had been a kiss. But the brotherly thing was even more opaque. She couldn't tell if they were the best of friends or if they wanted to kill each other.

She thought she might as well ask. So she did.

And found two pairs of intense midnight eyes staring back at her.

"Both." Quinn sounded faintly offended at the question. "Obviously."

"Normally I fall more in the want-to-kill-him camp," Bowie said with great cheer. "But then I think about what that would mean. For me. If I offed Quinn, I'd have to take over some of the duties that make him so boring. And I don't do boring."

"Bowie claims to run a charter air service," Quinn told Violet, while he stood by the door with his arms crossed and thunder all over his face. Which in no way dimmed his growly beauty, she couldn't help but note. "But mostly that means he likes to see how much he can tempt fate."

"It's not fate I'm worried about," Bowie drawled. "The

Alaskan weather, on the other hand. Well. That's always the real challenge."

"I would have thought the fog would keep you grounded," Quinn said. "Why didn't it?"

"The weather was fractious, I won't lie. But when I heard the news I had to come home to see for myself."

They both looked at Violet, who started. Because, like the floozy she apparently was now, she'd been contemplating the incontrovertible evidence that splendid abdominals were apparently a genetic gift to the Fortune family. *A fortune indeed*, she thought.

But Bowie's words penetrated the red flush consuming her. "Wait. I'm the news?"

"I'm afraid so." Bowie sounded amiable, but there was still that cool assessment in his gaze, a counterpoint to his grin. "It's the most excitement we've seen in Lost Lake since old Beatrice Fox formed herself a streaking club."

"Violet," Quinn said then, a considering sort of look on his face. "Why are you holding bear spray?"

She looked down at the canister she held as if she'd never seen it before. "I thought I heard a bear."

"She thought I was a bear," Bowie corrected her.

"Looks like she's still on the fence," Quinn observed.

"I can be wily and treacherous," Bowie agreed. Violet watched his gaze move from her to his brother, then back to the sleeping bags, before returning to Quinn. "But you're sure taking that to a whole new level."

"I have no idea what you mean."

Violet thought Quinn's voice sounded strange. Stiff and ferocious. It made her stand a little straighter.

But his brother only laughed. "I think you do."

"Thanks for dropping by, Bowie," Quinn said with exaggerated friendliness. "Feel free to go out the way you came in."

"My brother is no gentleman," Bowie drawled, looking at Violet. "Luckily, I'm not similarly afflicted. My mama raised me right."

"The only thing I know about your mother is that she's good at chess," Violet offered.

"Violet," Quinn began, frowning at her.

But Bowie looked delighted. "That she is. Always thinking six or seven moves ahead, that one. She's terrifying. And one thing she taught me a long time ago was that it's impossible to play chess if you don't know all the pieces on the board."

Violet heard Quinn mutter something, but she was too focused on his brother to pay as close attention as she should have. "I know the pieces on the board. If we're talking about an actual chess set."

"The thing is, Violet," Bowie said, but he was looking at his brother, "you do know that this isn't where Quinn really lives, right?"

Six

❧

Quinn was tempted to pick Bowie up and toss him out the front door. Face-first into the snow, preferably.

He would have, too, but he was busy watching Violet's face for her reaction.

"What do you mean?" was all she asked.

She was clearly thinking it through, that encyclopedic brain clicking away. Quinn wished he knew why he found that so . . . intriguing.

Bowie lifted a lazy finger and waved it around in a circle, obviously enjoying himself. "We like it rustic out this way, but this is extreme." He waited, while Quinn contemplated homicide, but all Violet did was blink. "Quinn doesn't live in a one-room shack, I'm sorry to tell you. He's putting you on."

"Okay, Bowie," Quinn muttered. "Thank you. You can go now."

But he was watching Violet and the crease between her brows. It deepened, she pushed her glasses up her nose, and he could not for the life of him understand why he found these things captivating. How was she driving him to the brink when he could tell she wasn't even trying?

"Putting me on?" she asked. "In what way?"

Bowie leaned back against the wall like he was settling in and did not appear at all fazed by the way Quinn was glaring at him. "This little old shack is a monument to the great and glorious Fortune past. Quinn, in many ways the self-appointed lord mayor of our small community—"

"Not self-appointed. Actually appointed. By virtue of my birth, as you are well aware."

Bowie shrugged that off. "Whatever. Quinn, *by virtue of his birth*, is filled to the brim with all things family in specific and Lost Lake in general, but even a martyr of his caliber draws a line at bunking down in a museum that we usually only use in the summer. Very sparingly."

"Unlike some people, I have responsibilities," Quinn bit out. "I'm not a martyr."

"Of course not. You just like to carry that cross around with you, no big deal." Bowie focused on Violet again. "He has a decent cabin about a mile away. This is . . . some kind of reality show, I guess?"

Quinn expected her to flush again now, the way she sometimes did. To look embarrassed that she'd been tricked, which was a reasonable reaction. He'd been dreading this moment of truth, because when he'd set out to fool her, she hadn't been *her*, had she? Not the way she was to him now. She'd been nothing more than the only Outsider foolish enough to actually track him down where he lived. Foolish or brave—that was the question.

He'd been asking it ever since they'd gotten here and he still didn't have the answer.

Because he didn't think he was going to get over it any time soon, the way she'd tilted back her head outside as if she'd wanted the aurora to sweep her away. She had spread out her arms as if she were already falling, tumbling off the snowy crust of the earth beneath her feet and flinging herself into the heavens.

Or inside, later, when she'd lain down in their little pallet, whispered his name, and then fallen asleep with her arms still outstretched on either side, still waiting to take flight.

Maybe the only fool around here was him.

Violet was still processing what Bowie had told her, clearly. It seemed to take her a very long time to turn her frown from Bowie to Quinn. "This isn't your actual house?"

"In a sense, it is my house."

Because the shack belonged to the entire Fortune family.

"No," Bowie said. "It's not. If you mean his house in the sense of, you know, the one where he actually lives. Because maybe you've noticed, this place is really, really small. And remote. And completely off the grid."

Violet adjusted her glasses. "I thought small and remote and off the grid was the point. Isn't that why you all live out here?"

"I promised her an authentic experience in the Alaskan bush, Bowie," Quinn said. Tersely. "I didn't promise her that it would be in my home."

"That's true," Violet agreed. "You didn't."

"I come to you today as a giver of truths," Bowie said, with his usual fatuous grin. Quinn reminded himself that they were grown men and he really probably shouldn't attempt to wipe it off his little brother's face the way he would have if they'd still been kids. But Bowie must have sensed his peril. "Don't shoot the messenger."

"Are you actually delivering a message?" Quinn asked, his voice hard. "Because as far as I can tell, you flew over, saw smoke where you didn't expect to see it, and decided to come make trouble."

Bowie inclined his head, meaning Quinn's assessment was correct.

Violet was no longer frowning at either one of them. "I'll be honest with you. I just assumed this was the standard off-the-grid, frontier experience. All lanterns and outhouses."

Quinn nodded. "It is. More or less."

"There's off the grid and then there's off his rocker," Bowie chimed in. "And this is pretty much the latter."

"Right. You can go now."

Quinn took a step toward Bowie, who must have read more murder on his older brother's face than usual, because he laughed. Then raised his hands in mock surrender. "I'm going, I'm going. But I actually am here to deliver a message, believe it or not. Mom wants to meet this Outsider you've hidden away out here before she runs screaming back to the Lower Forty-eight."

"I don't run," Violet said. "Or scream."

But Quinn glared. "Too bad."

Bowie rolled his eyes. "I'll let you deliver that response in person, assuming you have a death wish."

As Quinn did not, in fact, have a death wish, he could only seethe.

Bowie smiled. "Tonight. She said you're deliberately ignoring your radio."

Quinn shot a look at Violet, who was still frowning—no doubt over the running-and-screaming comment—but had yet to turn the spectacular shades of red or pink he was pretty sure would signal temper. Or shame, maybe, if she was embarrassed at being tricked. He wasn't sure he'd be able to handle that last one. Not if he'd been the one who put it there.

But at the moment, only her clothes were pink.

He glowered at Bowie. "If I'm deliberately ignoring my radio, you can be sure I have a reason."

"I'll tell Mom that I delivered her orders in person, then," he replied, smirking. "You're welcome. And enjoy the fallout of your little game."

And since Bowie had always liked himself a good exit, he nodded at Violet and then let himself out. Letting the cold rush in and the door slam heavily behind him.

Leaving the two of them alone once more. In the shack that seemed a whole lot smaller than it had before.

Quinn braced himself for Violet's reaction. "I wasn't deceiving you. Not really."

And there were any number of ways she might react. Maybe she would yell at him. Maybe she would try to use that bear spray on him. Maybe she would get truly emotional, and then what would he do?

What he didn't expect was for Violet to throw her fists in the air with a whoop.

The universal sign of victory, if he wasn't mistaken.

She took her time dropping her arms, and she beamed at him when she did. *Beamed* at him, as if she'd never been more delighted.

"You did not expect me to be this amazing, did you?" she demanded happily. "You expected to snap me like a twig. You made snide comments about pink clothes, you thought a shack would break me, and yet here we are. I'm not broken and I'm pretty sure you owe me that beer."

Something in him thumped hard. A current of heat wound around and around inside him, pulling tight. "I wouldn't get ahead of myself."

"I didn't realize this was a real challenge," she was saying, as if she was marveling out loud. Which was good, because he had no idea how to respond to this. Not when he'd expected angry tears and maybe a stamped foot. "I thought this was just some of that Arctic mountain man stuff. Prowling around and taking pride in how hard everything is here."

Quinn probably should have objected. He didn't know what *Arctic mountain man stuff* was, and he certainly didn't *prowl*. "It is hard here. That's why mostly, no one really lives here."

But she wasn't paying any attention to him. "Although to tell you the truth, it all makes a lot more sense now. How did you get my email in order to ignore it in a shack without a computer—or any power? Where are all your clothes? Your *things*? It's one thing not to have any entertainment and another not to have a life. I was thinking you were a strange sort of Alaskan monk, baptism by snow and what have you. And who am I to judge how someone else lives? I was observing the hardship, but it's much more fun that it was a challenge all along." She smiled again. With far too much satisfaction. "A challenge that I dominated."

Quinn felt like he had whiplash. He'd woken up this morning to find her sprawled over him in a way that he should have discouraged. Right from the start. The fact that he hadn't—and that, if he was honest, he looked forward to all the creative ways she'd wind herself around him in her sleep—was a problem. Everything about Violet was a problem and nothing about this situation was solving it.

She didn't seem overwhelmed in the slightest. On the contrary, she'd seemed remarkably comfortable in the shack from the start. She'd accepted it all. The outhouse, no water, eating dinner by lantern light, sleeping on the floor . . . Violet had seemed to adapt without a hitch.

It was tempting to imagine that she belonged in a place like this. With a man like him.

Only he knew better. He'd learned that lesson the hard way once already. Like every other Outsider he knew, Violet wanted something from him—but that didn't mean she wanted *him*. If there was a fool in the room, Quinn knew it wasn't her.

And besides, she knew she wasn't staying here. This was temporary. Anyone could do anything if they knew it had an end date. That was how he'd made it through all his years of school away from here.

He'd left her sleeping this morning because he'd needed to get his head on straight and that wasn't likely to happen when he could reach out and touch her. He'd hiked the mile back to his real cabin and had reminded himself, the way he always did, who he was. What he was doing. That he was lucky to have a purpose to his life the way his ancestors had before him. He was a Fortune.

Not only a Fortune, but as his brother had said, the unofficial mayor of Lost Lake with the law degree to prove it.

It didn't matter that Violet was pretty. That she listened to him and seemed fascinated by the smallest things, like every last mundane detail of life here. He liked all of that about her, sure. But that didn't make her suited for Alaskan frontier life.

And he shouldn't have been considering that train of thought in the first place when he knew she wasn't here to stay.

He'd seen his brother's plane fly overhead, and he'd known his time with Violet was coming to an end. Because they all lived out this way because they liked the peace and the ability to do as they pleased. Except when they could meddle in each other's lives.

He'd known exactly what Bowie was going to do.

What he hadn't anticipated was Violet's reaction.

As he watched, she began to dance around the cabin, fists in the air again.

Everything about her was soft and ridiculous. And he wanted her bad, all the same. Beneath him. Above him. However she wanted his hands on her would do. "Looks a lot like a premature victory dance to me, darlin'."

"Nothing premature about it," she replied, almost like she was singing. "I'm an Alaska natural. Just like I told you I would be."

"It hasn't been a week, Violet. This is the interior. When the weather changes, it changes fast."

And the same went for people's feelings about the place, particularly when they weren't from here. He knew about that firsthand.

Violet stopped her little dance, and that was too bad. He could have watched her do that all night. He would have liked to watch her do it naked. She faced him then, flushed and happy and pretty clearly drunk on her own success.

She made his chest hurt.

She made him want her in more ways than one, and that was nothing short of dangerous.

"It seems to me the primary barrier to spending time here is the weather," she told him, readjusting her glasses before they slid off her nose. And she sounded like who she was. An uppity professor who spent far too much time with her nose in a book. "Obviously, I have that handled. Up to and including trips to the outhouse in the middle of the night when I don't even want to know how far below zero it is. My hypothesis is that it could be a week, it could be a month. Hell, it could be a whole season. I'm not afraid of Alaska, the end."

"You thought my brother was a bear, Violet."

"Bears have teeth and claws and consider humans food.

Or they could. Weather is just weather. It doesn't want to eat you, it just doesn't care if you die." She waved a hand. "Totally different."

"I think this is another example of your mouth writing checks your body can't cash."

"Says the man who's afraid to go to his mother's house for dinner."

Quinn didn't know he'd moved until he found himself across the room, standing much too close to her. And she wasn't backing away.

He was far too aware of her. That was the trouble. Every single breath she took. The peppermint-scented all-purpose soap she'd used to wash her hair today. The way those gold-mine eyes danced, too bright for a dark winter like this one. Too bright for a man like him, constitutionally incapable of walking away from things that shined.

"You think you can last the winter?"

He shouldn't have asked her something like that. The point of this was not to discover that she liked it here, but to convince her that she didn't. To get her to run screaming from the state and never return—or send him any more proposals. When did he lose sight of that?

"I know I can make it through the winter," Violet assured him, with all the confidence in the world. All of it unearned, and he was astonished she didn't seem to know that. "Even if you feel you need to keep me here in this shack, for whatever nefarious purposes you have yet to disclose to me. It doesn't matter to me."

"You think this is about the shack." And it was an act of supreme will not to simply stand where he was, looking down at her and marveling at the way she could radiate defiance and delight all at once. And that confidence he wanted nothing more than to taste. "But it doesn't matter where you spend a winter in Alaska. It's a winter in Alaska.

The dark is relentless. The cold is worse. It's not a sprint, darlin'. It's a long, grueling marathon."

"And let me guess. I'm much too pink and fluffy for a marathon."

"You said it."

"As it happens," Violet said loftily, "I quite like a marathon. Or I would. If I ran."

"You wouldn't make it to the first mile marker."

"What if I do? Would you listen to my proposals then? With or without that beer?" When he only shook his head, she smiled. "I'll remind you that you didn't think I'd make it through that first hike."

And that was how Quinn found himself agreeing to extend this foolishness—and making it worse by taking her home—when that hadn't been his original plan at all.

Though he took a roundabout route.

"If you're staying for the winter, you might as well see the lay of the land. So you can get a sense of what you're signing up for." He laughed as he loaded her up onto his snow machine. "Excuse me. What you've already signed up for, full speed ahead, in a manner that a casual observer might call reckless."

She sniffed from behind her scarf. "I think you'll find it's not reckless to know yourself well."

He took her on a tour along the lakeshore, pointing out the different cabins that made up this part of the lake. The best part, in his opinion. Starting with his private inlet, then across to where Bowie and Piper lived. Bowie in the cabin he'd built alongside the hangar for his planes, and Piper up closer to their parents' place in what she liked to call her cottage and its makeshift greenhouses.

Finally, he rode them into the compound where he'd been raised.

"You might as well get the initial meeting over with

now," he said as they both climbed off the snow machine in front of the main house. "Far better chance of enjoying your dinner that way."

"My favorite thing about the people I've met in Alaska so far," Violet told him in a confiding sort of way, "are all the veiled threats embedded into everyday conversations."

"There's no veil," Quinn assured her.

But she only laughed.

He took her up the steps of the big house, pointing out the various highlights of the property. From the generator building, roaring away, to the sauna, to various other little huts and cabins scattered about.

Quinn had always found it beautiful here. He still did, though he supposed that to an untrained eye, it was too rough-and-tumble and functional to qualify. But then, that was what he liked about the Great State of Alaska itself as well as the first home he'd ever known. Nothing was for show. The beauty was the utility. Function over form, because pretty wouldn't keep a man warm through the cold months.

The original house that had been built on this site was still visible as the main part of the current structure, though subsequent generations had added their bits here and there. Mostly they'd taken care of the finishing touches and expanded the cramped parts, so that what was once an expansive log cabin, especially in comparison to the shack, was now something more like a lodge. Nothing pretentious, mind you. But to Quinn's mind, it was beautiful all the same.

He'd spent the summers of his childhood practically living on the wide, wraparound porch, with its views of the lake or the woods laid out before him. He knew every inch of this place like he knew his own body. Every log, rough or smooth, and what each one sounded like beneath his feet, depending on the season.

He led her into the arctic entry, which his mother liked to say was just Alaskan for "mudroom." Then, after they stripped off their outside layers, he ushered her inside the house. Where he looked around and realized he had no idea what his family home could possibly look like to a professional intellectual from California. All he saw were the memories overlaid onto the thick rugs, the wood floors and walls, the pictures on the walls, and the scent in the air.

But when he glanced over at Violet, she was looking around the front hall that led into the rambling family room in that same, spellbound sort of way she'd gazed at the Mine. As if she'd never seen anything so wonderful and, more, hadn't known that such marvels could exist.

She looked at everything that way, Quinn reminded himself. It was hardly meaningful. But he felt a little warmer, all the same.

He led Violet back through the house, to the big, rambling kitchen where he knew he would find his mother. And sure enough, Lois was there, one of her projects spread out across the utility table that lived on the porch in good weather while she muttered down at it. Like it was giving her lip. Not that anyone would dare.

Lois was dressed in her usual uniform of overalls, but with a winter sweater thrown on that she'd likely knit herself. Her hands were covered in grease and oil—she'd clearly wiped at her cheek at some point—and she didn't turn around when they entered.

Not when there were snow machine engines to fix.

"Heads up, Mom," Quinn said. "We have company."

Lois turned then, unsmiling. She looked from Quinn to Violet.

Violet, who had stripped out of her pinkest layers but was still beaming out the kind of girly femininity Lois had always professed to find baffling.

"You know anything about engines?" she asked. She was speaking to Violet, of course. She already knew what Quinn knew about engines. She'd taught him herself.

"As a matter of fact, yes," Violet replied. Buoyantly.

Quinn figured that was more of that wild confidence of hers. He couldn't tell if he wanted to shake it—or bathe in it. "You do?"

Violet rolled her eyes without even bothering to look at him. "My knowledge is more theoretical than practical, but I'm happy to put that to the test."

Lois smiled slightly. "No need to get your hands dirty."

"They're already dirty," Violet replied, holding her hands out. "What's a little grease on top of three days in the shack?"

At that, his mother laughed. "I have it under control. But thank you. Didn't realize professors were much good outside of their books."

"Technically, I'm not a professor." Violet sounded more like she was confessing than correcting Lois—which was a good thing. Quinn didn't like to think what his mother might have done with a correction from an Outsider in her own kitchen. "I have some of the qualifications to be a professor, but I don't teach. I wouldn't want you to have the wrong impression."

"I appreciate that," Lois said, and that time she really did smile.

"That was a test," Quinn told her. He wished he could read the gleam in her golden gaze. He wished he didn't spend as much time as he did thinking about all the colors that made up a woman named Violet and how little he seemed to be able to ward her off.

Here in this house, his failure on that score seemed to echo a little more loudly, laced through with all the memories he preferred to ignore.

"Apparently Alaska is filled with tests." But Violet grinned. "Good thing I'm really, really good at them."

Lois put her wrench down, then wiped her hands with a rag. "I like a woman who knows her own worth."

Violet's grin widened. "Beats the alternative."

To Quinn's shock, his mother smiled again. Making it clear the first time had been no mistake. "That it does."

"I love all these windows," Violet said with the blissful lack of awareness only someone who didn't know how prickly his mother usually was could possess. *She* had no idea that Lois was famous for ignoring new people for whole years, because, she liked to claim, there was no point wasting her energy until they'd lived through a few winters here. "It brings the lake in everywhere."

Lois made a noncommittal noise, though Quinn could tell that underneath her customary gruffness, his mother was not unpleased.

He decided to take Violet on a little tour of the old house before Lois remembered herself and got back to proving her bark and bite were nothing to scoff at. He showed her the banister his grandfather had carved. He pointed out the stuffy old paintings of his great-grandparents that stayed on the walls because they looked so somber it made their descendants laugh. There were the kind of hunting trophies he doubted graced the walls of wherever she lived in la-di-da San Francisco, a parade of embarrassing photographs, and his childhood bedroom that still looked like a fifteen-year-old might turn up to claim it.

"It's nothing fancy, but it's better than the shack," he said when they were sitting in one of the bay windows on the second story, with views that seemed to stretch on into forever. The glory of the lake in winter, beckoning and welcoming, the way it always did. Whether the water was solid or fluid, it called his name.

From the look on her face, it seemed it might do the same for Violet.

Something in him shuddered, deep and low.

"I actually liked the shack," Violet told him, sounding almost shy. Unlike herself. But when he looked at her, she was looking out at the frozen water, her face gone dreamy. Because that was what happened when a person looked out at this much unspoiled beauty. That was what happened when the sun was already going down, making the world turn pink like it was trying to impress Violet specifically.

He reminded himself, again, that this was temporary. Everybody felt called to the pretty places they discovered on vacation. Real life was something else.

Quinn knew that better than most, and that was a kick in the gut. He couldn't remember the last time he'd thought about Carrie. Or maybe he went out of his way not to think about her—but either way, the ghost of his ex was unwelcome.

And unnecessary, he assured himself.

"You were in the shack for a couple of days," he said dismissively. And maybe too harshly. "And not on your own."

Violet, as ever, didn't react the way he expected her to. She turned to gaze at him, her lovely eyes dancing. "Don't worry, Quinn. I'm not claiming that I should lead guided tours into the hinterland, never fear. I expected to crush it because that was what was required. And as I told you, I'm really good at tests. What I did not expect was to like it so much."

"That was an entry-level test. And surviving isn't the same thing as thriving, darlin'."

He sounded as dour as one of his painted forebears. Like he was already halfway as dead and gone as they were.

Violet reached over and punched him on the arm. "If

you could hold off being disdainful of my wilderness achievements for four seconds, what I'm trying to say is that while I really liked the shack, this house is amazing. Just amazing."

She let out a sigh that sounded not only happy, but unaware of the way he was gazing down at the point of impact. In astonishment. It had barely tickled, but that wasn't the point. The point was that most folks were a lot more careful around him.

He'd had no idea how hot it was to meet a woman who didn't appear to be the slightest bit impressed by his whole thing. It made him wonder why he hung on to that whole thing in the first place. *You have responsibilities,* a voice in him chimed in. *But that doesn't mean you have to act like you already died and are currently glowering down from a bad oil painting in the hall.*

Quinn felt something a little too close to winded.

Violet was sitting in his mother's favorite cozy chair in the house where he'd grown up. She'd crossed her legs so she could sit up higher and had her hands wrapped tight around the mug of coffee he'd given her on one of their passes through the kitchen. And whether this was all calculated on her part—the better to get him to do what she wanted him to do with the land and the mine—or whether she really was that captivated with the frigid beauty before her, it didn't really matter. Because her dark hair curled gently over her shoulders, her eyes looked dreamy, and he was . . . stupid.

Stupid and getting stupider by the moment.

She sighed. "You don't know how lucky you are."

"That's where you're wrong," Quinn replied roughly. "We were raised to know exactly how lucky we are. Exactly how much this land means. And the thing about Alaska is that fighting to live the way we want to live here never gets easy. You can never be complacent. This land is tough, and brutal, and it's only when you can handle what it throws at you that you can truly understand the price of all the beauty."

Violet looked away from the lake and settled her dreamy look on him. "Some would say they'd pay anything for beauty."

Everything inside him seemed to seize at that—but he caught himself. He knew she wouldn't stay. He knew it, maybe better than she did. After all, he'd done this before.

"I can't tell you how many people get seduced by their fantasy of what the wilderness is like. There's a whole out-door industry dedicated to convincing soft, comfortable folks in pleasant, boring little lives that if they just buy enough gear at REI, they could take on the frontier with their bare hands and a couple of hiking poles."

Violet, being Violet, laughed. "REI did nothing to con-vince me, personally, to take on the frontier. I decided that on my own. What they did do is make sure I could look fantastic while not dying out here."

He wanted to smile—but that was a sure sign he shouldn't. Their time in the shack had been specifically tailored to convince her to run back down south. He needed to dampen whatever fires were burning here, not throw gas on them.

"I met a girl my final year of law school," he told her abruptly, because he was already thinking about Carrie. Why not share the story where it might do some good? "Native Alaskan, though she spent a lot of her childhood in Hawaii. Half the reason we got together was because we were both fired up about all the ways we could give back to rural Alaska communities, like the ones her parents came from farther down the Kuskokwim near Aniak. She spent

her summers there, running around with her cousins. Together, there was no ceiling to the things we thought we
could do to improve some lives out here."

Beside him, Violet was still. Listening intently, with her
whole body, which shouldn't have struck him as sexy—but
it did. He took the opportunity to stare out the window, letting the lake ground him. Letting the stretch of glimmering
ice in the falling dark remind him.

"I brought her home after we graduated, figuring I'd
jump right in. Marriage, kids, the whole deal. But my father
sat me down, man-to-man, and asked me to give it a year."

"A whole year?"

"My exact question. Except I was ruder." Quinn ran a
hand over his jaw. He needed a shave. More than that, he
needed to get this over with so he could get back to his
normal life. Before he got unpardonably stupid. "I ranted
about how perfect Carrie and I were for each other, but my
father felt strongly about it. And he's not a man to speak
just to hear himself talk." He shook his head, remembering
mostly how young he'd been, though he would have argued
against that at the time. He had argued. "I could have ignored him, grown man that I was, but I was settling into my
new position here. And I figured, what was the harm? If
you plan to be with someone forever, what's another year?
Besides, it gave Carrie and me more time to see how we felt
about the practicalities."

"You mean wedding planning?"

Quinn didn't tell her exactly how funny that was, because that would take a broader explanation of how laid-
back folks were around here. "Neither of us were big on
ceremony. I mean where to build. What kind of cabin to
build. Most of my family is settled on this side of the lake,
but with Carrie likely to want easier access to her family,
maybe it would make more sense to be closer to the Mine

or even down in Hopeless for the river access. Practical considerations."

"I'm guessing that this is a cautionary tale," Violet said when he was quiet for a moment. "Not a lovely story involving rainbows and happy-ever-afters. For the record, I'm not much for warnings. I have a terrible habit of taking them as personal challenges."

Quinn found himself standing, his hands shoved into his pockets. He put his back to the view and kept his gaze on Violet. "Everything was great until it started getting dark that fall. Come Christmas, Carrie went home to see her folks in Hawaii and she never came back."

Violet looked startled. "Never? Not even to pick up her things?"

"I mailed her all her things." Quinn lifted a shoulder. "She never spoke to me again. And last I heard, she's never been back to visit her cousins, either. It's like a taste of real Alaska cured her of wanting any more of it. Forever."

"That's awful. A person should at least have the decency to change their mind face-to-face."

Quinn needed to remember to chase that up, given the dark look on her face, but this wasn't the time. "It hurt back then, but I learned a valuable lesson. Anyone can say that a winter here sounds great. Living through it is something else. Most people can't handle it. Outsiders believe that they can bend the weather to their whims, and that's a good way to get yourself killed in Alaska."

Violet blinked a few times, in a way he recognized meant she was pondering something. When she frowned at him, he figured she was getting his meaning.

"The truth is, most people who want to get their hands on land up here have no idea what they're getting into," he told her. "How could they? Alaska's big. Really big. The terrain varies wildly and the weather is fickle at best. Still, you always hear about some Outsider buying up some land, thinking he's going to live off-grid out here somewhere. Only, best-case scenario, to limp back out after a tough season. A lot of the time, they don't make it out."

"I'll keep that in mind should I take it upon myself to relocate," Violet said, and he knew that note of primness in her voice meant her temper had kicked in.

"There used to be a road up from Hopeless," Quinn told her. "You have to have a road to bring in mining equipment. But there isn't one now. Do you know why?" But he didn't wait for her to answer. "They did it in gravel. Gravel is warmer, so it was always sinking and filling up with water. It was wiped out so many times by the permafrost heave and melt that eventually, they gave up. The wilderness always wins up here, Violet. Always."

"Luckily, I haven't bought any land just yet."

"You haven't," he agreed. "As far as I know. But here's what I have to ask myself, Violet. You seem to have an awful lot of free time on your hands. You didn't know if I'd see you at all when you turned up at the Mine. You didn't know I'd dare you to try a week off-grid, much less the whole winter. Yet you were fine with both. As far as I know, you didn't even make a call. How can anyone block off an undetermined amount of time to go chase down a potential conversation in the middle of nowhere if they don't have ulterior motives?"

"The good news about the kind of work I do is that I take all I need to do my job everywhere I go," she replied lightly, but her eyes had gone cool. She tapped her temple. "I have everything I need right here."

"Maybe you're telling yourself that you're here to talk me into putting our land into a new trust. Maybe you want to get your hands on a mine that our ancestors bled for.

Maybe that's why you came, but I doubt it's why you stayed. You could have kept right on emailing me."

Violet stood, almost gingerly. She placed her mug of coffee down on the table between the chairs, very precisely. Her gaze never left his. "You're not big on answering your email, Quinn. You prefer to issue beer-soaked challenges, then renege on your part when people actually take you up on them."

He wanted to touch her. He didn't know how he kept himself from it.

"There are only two reasons people turn up in Alaska and look like they want to set down roots." Quinn searched her face, looking for a pink flush, but she was paler than he'd ever seen her. He didn't let that stop him. "One is because they've run away from something back down there. Is that you?"

"I already told you I don't run. Unless there are marathons on offer. I like to excel in all things, you understand."

Quinn leaned in. "I think the idea of Alaska's gotten into your blood."

She swallowed hard. "Why is that a bad thing?"

He shook his head. Downstairs, he heard his father come inside, stamping off his boots. He heard the sound of a snow machine outside, and knew his siblings were coming. And it didn't matter that Violet was the only stranger in living memory who Lois hadn't hated on sight.

All of this was temporary. Violet wouldn't stay. No one so soft, like the flower she was named for, could ever bloom in all this icy dark.

She might not know that. She might wish it was different.

But Quinn knew better.

"It's not that it's bad," he told her. "It's that it's only going to hurt you."

Violet scowled at him. "I'm not so easily hurt. I—"

Quinn reached over and took her chin in his hand. He waited until those golden eyes met his.

And he got his face in hers, because he needed her to understand that this was hopeless. That it was doomed. That it could never be anything else no matter how long she stuck it out here.

"Just because you fall in love with Alaska," he told her, rough and low, and he assured himself he was talking about this place and only this place, because what else could he be talking about with this impossible woman, "that doesn't mean Alaska will ever love you back."

Seven

❧

Violet was grateful that Quinn had reminded her of reality—and her purpose here.

Filled with gratitude, she told herself briskly. *Riddled* with it, even.

Maybe if she kept telling herself how grateful she was, it would feel true. Because gratitude was certainly better than all her uncomfortable, unnameable feelings, all of them entirely too messy as they stormed inside her. And, she was painfully aware, really not all that rational.

Quinn hadn't said much after that moment by the windows. He'd taken a while to release her chin, but once he did, she could still feel his strong fingers there as if he were still holding on. Like he'd marked her deep.

She turned the things he'd said around and around in her head when he brought her pack inside, showed her to the sprawling shower-and-bath complex at the back of the house that had clearly been built with extended houseguests in mind, and gruffly suggested she shower off her few days in the shack.

Violet did exactly that. With a certain briskness that was, possibly, a little more testy than truly grateful.

When she was done, and *fired up* with all that gratitude, she found her way back to the kitchen and into the middle of a raucous family dinner.

She had attended any number of group dinners over time, obviously. Her parents liked to throw events and grudgingly included her if she happened to be present. And dinners with her colleagues, no matter how pleasant, varied from grabbing something after a day at the office to convening at conferences, but they were all work-related.

Violet realized as she sat at the long, handmade wooden table in a dining room in the middle of a spirited discussion about the fishing industry, that this was probably the first real family dinner she'd ever had. Because stilted meals involving her angry parents certainly didn't count as *family*.

Piper and Bowie had been there when she'd gotten out of the shower, laughing and squabbling while supposedly helping out in the kitchen. Which had looked to Violet like less actual help and more hanging around. She'd met the tall, broad-shouldered Levi, Quinn's father, with gray in his hair and beard and a quiet intensity about him, and knew without a doubt that she was looking at Quinn's future. Right down to the way his father frowned while he talked, rubbing his hand over his beard as thoughtful punctuation.

Quinn already did that. Violet had to actively keep herself from fiddling with her own chin, where she could still feel his fingerprints.

Sometime after dark the big, brooding man she'd last seen at the bar in the Mine appeared, exuding the kind of watchfulness that Violet associated with the military men she'd met in the course of her work at the Institute. He introduced himself as Noah, studied her a little too intently for comfort, then went to have a beer with Bowie.

Everyone seemed to join in on the cooking and when it was done, they brought out dish after dish, filling up the table before they settled down and settled in.

And it took Violet a while to realize that the purpose here wasn't to eat the food, as hearty and delicious as it was. It was everything erected around the food. The funny stories that Bowie told about the places he flew and the stunts he pulled all over Alaska. The way Piper talked about her plans to build a pioneer empire from her cottage, waving away her older brothers' skepticism with a long-suffering air. It was Levi and Lois, who sat catty-corner at one end of the table, held hands when they weren't eating, and often finished each other's sentences. Noah, who certainly wasn't as chatty as the rest, but whose shoulders seemed to bear a little less weight the longer they all sat there.

It was the way even Quinn laughed, like it was something he did freely only here.

Violet had always dispassionately concluded that the family dinner was a myth perpetrated by television shows. That no one really engaged in it outside of the holidays. She thought it was one more way that the myths people were force-fed were used to beat themselves up. Because if she really believed that out there, somewhere, people were settling in around tables groaning with food for the sheer purpose of enjoying each other's company, then what? She might start viewing a life shared only with a rabbit named Stanley as somewhat lonely. She might even reflect on the bitterness that had always marked her interactions with her mean-spirited parents and find it all a bit . . . unbearable.

And who wanted to feel that their life was lonely and unbearable? She had gone to a lot of trouble to make sure she didn't, but this dinner was making that hard.

It wasn't that the Fortunes agreed on everything. They clearly did not. Bowie and Quinn poked at each other, each grinning when they got a rise out of the other. They both liked to needle Piper, who often returned the favor. And she was the only one who seemed to get a rise out of Noah. Levi appeared to be a huge fan of asking provocative questions, then sitting back, clearly entertained, while everyone else argued the point. Lois, by contrast, seemed to prefer selective directness like a sledgehammer.

Each and every one of them, to Violet's mind, was an intense personality in their own way. Taken altogether, this dinner should have been a war zone. But instead, there was more laughter than fighting. As if the squabbling and debating were part of the laughter, really. And it occurred to her that there was another difference between these people and any of the other families she'd observed. The Fortunes seemed to know each other on a much deeper level than most. When Violet had been given to understand that it was typical in families to feel as if everyone you happened to be related to was a complete stranger.

It wasn't until dinner was cleaned up and everyone wandered into the big, comfortable living room—deep couches and endlessly cozy leather chairs arranged around the big stone fireplace—that she got it. There was no television in this room. No one seemed anxious or antsy. Instead, they just . . . sat around and talked.

She kept expecting someone to end it, but no one did. And then, suddenly, it was like a light going off inside Violet. This is what the Alaskan winters did. It created closeness in isolation. This family knew one another far better than their average suburban counterparts, who were forever juggling distractions.

This far away from everything, there weren't any distractions.

There was only family.

Something in her went a little seismic at that. She couldn't

have said what it was, only that she suddenly thought
that she would rather die than let anyone in this room—but
especially Quinn—see anything on her face but polite interest.

And that gratitude.

"You don't seem to have a lot to say for yourself," Lois
said then, cutting into Violet's lightbulb moment.

The way everyone turned and stared at her, it was clear
that she was supposed to be cowed by Lois and her directness. She wasn't. But then, even if she had been, she would
have hurt herself to pretend otherwise. Violet beamed at the
gruff older woman.

The Fortunes might have learned how to nurture their
roots and let them get and stay tangled. But all the lessons
Violet had learned in the battle zone of her parents' endless
war involved disarmament.

"I have a lot to say for myself, actually," she replied easily. "But I don't know that I have anything to prove. So I'm
perfectly happy to wait and speak only when necessary."

"I see. One of those *I don't care what anybody thinks
about me* types?" Lois nodded, but her gaze was a little too
canny for comfort. "Those come in two stripes, as far as I
know. One version cares a lot but pretends she doesn't, usually because she's hiding something. The other is lying."

Violet thought about the Institute then. Her friends and
colleagues, and how disappointed they'd all been with her
and her scandalous floozy ways. That was why she was
here, after all. "I don't pretend I don't care what others
think about me. I do. And I have to think anyone who
claims they don't has probably alienated everyone already."

The rest of the room had gone quiet, but Violet kept her
gaze on Quinn's mother. Like her children, she had deeply
compelling eyes and dark hair. She had changed for dinner,
into a pair of jeans and another cozy-looking sweater. Un-

like Violet's mother, who was terrified of aging and fought it at every turn, it looked as if Lois Fortune welcomed her years. She had the kind of lines on her face that could only come from laughter, not sorrow. And the look she trained on Violet was steady.

More directness that Violet bet most people found intimidating but she found refreshing. Especially after a few rounds with Quinn.

"Word is you think you have better ideas about what we can do with what we own than we do," Lois said. Conversationally.

"Way to go right for the jugular, Mom," Bowie said, but not in a chiding way. More like he admired her for it.

Violet laughed and the sound echoed around the big room. All around, everyone was focused on her with varying degrees of intensity. Was this the reason Bowie had come to the shack this morning? To make sure she showed up for her third degree?

Handy, then, that she was more than happy to have this conversation. She'd trekked all the way into the Alaskan bush, in January, to have this conversation.

"Glad you think it's funny," Quinn said from beside her on the couch, not exactly hostile. But not brimming over with friendliness, either. "I can tell you, darlin'. We don't think it is."

"I'm sorry." Violet tried to school her expression. "I was laughing at the notion that any idea I had could contradict yours. The truth is, nobody knows what you all plan to do with this area. The land and mineral rights haven't been allocated to the Native corporation in this region because, unusually, you all own both. You have that gold mine. There are no shortage of outside companies that would love to come in and see if they could find more gold than the original miners here did, and all of them have been attempting to cozy up to Quinn for years. I'm sure I don't have to tell you the environmental consequences if you were to hand over your rights."

"We know the environmental consequences," Quinn replied, in that same impenetrably stern manner. "We live right here in the actual, local environment."

"Seems like the major consequence folks like you don't want to consider is money," Levi added. "Real easy to sit in places like California and fill up on opinions about how other people should handle their money. Maybe you haven't noticed, but folks up this way live pretty close to the bone. If we lived in cities, they'd probably call us poor. Dirt poor. Could be that the money the land could bring in could make things a whole lot easier for us."

"Plus jobs," Noah said in his low, deliberate way. "People here aren't afraid of hard work. They just don't get the opportunity to do much of it so far from the city. Could be this is a chance to change that."

After the conversation over dinner, Violet knew that when the Fortunes said *the city*, they meant Anchorage.

"I didn't know I was going to get to have this conversation tonight," Violet said, brightly enough. "You have to give me a minute to shift gears. I was told I needed to have a beer in my hand in Quinn's favorite bar in order to discuss these things."

"Quinn is the one who gets to make the decisions." Piper smiled with a sweetness Violet didn't quite believe. "There are four families who stayed here and banded together to buy the surface and the mineral rights from the mining company. They made it so the oldest in each new generation takes on the leadership role for the community. That way there can be no fighting for the position. But he has to base those decisions on our collective opinions, you see. We come to a consensus or everything remains as is."

"You're welcome to your opinion, Piper," Quinn rumbled at her. "Like anyone."

"Vote's coming up," Bowie drawled—but this was clearly not news to anyone in the room except Violet.

"They have a big meeting every quarter," Noah told her. "Everyone with a stake in the land, so the Fortunes, the Saskins, the Barrows, and the Foxes. They fight about everything and then, somehow, agree in the end."

"They? Not you?"

"I'm a transplant. I can observe and comment, but I don't get a vote."

"Marry one of those Saskin girls and you can vote to your heart's content," Lois advised him. Though Violet noticed she was looking at Piper.

"Not the marrying kind," Noah replied, easily enough.

And that time no one looked at Piper, but it seemed more pointed, somehow.

"Shifted those gears yet?" Levi asked Violet, genially enough. Just in case she'd imagined they'd get sidetracked.

Violet already had her knees up in front of her on the wide, low couch where she was sitting entirely too close to Quinn. But she couldn't let herself concentrate on his proximity—and certainly not in the presence of his family. She wrapped her arms around her knees now as she went into full work mode. It was something of a relief after what she'd been doing all night, which was attempting to parse all the *feelings* inside her.

Feelings that were not gratitude, despite her best efforts.

"I know that selling what you have and allowing new gold mining must make a lot of sense," she said, and though she would have started off like that anyway, she meant it more than she had when she'd practiced this sort of speech on the plane. It was different now that she'd actually come to Alaska. Now she actually knew some of the people involved. But she shoved that aside and went back to her script. "It's a lot of money and it could change people's lives. I'm not denying that. My argument is that the money from selling would be a finite gift to this community."

Someone cleared their throat, but when she looked around, all she saw were these people she'd shared a meal with . . . listening to her. Not jumping in to argue with her. Not distracted by their phones or computers. Just listening. It felt novel.

"Sooner or later, mines tap out," Violet said. "If you did sell, do you think that the money you all would make would be enough, handed down over time, to allow your descendants to move to a place that's as unspoiled as this? And that even if it was, would you be sufficiently happy with moving?" She thought of her days in the shack and the things Quinn had so grudgingly told her about his family. "Or do you believe that your identity is wrapped up in this particular lake? This particular land?"

"No one can tell the future," Levi said into the silence that followed that question. "Especially not in Alaska."

Everyone else laughed.

"The weather," Quinn said, and she chose not to have any feelings whatsoever about the fact that he knew she didn't understand the laughter. Just like she had been decidedly not feeling anything while sitting there on the same couch with him, now conversant in what his muscled thighs looked like in faded denim. "It changes just quick enough to ruin any plans. That's about the only thing you can count on."

She told herself her mouth was dry because she was too far north in the middle of winter. Certainly not for any other reason. "Conservation initiatives are about preserving a space for the future to inhabit," she said, ignoring the dryness. And the thigh closest to her. And that fever inside her. "Of course no one knows what the future will hold. A conservation land trust establishes only that if what you value is the pristine nature of this land, that will be protected. That's all."

"Why do you care what we do with our land this far from anywhere?" Lois asked. "Seems like California has its own troubles. Why borrow ours?"

"It's not lost on me that it's very easy to have opinions from far away," Violet said carefully. "But it's been a real gift to come here. To see not only why it is that people might love it here enough to be determined to keep it safe from outside influences, but also why a mining company that could bring in jobs and money and even some infrastructure must be incredibly appealing."

Somewhere down in California, she thought, Irving Cornhauser was having a cardiac arrest. He would be horrified that she could profess to see the side of any mining company, even in theory. She would have been appalled herself before she'd come here.

But she couldn't parse through what all of that meant. Not now. Not here on the couch where she was *this close* to Quinn, yet watched by his family from all sides. It wasn't quite the same as waking up in the middle of the night to find herself using his bicep as a pillow—but her body didn't seem to know that. She was much too hot. Everywhere.

"That's a lot of pretty talk," Bowie said with a laugh.

"She's real good at that," Quinn replied, though the look he shot her way made her pulse pick up. "Pretty sure that's why she's the professor."

The rest of the family seemed to be content to study her. In silence.

"I think private land is always tricky," Violet said, though she was straying even farther from her prepared script. But this was the wilderness. Maybe straying was called for. And maybe meeting the people who carved out a life in this particular wilderness made scripts as superfluous as her bear spray apparently was. "Especially in places like Lost Lake, where families have lived here so long and it's a generational concern. Because whatever you think you might be talking about, the reality is, it's always about feelings. Nostalgia. Memories and hope."

There was silence for another moment, and Violet's throat was too tight. Too thick.

But when Bowie spoke up again, it was to change the subject, and after a while, everyone was involved in another rousing debate—this time about a local resident in her eighties who viewed the spring breakup, that being when the ice and snow melted, as a Klaxon call for her to partake in what she claimed was her passion. Streaking.

"I don't care if she has dementia or doesn't," Levi was saying. "What I'd like is to make it through spring at least once without a forced contemplation of Beatrice Fox's privates."

"Dad." Piper sounded scandalized, though she was grinning. "She's *expressing* herself. You shouldn't try to police her self-expression."

"If a person's self-expression hinges on me having to witness it, it's more of a performance," Levi retorted. "And I did not buy a ticket to Beatrice Fox's performance."

Meanwhile, outside, the night was kicking up a ruckus. From her corner of the couch, Violet could hear the wind at the windows and the side of the house, and sometimes down the chimney, too. Later, a check of the weather showed that the snow was coming down hard and the wind was high, making it safer all around if everyone bunked down here.

"Is that normal?" Violet asked Quinn as he led her up the stairs to the top floor. "Suddenly having to sleep over places when you expected to go home?"

He glanced at her over his wide shoulder, which didn't help her any with her temperature-control problem. "When people talk about being prepared here, they mean it. You have to be ready to bunk down wherever you find yourself. You never know if you'll make it home. Weather reports can only go so far."

The top floor of the house had a pitched roof and was divided into small rooms off a small central area. Quinn led her to the room farthest away from the stairs, then nodded that she should go inside.

"Wow," Violet said when she walked to the door and peered in. It was a cozy room, with a bed on one wall, a thick rug beneath, and prints of flowers on the wall. "A hot shower, a great dinner, and an actual bed to sleep in? I feel like a princess."

Quinn only shot her a dark look. "I'll get you your pack."

Then he stalked away, as silent as ever.

Violet caught herself as she stood there, staring after him. *Enough.* She went and sat on the bed, trying to look out the little porthole window, though there was nothing to see but the dark.

She didn't know what she was doing. She was still a mess of feelings and she had no idea what to do with any of them. Violet had thought, earlier, that she ought to have felt like herself again as she talked about the very thing she had come to Alaska to discuss . . . but she hadn't. Conservation of pristine land. She hadn't even gotten to the preservation arm of her proposal, which involved applying for a historic designation for the mine itself, like the abandoned Kennecott Copper Mine to the south and east. Instead, she'd found herself hyperaware of Quinn. The way he looked at her or didn't. Whether his muscled thigh looked tense. What his voice sounded like when the conversation moved on and whether that gruffness she heard meant he wished he'd left her marooned in the shack . . .

Though the truth was that even in a room filled with others, it had still felt to Violet as if the two of them were on their own in that one-room cabin. He was that . . . *big*. It was as if there were no other oxygen around when he was beside her.

And that wasn't even getting into the story he'd told her about his ex.

Or all those tangled feelings that were in no way *gratitude*. Violet hadn't wanted a lecture on how she didn't belong here. She hadn't wanted to hear that yet one more thing in this world wasn't going to love her. It had felt like a deep betrayal that he'd said those things to her with his hand on her.

When she'd dreamed of his hands on her, but not like that.

She jolted when the door opened again and Quinn came in, carrying the pack she'd left in the shower room. He set it down on the end of her bed, too carefully.

And suddenly all she could think about was the bed. And the two of them *right here*. And no matter how many times she told herself not to be silly, that they had slept in one small space together without any ravishment of any kind occurring, it still seemed as if the beat of her pulse took over the room.

You're a child, she lectured herself.

But she didn't feel like a child. She felt like a fully grown woman standing in a small bedroom with a fully grown man, and the fact that she hadn't done any of the things currently crowding her head didn't mean she didn't want to try.

All of them.

Even if his entire family was in this same house.

Quinn was so tall, dressed tonight in a henley that made her want to weep over his torso and the faded old jeans that she had already spent hours appreciating. He had to stoop away from the steep pitch of the ceiling, but that only added to the notion that he was taking over the sky.

The world, maybe.

And his dark eyes seemed fixed on her. Almost like he couldn't bring himself to look away, either.

"Not everybody could hold their own tonight," he said. "You were impressive."

"I told you," she began, though she felt a little light-headed. It was the praise. She was a sucker for a little praise.

Especially from stern, taciturn Quinn, who seemed allergic to it.

"You're good at tests. Yeah. I got that. Still, it mattered to everyone here tonight that you understood both sides." He looked something like grim. "It mattered."

To me. He didn't say that. She added it on in her head, and maybe he hadn't meant that at all. Even if he was looking at her the way he sometimes did, as if she confounded him. *As if he feels affectionate*, something in her whispered, but what did it know? That was probably wishful thinking.

And since when had she been about *wishes*?

If wishes came true, she would have had a family like his.

Violet stood up in a rush. But that was worse. Standing made her entirely too aware of her treacherous knees and their sudden precariousness. And everything seemed breathless. Because the room was small, the roof was slanted, and everything was too close, suddenly.

But not close enough.

"About earlier," she said stiffly. "You don't need to warn me. Really. I understand that you might have confused me for a woman of action in all things."

"I don't think I'm the one confused about what kind of woman you are, Violet."

And she knew that she was breathing too heavily. She should have been embarrassed, but she wasn't.

"I am, as I proved beyond a shadow of a doubt since I got here, *absolutely* a woman of action." She scowled at him and his obvious doubt and that dubious yet amused expression on his face. "But I like to precede any action with research. Copious research. There is no possible scenario in which I would move from my block to the next without *significant* consideration in advance. I would never move to another state. And especially not this one, that sometimes feels like it's on a different planet. So thank you for warning me off, but I can assure you, I'm not planning to sneak back to that shack and set up house."

Something changed on Quinn's remarkable face. And even after an evening spent surrounded by the Fortune family and its collection of operatic cheekbones, his were the only aria she knew by heart. And the song that was his soared inside her.

His midnight gaze seemed harder, but brighter, and it was like a pressure in her chest.

Quinn reached over and hooked his fingers around one of her curls. He pulled on it slightly, then released it.

Violet thought her chest might shatter into pieces.

"Maybe," he rasped at her, "you're not the person I was warning."

And when he bent his head and touched his lips to hers, Violet was surprised she didn't burst into flame where she stood.

But she was fiercely glad she didn't, because she didn't want to miss a moment.

There was the touch of his lips and the heat of it, rushing through her, as bold and ruthless as the man himself.

Then he angled his head, and the flames leaped high.

Quinn took the kiss deeper, hotter.

His tongue found hers, and it made her shudder, every-where.

It was like molten gold, running through her veins. It pooled low in her belly and rushed between her legs, where she seemed to pulse with a shocking need.

She felt . . . greedy.

Pure, golden greed, without a thought in her head but *yes. This. Him.*

Violet surged toward him, her hands reaching for his midsection, which was even better to touch than it was to admire from afar. One of his hands was on her jaw and the other streaked down to grip her hip and haul her closer.

In a thousand different fantasies, it never would have occurred to her that simply feeling the way this man wanted her, hard against her belly, could make her want to sob. She felt hollowed out and filled instead with a sensation that felt a lot like fate.

And Quinn just kissed her, long and hot and deep, as if all he wanted was this.

Their mouths together, the delicious feint and parry of their tongues, told her things about her body she'd never known before.

Things he already knew, she could tell. Things, in fact, she suspected he might be an expert on.

Violet wanted nothing more than to make herself his most dedicated student.

He pulled back, and his eyes looked almost black as he searched her face.

She felt as if she'd been knocked off her feet. As if all the breath had been jolted straight out of her body. And as if, as she came back to herself slowly, it all seemed to fit differently.

Because she'd been looking at this very same recklessly male face for days and she understood now that the things she'd imagined in that solitary cabin had been gauzy and silly. Based on imagination and wonder and books she'd read, not the inarguable physicality of his tongue in her mouth. His big hand on her hip. His need a hard rod against her stomach.

And the overwhelming, inescapable thing she had learned, just now, about Quinn Fortune was that he was real in a way she'd never experienced before.

Not a smile on a screen. Not words on a page or in an email. Not a book or a thought.

He was flesh and blood, greed and glory.

Violet understood she would never be the same.

She felt as if his mouth on hers had torn away a wall she hadn't even known she'd built between herself and the world.

But now she knew. She *knew*. Violet wanted to keep on feeling . . . all of this. Anything. Everything. Maybe she just *wanted*.

"Sleep well," Quinn rasped out.

And in case she thought she'd imagined what had just happened between them, he reached over and ran his thumb along the seam of her lips.

Such a small thing, and yet that same dark yet too bright sensation jolted around inside of her again and it was almost worse this time. Because it was so *hot*.

Because it was Quinn.

He let her go. He turned and let himself out of her little room, shutting the door behind him so quietly it almost hurt.

He didn't look back.

Violet wanted to run after him and tackle him. She wanted to demand that he keep going, that he teach her everything he knew. Because it seemed obvious to her now that she had no idea what her body was *for*. Every part of her felt alive and bright and *wild*, and she wanted to find out what they could feel together.

She went over to the bed and sat down hard, only to find herself laughing, her fingers pressing against her own lips as if she could trap the sensation she still felt whirling around inside of her there.

She laughed until she cried a little, then she cried until she laughed some more, and at the end of it she curled herself up into a cozy bed that felt lonely without him, did not try to think of any kind of action plan or really *think* at all, and drifted off into sleep with his taste in her mouth.

Where dreams of him waited, brighter and hotter than before.

As if he'd done this to her on purpose.

Eight

❧

Kissing her was a mistake.

A terrible mistake, in fact. He'd spent far too much time in the shack wondering how she would taste. He'd told himself—repeatedly—that reality never matched up to fantasy. And that it was just as well he'd never know.

But now he knew.

And there was no sleeping afterward. He'd gone downstairs to his childhood bedroom and glared at the ceiling, knowing she was right there above him. And wishing it wasn't storming outside, because he would have far preferred to throw stones at the moon than to lie awake, reliving every too-hot second upstairs. It would have been more productive, certainly.

So far his plan to scare the soft, pink Outsider away from Lost Lake was not exactly a rousing success.

Quinn eventually fell asleep. Then woke up early. It was so dark that he almost forgot where he was, but the fact that the soft weight of a sweet-smelling woman wasn't happily pinning him to the bed beneath him was the first clue that it wasn't the shack.

And in the next moment, all he could think about—again—was that kiss.

That impossible, glorious, gut punch of a kiss.

He greeted the day, dark outside though it was, by cursing himself out. Fluently.

At which point he figured he might as well get up and go curse the weather that had stranded them here last night. Better to blame the snow. So he didn't have to face the fact that he'd liked sitting on his favorite couch in his parents' deeply comfortable living room with Violet curled up on the seat beside him. Or that he'd also liked what she had to say about land and legacies, without a PowerPoint presentation in sight.

Maybe the real problem was that he just liked her.

But that was a can of worms best left unopened. And unkissed, but it was too late for that.

Dumbass, he growled at himself.

He pulled on his jeans and the henley he'd been wearing yesterday, but he felt colder than he had last night so he tugged his hat on, too, then headed down to the kitchen to throw some coffee on his mood and see how it shook out.

The house was quiet, though that didn't mean everyone was sleeping. He knew that most of his family liked to get up early in the winter so that by the time daylight turned up, they'd been up for hours and could enjoy it more.

Quinn fixed himself some coffee and settled in for an epic brood in the cozy kitchen with its woodstove in one corner, the old couch on one wall, and his mother's collection of mugs from places she'd never been. He liked the view out toward the lake, even if he couldn't see it yet. He could conjure it up in his mind, gleaming and inviting.

He heard a sound behind him and expected to see his mother, but when he looked around, it was Piper.

He took one look at his baby sister's cranky little face and handed her his own mug of coffee, because emergencies required swift action. Only when she took it did he head back to the coffeemaker to fix himself another cup. Easily done on a day like today, when there was power. On the days the generators got to feeling unruly, they had to do it shack-style on the woodstove.

And there were things about living that far off-grid that Quinn couldn't help but admire, like its simplicity, but he couldn't deny that he liked not having to wait for snow to boil to drink his coffee.

A few moments later, Piper sighed, her caffeine crisis clearly averted. She even smiled at him, however faintly, before hiking herself up onto the counter.

"I appreciate you understanding that waiting even one more second for my coffee infusion would have killed me."

"What are older brothers for?"

Piper swung her legs, her heels making a soft little drumming sound against the cabinets below her, reminding him of when she'd been little. Sometimes he forgot that she'd gone ahead and grown up, too. Or maybe he wanted to forget that part because it was inconvenient. When he looked at her he saw the tomboy she'd always been. The overly precocious kid who was so used to spending her time with adults that she'd been outraged at any indication that she wasn't already one of them. His knee-jerk reaction to all things Piper was to pat her on the head—a move that might make her bite him these days.

He remembered what she'd talked about the night before. "You're really going to start selling canned goods? On the internet?"

She smiled at him in that way she did, like she was merely tolerating him. It effectively put his teeth on edge, which he figured was the intent. "Why not?"

"Is there an audience for that?"

Piper laughed. "The worst-case scenario is that I don't sell anything and we have a surplus of canned vegetables to eat all winter. I don't see a downside."

He did. "Will you be sending what you sell from here?"

"Yes, Quinn, I'm aware that you don't like the fact that I might publicize the existence of the place where we live." She sighed. "The truth is, I could issue specific invitations with hand-drawn maps and people still wouldn't come here. It's literally the middle of nowhere. It's our nowhere, and I love it, but let's not pretend it's easy to find."

"I would have agreed with you before Violet showed up."

"No matter how many things I post on the internet, I'm not going to create a sudden booming tourist trade in Lost Lake, Alaska," his sister said with a laugh. "But let's talk about Violet. Why would someone come all the way out here on a dare? That's a whole lot of commitment. Or very, very foolish. You know her better. Which is it?"

Quinn wasn't sure he liked the speculative look on his sister's face. Especially when it connected to the guilt and heat still storming around inside him because of that kiss.

"It wasn't a dare. It usually functions as a brush-off."

"Six of one, half a dozen of another, I guess."

Quinn stayed silent, the sort of silence that usually indicated to anyone else that they should move on. And fast. But his little sister wasn't just anyone. She'd been artfully ignoring his cues, verbal and nonverbal alike, for the entirety of her existence.

"All I'm saying is, you brought a girl home." Her gaze was much too bright. "It's been a while."

It was one thing for him to bring up Carrie. Quinn still wasn't entirely clear on why he'd felt the need to do that. But it was completely unacceptable for anyone else to mention her—especially Piper, who'd still been a teenager the year Carrie had come home with him, then left him. What did a nineteen-year-old know about anything?

"You seem to misunderstand my responsibilities," he said sternly. She was visibly uncowed, but he didn't let that stop him. "Violet isn't the only person who's interested in our land, she's just the only one who actually turned up here. I spend half my life fending these people off."

His sister took a long, serene pull from her coffee. "No one misunderstands your responsibilities, Quinn. Mostly because you talk about them a whole lot."

He wished that Piper were bigger and a guy, like Bowie, so he could respond the way he wanted to. "You have no idea what you're talking about. Not surprising. You're still young."

Usually mentioning her age was enough to set her off, but she only smiled, entirely too calm, to his mind. "I'm six years younger than you. And you are no spring chicken, so."

"I lived in exile for seven years," Quinn gritted out. "*Seven years*. I will not throw away the commitment that I've made to this place, or the time I've spent becoming what it needs, on some . . . Outsider."

The way Piper looked at him just then reminded him of their mother. Too direct. Too knowing. "You should think about the fact that people who've only been as far away as Juneau on a school trip that one time may not be the audience for how persecuted you feel that you got to go off and have an education. Two educations, in fact. Some of us just have to live vicariously through your endless complaints."

"I'm not complaining."

"Aren't you?" She slid off the counter and landed lightly on her feet. Then, with a lofty sort of expression that made it clear she intended to ignore him from here on out, she glided over to fix herself another mug of coffee.

Leaving Quinn with the unusual sensation of being entirely in the wrong. And more, like his little sister had just delivered him a kick upside the head and a wake-up call, neither of which he'd really intended to entertain this morning.

Not when the only thing he could think about was Violet. More specifically, the soft and greedy little sounds she'd made while he'd learned the taste of her mouth.

He gritted his teeth.

But before he could rustle up the right words to apologize to his sister the way he knew he probably should, Noah came into the kitchen dressed in a T-shirt and sweatpants that indicated he'd been in the gym area at the back of the house near the shower room, getting a workout in.

"Thank God you got your sweat on," Piper said, sharply enough to have Quinn glancing over at her, then at Noah. "After all, you ate carbs last night. The world might end if you didn't burn them off."

"Maybe if you got a run in yourself," Noah replied with his Texas drawl, "you wouldn't need to run your mouth so much."

And before Quinn could comment, or maybe choose not to comment, Bowie shuffled in. Already grinning.

"I didn't realize we were having a party," he said.

"Because nobody is having a party, Bowie," Quinn retorted. "It's always just you."

"Look at you." Bowie grinned. "Making grumpy into an art."

"Better than making sheer laziness a virtue," Quinn shot back.

"This is why I prefer to stay in my cottage," Piper said, to no one in particular. "It's blessedly free of all this testosterone."

"But filled with canned beets." Bowie tousled her hair as

he passed and laughed when Piper punched him on the arm. "You're really winning on that one."

"I could try canning your nonsense," she replied, with fake sincerity and that big smile of hers. "Oh, but wait. There's no market for that."

Bowie smirked at her as he poured himself some coffee. "I think you know better, little sister."

"What I know," Piper said then, opening up the cupboards nearest her, "is that it's a family tradition to have pancakes when we're all home. And since neither of you ever seems to remember a family tradition unless it suits you, I guess it's on me."

"Way to get yourself some family martyr points," Bowie drawled.

Noah raised his brow in Quinn's direction. Quinn shrugged. "I didn't realize there were points."

Bowie's gaze gleamed. "I guess it's hard to notice the competition when you're always winning, am I right?"

And it was somewhere in the middle of the commotion, as Piper started mixing up batter and issuing orders to her brothers and Noah while she did it, that Quinn looked up and found Violet standing in the doorway. Looking in on the big, cozy kitchen that featured prominently in too many of his childhood memories to count. A strange little counterpoint to the images of her that were currently dominating his thoughts.

And yet something in him stilled at the sight of her.

She looked beautiful. She was wearing little more than a pair of leggings and a long-sleeved T-shirt—the leggings shocking because they weren't pink and the long-sleeved T-shirt a relief, because it was. The bulky socks she wore looked appropriately Nordic and woolly, like everyone else's.

It took him a minute to realize that something in her

expression was poking at him. He was tempted to call it wistful, and it wasn't aimed at him so much as the kitchen as a whole. He remembered what she'd told him about being an only child, and her parents, and he figured she'd never experienced this kind of loud family morning.

What he couldn't figure was why that made his heart kick a little bit against his ribs.

"Don't just stand there," he told her. And he liked it far too much when her gaze snapped to his. "Pancake mornings around here are an all-hands-on-deck affair."

"Tell me what deck you want my hands on, then," she replied at once, her eyes brightening up with all that enthusiasm that really should have made him grouchier.

But somehow, he didn't feel the least bit grouchy any longer.

Someone turned on music, the old stuff Levi and Lois had listened to when they were small. Eighties rock songs and some folk to get his sister singing.

And when his parents finally reappeared, bringing the cold in with them, the whole house smelled like bacon and syrup and the thick pancake batter that had been their grandmother's recipe.

"Glad to see you still use every single pot and pan we own," Lois groused, the way she always did. But she wore a big smile on her face as she went over to the stove to critique the way Noah was flipping pancakes. "I don't want to hear about food comas when it's time to wash them all."

Bowie slid a cup of coffee toward Levi, fixed the way he liked it, light and sweet. "How's it look out there?"

"Not too bad." Levi held the mug between his hands, a pleased gleam in his dark eyes as he watched his people move around his kitchen. "Storm moved on."

Which meant they could all head home.

Home. The notion of what that meant ricocheted around

inside Quinn as everyone loaded up their plates with pancakes and moose sausage. Then sat where they liked at the table, most of them talking at once. Noah and Piper continued to snipe at each other. Bowie continued to be ridiculous. Lois cracked herself up the way she usually did, especially when joining in on whatever good-natured sniping was going around. And Levi sat back and waited for the perfect opportunity to jump in with one of his sucker-punch questions.

The pancakes were fluffy, the moose sausage was cooked to perfection, and life was good.

And still Quinn found himself watching Violet. The way her eyes got big and wide with an extra sheen as she sat there in the middle of it all.

"Not used to a crowd, are you?" Levi asked her.

She smiled as she shook her head. "The kind of commotion I'm used to doesn't come with pancakes. More, you know, broken glasses on the floor."

"Lois is a thrower." Levi grinned when Lois protested from beside him. "Not afraid to share her temper."

"As you're about to rediscover," Lois promised him.

Quinn wanted to ask Violet some follow-up questions about broken glasses on the floor and the kind of commotion she knew—but stopped himself. She wasn't his date. No matter what response his body was having to the notion of carrying her off to his cabin.

It brought a whole new meaning to the idea of *home*, didn't it?

Not that he was going there.

He reminded himself that he was in something of a drought, that was all. Because otherwise, he would never mix business with pleasure. He never had before.

You've never put that to the test, a voice inside him remarked. Since most of the people he did business with were corporate types who never wore pink, were only enthusiastic about their own profits, always seemed unhappy that Quinn had that law degree, and certainly didn't show up here at the lake smelling like apples and honey.

After breakfast was done, Violet led the charge on the dishes, leaving Quinn and his father sitting at the table together.

"You sure you know what you're doing with that one?" Levi asked, jutting his chin toward the sink in the kitchen, where Violet could be seen attacking the piles of pots and pans with a ferocity that Quinn shouldn't have found so hot.

Especially in the presence of his entire family.

"I wouldn't say I'm doing anything," he replied, hoping he sounded as casual as he intended. "I'm more . . . allowing the bush to do the talking."

"She looks like a wilting flower, but I don't see any wilting. Made it through a few days at the shack easily enough." Levi laughed. "I don't think that I'd want to spend a few nights in January on the floor of that place."

"She wants to stay through the winter. Just to prove she can. But I doubt she'll make it."

"Maybe it's good that she's here. She can bring her case to the collective herself, keep folks from grumbling about your interpretation of offers."

Quinn shrugged. "Let them grumble. That's part of the job."

That was how it had always been done. Back in the day it was Levi who'd brought offers and ideas to the people of Lost Lake, gave them his impressions, and put it to the vote. Just like it was Levi who had told Quinn a long time ago that it was tempting to take the grumbling to heart, but it wasn't personal. *Folks like a villain,* he'd said. *If they can pretend it's you, good, because you can talk them down. The real villains won't bother.*

Normally Quinn had no qualms taking the heat for whatever current villain got the community riled up. But his gaze kept returning to the kitchen, where Violet was talking so animatedly to Piper that when she waved her hands in the air over the sink, suds went flying.

He cleared his throat when he realized his father was watching him . . . watch her.

"I think a few days in Alaska could turn anybody's head." He didn't guiltily look away from Violet. He frowned instead, like she was a problem he was in the process of solving. The way she should have been. "But you and I both know that week after week of winter darkness can wear on a person. I doubt she'll make it through the week. No way she makes it to the end of the month. So I don't think it's likely she'll be around for the vote."

Levi kept his gaze on the scene at the sink, too, though it was impossible to say what he was actually looking at. "Not sure it's part of your job description to take in every Outsider who shows up. You sure it's wise?"

Quinn was 100 percent positive that it was the very opposite of wise.

"I can handle Violet, Dad," he said.

His father sat with that a moment or two. "Seems like maybe the job has some more perks than I remember."

All that heat and guilt and desire ignited inside of Quinn. "I'm not having sex with her, if that's what you're implying."

Levi laughed and clapped his elder son on the shoulder. Hard. "Maybe you should. Maybe that would lighten you up some, because, hear me on this, Quinn. Your role in the community is supposed to be an honor. Not a trial." His gaze was steady. "Not a *job*."

Quinn was still chewing on that later, when everyone was either headed to their own homes or getting ready to take off. He stood in the front hall, stared at the portraits of his infamously sour-faced relatives, and wondered when he'd decided to become one of them. Would his own face hang here one day soon? So future Fortune kids could tell one another stories about who he might have been and laugh themselves silly right here in the Grumpy Gallery the way he and Bowie and Piper had done?

It felt less like an honor and more like a curse, if he was honest.

He heard Violet clomping down the stairs long before he saw her, her pack on her shoulders and that happy smile on her face.

And he wanted to . . . eat her alive, maybe. Kiss her again, certainly. He wanted to shake some sense into her while he was at it and tell her to go home. Maybe demand that she stop smiling all the time.

Because she was an offense to his sensibilities, that was the trouble. All that pink. And that flush on her cheeks that was infused with entirely too much delight.

For everything around her . . . when he wanted it all for himself.

The simple truth rushed through him like an icy wind.

"I don't know how you can scowl like that after breakfast," Violet said as she came to a stop before him, exhibiting the usual complete lack of awareness of her own peril. "That was the best sausage I've ever had and I don't mind telling you, I'm something of a sausage connoisseur." Her eyes were bright with mischief. "I like to know how it's made. Obviously."

Obviously. "In this case, Noah hunted the moose and portioned it out. And my dad made some of his famous sausages." She blinked as if she didn't understand. And suddenly, it turned out he was enjoying himself after all.

"This is the country, Violet. We do country things in these parts. Like hunt for our food."

She nodded, but she still looked like she was trying to take it on board. He figured that was a typical city response to the very notion of a hunt.

His grin felt a little dangerous, but he didn't let that stop him. "Please don't tell me you thought sausage came in supermarket packages, all vacuum-packed and pretty."

But she surprised him. Again.

"I know where sausage comes from," she said with a direct gaze. She shoved her glasses up her nose. "I was thinking that I don't know how to hunt. And in what way it would have altered the experience of eating the food if I did. Or if I'd hunted for it myself."

"It doesn't alter the experience. But it's a good thing to know where your food comes from. If you know what it eats, you know what you're eating, too."

"Knowing where your food comes from is a gift, though." Her voice was soft. Like a dose of pink straight through him. "Having access to that much knowledge about what you put in your body, what effect it has on you, and what to breed or grow differently in another season. There are a lot of people in this world who can't say the same."

Quinn rubbed at his chest, as if she'd gone ahead and swiped at him. Without even meaning to. She headed off to find her cold-weather clothes, completely unaware that she'd left him . . . disarmed.

Completely.

And she was still musing on the subject of game hunting, the acquisition of meat in general, urban-versus-rural approaches to the food supply as a whole, and other such highfalutin things, when Quinn pulled up on the snow machine in front of his cabin.

His real home.

"It looks like a postcard," Violet breathed as she looked up at it with what seemed like genuine pleasure.

Quinn had to face the fact that he'd been a little . . . Not worried. That wasn't right. He wasn't *worried* about bringing Violet to this cabin he'd built himself.

He told himself he was interested in her reaction, that was all.

The cabin was much bigger than the shack, if not quite the rambling masterpiece that his parents' house had become. Quinn had taken his time with it in the first year or two after it was clear Carrie wasn't coming back, when most of the time, things in Alaska got built in a rush come summer because winter was always closing in.

But he'd wanted to get the house right.

Long after he'd stopped missing a woman who hadn't done him the courtesy of saying good-bye, he'd dedicated himself to making this cabin as close to perfect as he could get it. And he'd lived in it on his own, perfectly content.

He didn't want to care what Violet thought of it.

Quinn led her up to the front door and kicked away some of the snow on his stoop before letting her in.

"It's going to be cold for a while," he told her as they took off their boots. Maybe a little too gruffly. "Takes a while for the heat to kick in."

He set about handling the heat and the power, but what he was really paying attention to was her reaction as she trailed after him, turning in a circle to take it all in.

Quinn had attached his shop with a covered walkway off to one side, so he could keep his living space apart from the inevitable snow machine engine on the kitchen table. And he liked a separate, cozy kitchen like the one he'd grown up with. He was a tall man who liked high ceilings, and he'd spent a good long time on the big hearth in the center of things. It was double-sided, separating the kitchen and his comfortable living room.

And despite everything, he was an optimist, so he'd built more than one bedroom.

But in all these years, the only women who'd been inside were either related to him by blood or members of this community who had always been the same as family to him.

None of them had been snooty professor types from the Lower 48.

"This is absolutely beautiful." When Violet's gold-mine eyes found his, they were shining. "If I was going to dream up a winter cabin, this would be it."

That pleased him more than he wanted to admit.

"You're in here," he told her.

He led her across the living room with its deep red rugs, dark brown leather couches, and bookshelves, then into the small hallway beyond. The guest room had only ever been used by his sister, and Piper was the one who had given him an unsolicited list of critiques after her first night's stay. So now there was a queen-size bed and a night table with a light right there, because, as Piper had informed him, no one wanted to get out of a warm bed to turn off the light after they finished reading. *It's cruel and unusual punishment*, she had said. And unlike the rest of the house, it was blue in here. *Because,* Piper had announced when she'd showed up with bedding he would never have purchased, *not everybody is a weird male hermit who thinks brown is a fashion statement.*

Quinn still didn't know what that meant. But he had to figure it was all worth it when Violet smiled at him, looking nothing short of delighted.

"I'm not going to lie," she confessed. "I was expecting

more furs on the floor. And maybe a missing wall. With a tarp, maybe, for color."

"I can be as civilized as anyone else, Violet. If I feel like it."

"I'll make a note."

"We both know that you probably will. Make a note, I mean. I don't think you're supposed to say that if you really will make notes."

"You know it's bad, Quinn"—she shook her head at him—"if you're more pedantic than I am."

He left her then, happy to find that the house was marginally warmer. Sometimes it took days for the place to warm up again, and he opted not to question why he was so concerned about that, suddenly.

Now all he needed to do was figure out how on earth he was going to survive having Violet here, so close, in his own house.

His father was right. He really hadn't thought this through.

All you have to do is make it through the week, he assured himself. *Maybe two. Then she'll be gone.*

Because that was what he wanted.

That was the job. The *honor* was taking this hit before Violet wound up the rest of the community. He brushed aside the martyrdom comments his siblings had made, because what did they know? They'd never sacrificed anything, to his way of thinking. And certainly not for the good of Lost Lake.

Quinn was well on his way to canonizing himself by the time Violet emerged from the guest room.

"We need to talk," she announced, marching over to where he had found a seat at his kitchen table and was considering attaching a halo to his own head.

He paused the self-congratulation long enough to notice that she was wearing a pair of leggings he hadn't seen before and a little T-shirt that couldn't possibly be warm enough. But who was he to tell her to put a sweater on? He liked the view as it was.

But he did go and throw another log on the fire.

"I'm guessing this has something to do with that kiss."

Her head drifted over to one side as she considered him. "Is that considered *one* kiss? I've always wondered. Is it one episode of kissing but referred to in the singular? Or should each shift in angle become a different kiss? Because really, taken together—"

"It doesn't matter how many kisses it was." He sounded dour and stern and unamused, because it was that or he might pull her close for a repeat. "What did you want to talk about? Because if it's an apology you're after, you should know. I'm not much for those."

Funny thing was, he'd been thinking he should apologize. Set them back on track. Keep it distant. But then she'd come out of her room in a T-shirt that showed off all her curves and he'd stopped feeling apologetic.

Violet looked distracted again. "I didn't realize that was an option, as a grown adult, to unilaterally declare that you're *not much for apologies*. Do people in your life actually let you get away with that?"

"I kissed you. Deal with it."

"Deal with it?" She sounded outraged but her cheeks bloomed red, and he liked that far too much to tone down his behavior.

He took his time sitting back down in his chair and kicking his legs out. "Can't change the past. But we can make some ground rules for the future."

"Ground rules."

"The first rule will be no repeating things back and forth," Quinn said drily. "No one likes an echo."

Violet made a small pageant out of adjusting her glasses.

"I think you'll find people love echoes. Or they wouldn't always be out there shouting at things to see if sound bounces back."

"The second rule is no more kissing. Let's get that out of the way."

Maybe it was his imagination, but he almost thought she looked . . . Her jaw firmed. Her frown deepened. Her cheeks stayed red.

"Rule number three," she said after a moment, that gold gaze of hers darker than before. "No more games. All I'm asking for, all I've ever been asking for, is a chance to make my case if I make it through the winter."

Violet waited, her gaze steady.

And Quinn was too aware of the heat between them. The way she'd tasted, the noises she'd made, the feel of her lush form in his hands.

Just like he was aware, even if she wasn't, that she would never make it through the winter here. That it would be a miracle if she made it to the end of next week. She would be safely back home in San Francisco long before February made an appearance, the Alaskan wilderness—and him—behind her as if she'd never come here.

He should have told her that. He should have made it clear.

But he couldn't quite stomach the idea that if he did, he'd hurt her feelings.

"You make it through the winter, I'll let you make that case," he told her gravely, because he wanted her to beam at him the way she did then, all that sunshine and gold. "Over a beer, as promised. I'll even buy it."

Nine

❧

Violet should have been overjoyed that relocating to Quinn's actual cabin meant a return to the modern age. Because he had internet access. And that meant she was no longer cut off from the world she'd left behind.

Was it really only a few days ago that she'd boarded that plane in San Francisco? It felt like a lifetime.

"Great," she muttered later as she glared down at her phone and all the messages waiting for her once she was connected. "This is just *great*."

She had retreated from her deliciously unapologetic host to the admittedly lovely guest room that made her feel like she was at a B and B somewhere safe, if quirky. Instead of *forging a path* through the *implacable wilderness* and/or *battling the Alaskan elements*, Laura Ingalls Wilder–style. A bit of a letdown, really.

But that was nothing next to the cold-water-in-face sensation she felt when she looked at her inbox.

There were two messages from Stuart that Violet deleted without reading, which surely any self-respecting *woman of action* would do. With prejudice. Kaye had sent along pictures of Stanley enjoying his vacation and cuddling up with Kaye's haughty Abyssinian, like the traitor he was. *Then again, maybe being a floozy runs in the family*, she thought.

And she wanted nothing more than to ignore Irving's increasingly concerned messages demanding to know if she'd made it to her remote destination. If only because it was difficult to remember her life, much less what was left of her career, after a few days of sleeping in furs and riding through the snow on snowmobiles. She wanted to write her boss a quick, casual explanation of where she was and what she was doing, but everything she tried to compose fell flat.

How could she describe standing outside in below-zero weather, miles and miles away from any other living soul apart from Quinn, perfectly content to look up at the night sky until she grew too cold? How could she explain to sophisticated and decidedly indoorsy Irving that it was possible not to mind an outhouse?

After her fifth abandoned attempt to write something that captured her experience even a little, she gave up and called into the office.

It was already beginning to look like the light was fading outside Quinn's cabin, meaning it was coming up on four in the afternoon. San Francisco was an hour ahead, but, she reasoned, it was possible that Irving had already left for the day—

But no such luck.

"Violet. Finally." Irving actually sounded as near to panicked as she'd ever heard him. "I trust you've given up on this off-the-wall idea and are even now on your way back to the real world?"

"My trip is going very well, thank you. I appreciate you asking."

Her boss sighed. "I take it you haven't heard the news."

Violet already regretted this call. Deeply. She glared at the blue and white wall before her. "I haven't heard any news, Irving. This is the first time I've ventured anywhere near service since I left Anchorage." That wasn't entirely true, but Anchorage had more name recognition than McGrath. She screwed her eyes shut and tried to sound pious and professional. "You were my first call."

She could hear Irving's desk chair squeak. She could picture his office perfectly, having spent so much time in it, and yet it almost felt as if she'd dreamed it all. Him, the Institute, all of San Francisco, and the greater Bay Area, too. No matter how she tried, she couldn't seem to make what she knew was her real life *feel* entirely real to her any longer. Everything back in California seemed watercolored and airy, like a soft mist that disappeared in the light. While everything here was vibrant. Vivid. From Quinn Fortune's breathtaking kiss to the punch of the weather, the slow drip of the pink and gold sunsets, the glitter of the ice clinging tight to everything.

"It gives me no pleasure to tell you this." Irving's voice was grave, and Violet sat straighter as her stomach cramped. As if it knew, from his voice alone, that he'd gone red again. And that couldn't bode well for her. "But Stuart Abernathy-Thomason has started a rumor, placed ever so carefully in the worst possible ears, that you've been put on administrative leave pending review and potential termination. For attempting to steal *his* work and pass it off as your own."

Violet's head didn't go blank, exactly. It was more that there was a kind of whiteout. A surge of temper so intense it knocked her sideways. Out of herself entirely. When she came back, Irving was still talking, more and more nervously.

"Of course these allegations would be categorically denied if they were ever actually made directly," he was saying. "We have proof of our own research methods, drafts of our paper, and so on. But it appears that your—ah—that Stuart is not actually making any real claims. How can he? He's spreading rumors instead."

"That makes sense," Violet said, sounding as if she were speaking from under several avalanches, far away. "Rumors can't ever really be refuted, can they?"

Irving started to say something else, but Violet couldn't take any more. She felt as if she'd been slapped—and more than anything else, she was furious she hadn't seen this coming. And it was clear to her in the next moment that talking to Irving might send her over the edge, so she hung up.

Then sent him an email, claiming her service up here in the frozen North was unpredictable, which was probably true.

She sat where she was for some time, reacquainting herself with the surge of acid in her stomach that she hadn't experienced in days. Funny how the specter of Stuart could bring it all back. Violet stared down at the phone in her hand and then, gritting her teeth, went into her email, opened her trash, and froze there, her finger hovering over Stuart's first email.

She didn't want to read anything he had to say to her. But she also didn't want to stick her head in the sand and pretend this wasn't happening . . .

Actually, that was exactly what she wanted to do.

Violet blew out a breath. She reminded herself that she was a woman of action, and that making like an ostrich didn't count. She braced herself, then opened the email with a jab of her index finger.

Greetings and salutations,

I'll confess that I'm worried about you, Violet. I
expected to hear from you after our last conversation before Christmas. I know it must be difficult to
face the truth. I shall be here, as ever, to talk when
you feel able.

—S

"No one says *greetings and salutations*," Violet grumbled,
scowling at the phone in her hand. "Not even you, Stuart."

She tried to imagine Quinn saying such a thing and failed.
He would likely punch himself in the face first—and the
very thought of that made her laugh. And then laugh harder
when she tried to imagine explaining to him that anyone
actually said such things in the first place. He would glare
at her. He would say something gruff and surly. And he
would be far more likely to bend his head again and—

Violet sighed a little. And felt warm all over.

In a much better frame of mind, she opened the second
email.

Salve, Violet.

"Because Latin is obviously the only way to get *more*
pompous," she seethed at her walls. "*Salve*, for God's sake."

Please know that my thoughts are with you, even in
this difficult time. If you find it necessary to hole up
and lick your wounds, as it were, I understand. Still,
I remain willing to talk. Only if and when you're ready.
Please stay safe.

—S

Violet had been fooled by Stuart for an entire year. That was an unpleasant truth she was going to have to find a way to live with—though she rather thought that she'd been fooled more by her own creative interpretation of who he was than by him. It was comforting to assure herself that if they'd met up in person during the past year, even once, she would have seen right through him.

She very much wanted that to be true.

But either way, she saw him very clearly now.

There was no telling who else was hidden on the bcc line of those emails. People who would think he was the soul of graciousness to extend an olive branch to the spurned not-quite-a-lover who had tried to steal his work. A selfless paragon of virtue, too good for this world, etc. Assuming he claimed her as an ex at all, that was. Maybe she was the only one who'd ever thought they were dating.

Funnily enough, her stomach didn't react to the idea.

Because if Violet could come back to the Institute with Quinn ready to talk conservation and preservation at Lost Lake, it would be nothing short of a coup. Given that no one had ever been able to get Quinn to sit down for a serious conversation about this land, everyone would believe it had taken some doing. A year's worth of debate and drafting, even.

And why would she bother to steal Stuart's supposed research when she was out here working magic in the pristine Alaskan wilderness? Or anyway, that would be an easy rebuttal to any lingering rumors. Let Stuart make his claims. *She* would return bathed in glory.

First, though, she had to compose the perfect reply to all his gaslighting and insinuating and *salutations*.

Which was not, sadly, an invitation for him to explore a few anatomically impossible positions.

Though she wrote out said invitations a few times first

before deleting them because she was only human. And it was satisfying.

Dear Stuart,

One can only hope that any further discussions are conducted with you clothed, this time, as your naked heaving about was—

She deleted that, too.

Stuart! What a shock to hear from you. I was under the impression that your confession of treachery was meant to stand as the last word—

"Violet," she chided herself. "Concentrate."
She took her glasses off and took her time cleaning them. Then shoved them back on and applied herself to the task once more.

On a work trip to Alaska.

No *Dear Stuart*. And certainly no *Salve*, thank you. She hoped she wasn't quite that pretentious.

Looking forward to seeing you at conference if we don't chat before then.

Brief. Opaque. Certainly not emotional or deranged or whatever story he was selling out there. Open to whatever interpretation he wanted to give it, but then, that allowed her plausible deniability. With a hint of the glory to come.
Violet sent it.
Then she tossed her phone on the bed and went out into

the main room of the cabin, because she was still a little warm and she might as well look at the best view around while she fretted over things she couldn't change back down there in the real world.

Out in the living room, Quinn was sitting on his couch, a book open in his hands. Looking very much as if he spent a lot of time in that position.

Violet's heart stopped. Then started with a kick.

It all felt a whole lot more real than a few snide emails.

Especially when he looked up and met her gaze, all acrobatic cheekbones, unshaven jaw, and eyes like midnight. Midnight laced through with too many stars to count. The kind of midnight she'd only experienced here. Breathtaking. Heart-stopping.

Too beautiful to explain to anyone not lucky enough to see it.

"You all right?" he asked gruffly.

She nodded, not sure she could speak. And somewhere within her, a voice reminded her that she needed to approach the rest of her stay here with scrupulous professionalism, especially with Stuart running around telling lies about her—

But then again, this was Lost Lake.

Real-world rules didn't apply.

Because the real world was so far away it was tempting to imagine it wasn't real at all.

Quinn regarded her for what felt like much too long. Violet was sure he could see straight through her. She flushed, but tried to cover it by going over and standing by the hearth. Maybe he'd think it was the heat of the fire.

She could see from the way his mouth curved just a little, just there at the corner, that he wasn't fooled.

"Let me know when you get hungry," he said.

Violet swallowed. Hard.

"For dinner," he clarified.

And then, as she stared back at him, all kinds of *hunger* storming around inside her, that curve in his mouth turned into an unmistakable smile. Slow and edgy all at once.

She could feel it everywhere.

"Violet," he said in that same gruff and glorious way, "behave."

"Yes," Violet managed to say, with a stab at platonic professionalism that she suspected fell short of the mark. By miles. "Dinner. I'll be sure to—ah—let you know."

Then she stayed where she was as he returned his attention to his book.

Right there by the fire.

And burned.

The next day was market day, Quinn gruffly informed her when she got up that morning and made her way out to the kitchen.

"Meaning you do your shopping on Saturdays?" she asked, rubbing at her eyes and wishing this man could be more like a normal person and wake up of a morning looking like a troll. Instead of a god limned in the light from above. Even if it was more pedestrian electric light instead of a lantern, he blazed with male glory. It was unfair. Violet cleared her throat. "On a prearranged schedule? I'll admit that sounds distressingly normal and not at all what I'd expect from a mountain man hermit sort of person."

She didn't really mean to say that.

Quinn shot her a look she couldn't read, but the glitter there made her warm. "Not exactly."

It occurred to her that the challenging way he was looking at her was a kind of dare to keep asking him questions like that. With the editorializing that didn't exactly help matters. So she didn't.

Later, after a quick breakfast and a round of chores that Violet wanted to do to earn her keep here and Quinn didn't want to share, they bundled up and headed out into another gaspingly cold morning, bright enough to make her eyes water.

It felt like a decade or two since Violet had traveled the whole length of the roughly V-shaped lake, and this time, she had a better sense of the shape of it. Still, she felt like a different person as they headed back. She *was* a different person, she corrected herself as Quinn drove them over the ice and snow.

She didn't think she would hike off into the bush and set up her own off-grid cabin anytime soon, but the very idea of it didn't feel as overwhelming as it had when she'd been reading about it down in San Francisco, her rabbit in her lap. She'd already lived through lantern-lit nights and pounding storms. Nights that seemed to last forever and days that never quite took. She prided herself on the fact that no matter what, she had maintained her calm.

Even if only outwardly.

Well, maybe the bear spray incident with Bowie hadn't been *calm*, but she also hadn't screamed down the tiny cabin.

As far as she could tell, that was what being Alaskan was all about. Stoicism in the face of sure disaster. Or maybe taking what didn't kill you as an opportunity to crack a few jokes. Either way, she was feeling pretty pleased with herself as Quinn pulled up in front of the Mine that morning.

Not quite Alaskan, maybe. But *Alaskan-adjacent*, which felt a good deal like taking the sort of action she'd always felt she could. If pressed.

There were more snowmobiles scattered in the snow today, with the red buildings rising up above them, than she remembered from last time.

"Everyone comes to the market," Quinn told her, following her gaze. "From all around the lake, down in Hopeless, and any of the other communities along the river that want to brave the weather."

Violet followed him inside and she already felt like an old hand at peeling off her layers upon entry. She knew by now that it was wiser to strip off more while inside somewhere. If she planned to stay more than a few minutes, she needed to get out of her snow pants. Because if she didn't, she would begin to sweat. And the last thing she wanted to be was damp when she was ready to go back outside again. It could kill her.

The first thing she noticed was that there were more boots beneath the benches and coats hung up than before. She looked past the entry cubbies and pegs and, for a moment, forgot to remove her own boots because she was too busy staring around at the vast, rambling Mine.

Because it was crowded.

Violet knew that there weren't that many people gathered here, objectively speaking. She'd seen more people on any given street in San Francisco than were currently milling around on these old wood floors, but it was more people than she'd personally seen since Anchorage.

More surprising, she didn't know most of them. She'd begun to feel as if she was practically a citizen of this place because she knew so many Fortunes and had met a bunch of Saskins. Plus Rosemary and Abel from down in Hopeless.

But apparently there were a lot more people in this isolated place than she'd imagined. Certainly more than the twenty she'd been told actually lived right here in the old mining town.

Quinn lifted his chin at her, waited for her to smile, and then left her to her own devices. Violet didn't look to see where he'd gone, because she had some self-respect—or she thought she ought to, anyway. And because all of the stalls were open, all the little shops had people staffing them, and they'd all been replenished so that their goods were practically overflowing. She drifted over to look at some handmade silver jewelry when she heard a sound that was so ubiquitous in her usual life that it took her a moment to realize she hadn't heard it since she'd come here.

An espresso machine.

An actual *espresso machine* in Old Gold, Alaska, on the shores of Lost Lake, where there had to be far more moose than espresso drinkers.

Violet wheeled around and followed the sound over to a bit of counter space down from the diner area. Rosemary and her brother, Abel, stood there, manning a beautiful old espresso machine that gleamed like the beacon of civilization and caffeine it was.

Hallelujah, Violet thought. Reverently.

"Espresso drinks?" Violet asked when Rosemary glanced up. "I have to be hallucinating this. It was my understanding that there were no lattes to be found outside of Anchorage."

"This espresso machine is always here," Rosemary told her. "It's just that Mia refuses to operate it. She says she can't be bothered on a normal morning, so Abel and I have the honors on market day."

"Mia does not take coffee seriously," Abel told Violet. With an intensity that made it clear he, by God, did not suffer from the same deficiency.

"I heard that, Abel Lincoln," said Grand Mia Saskin herself, sliding two overfull plates onto the counter in front of a couple of customers, also strangers to Violet. "If you want to take coffee seriously, you need to move somewhere

where folks are perfectly happy to throw their money away on too much foam."

"Grand Mia had a cappuccino once while she was visiting her sister in Tacoma," Rosemary said in an undertone. "She was unimpressed."

"I like real coffee," Grand Mia replied. "If you can't stand a spoon upright in it, what's the point?"

She waited for the couple with their plates of food to make assenting noises, then marched back into her kitchen. Abel watched until she was gone, then slid the lattes he'd just made before them, complete with foam art on the top.

Violet certainly wasn't the only one wandering around the market with one of the mismatched, oversize mugs that shouted out her allegiance to designer coffee. The cups were rejects from the local potter, a member of another Old Gold family, the Barrows.

"You might think that Camille Barrow makes more discarded pieces than she sells," Abel said. "And you would be right, but don't tell her that."

"Camille is an *artist*." Rosemary smirked. "Just ask her."

After Violet went back to get her third round, delighted that her heart was pounding about something other than Quinn Fortune for once, she carried the giant mug to one of the cozy armchairs and sat. She pulled her feet in their bulky socks up beneath her and wished she'd thought to liberate her guidebook from her coat.

She would have to remember to write all this down later. Because sitting here, watching these people, it became clear that the feeling she'd been having since she'd walked in today was what she imagined engaging in time travel might feel like. As if she'd tumbled back into a different era.

Where people came as much to gather and catch up as to buy things. Like this grand old building, done up with fairy lights that made it seem all the more magical, was like an old-timey market square.

Piper found Violet sometime later, her arms filled with a selection of her canning bounty. She might have told her brothers that she intended to sell her stock online, but she'd confided to Violet that she already did a brisk business here at home. *The fancy stuff,* she'd said while they'd washed dishes. *Everyone here knows how to do their own canning. They think what I do is self-indulgent and hoity-toity and they mutter about it all year long, then come and buy it anyway.*

"I can't believe that everyone gets along so well," Violet said, gazing out at the crowd.

Piper laughed, wrinkling up her nose as she looked around. "Do they?"

Violet waved her mug at the people milling about before her. The man selling custom-cut Styrofoam toilet seats, the better to warm your trips to the outhouse. The mother-and-daughter team in a nearby stall selling carved Native masks. Pottery, jewelry, hand-knitted garments. Piper's canned delicacies. "It seems like everyone who lives within a hundred-mile radius of the Mine is here. Perfectly happy to chat, catch up, and *act* friendly enough."

Piper shifted the weight in her arms. "No one actually fights on market day," she agreed. "It would defeat the purpose."

She headed off to her stall and Violet found herself thinking that she understood all kinds of things differently now. Things that would never have been clear to her back in San Francisco. Not just the weather here. The vastness, the distance, or how truly far away it was. But things like the divide between urban and rural communities that people she knew were always talking about, as if one was inherently better than the other. When it was simply rationing solitude and community in different amounts depending on where you were.

Violet would have to think about that kind of rationing more, and her fingers itched to jot down her impressions—because surely there was a paper there. But first there was the phenomenon of this market day to consider. There was something about this community that made her wish that she was a part of it. The good cheer, maybe, mixed in with a kind of exasperated familiarity. The stories she could hear being told and retold, as if facts were only considered facts when they'd been agreed upon and embellished by everyone within earshot.

She had the strangely dizzying sensation that it had always been like this here. That she could have come on any Saturday in any month, in any year, and found a scene much like this one. Children running underfoot, both benignly ignored and mildly parented by anyone nearby. Groups of men and groups of women talking about subjects she thought groups of men and women had been concerned with since the dawn of time, mixing and separating according to whim and crying children.

Violet felt connected and apart from it all at once.

It wasn't until the crowd shifted and she found Quinn Fortune staring at her, his back to the bar and his gaze intent, that she understood.

This felt like home.

When she had never, ever had that feeling in any of the places she'd lived. She'd been content in San Francisco, there in her little apartment with Stanley and the Institute, but it didn't feel like this. There wasn't an ache and a sweetness to her life down there. She never sat back and witnessed it, reveling in its richness. Instead, Violet had grown so used to never quite belonging that she'd long since stopped trying.

Maybe she had never tried. Not really. Maybe that was a consequence of being shuttled back and forth between endlessly warring parents, never really able to get a foothold with either one of them. She would have said she liked her isolation.

She had liked it. She knew she had.

But sitting curled up in her chair, Quinn's gaze upon her so that she felt as if all of that midnight was tumbling around inside her, she understood that Lost Lake had the perfect balance. All that delicious quiet, out in the wilderness, alone. And then days like this to take the edge off. A rambling, beautifully bright room filled with oddballs and hermits, all of whom preferred their own company but were happy enough, once a month or so, to have a taste of maybe too much extroversion.

Maybe she had to reconsider her ratios, she thought when she could breathe again. When the crowd shifted and she no longer felt torn asunder by Quinn's gaze. Not directly, anyway.

As the afternoon wore on, various residents picked up instruments, or made their own from materials they found lying around, so there were songs. Some that were haunting and lovely, winding through the crowd like regrets. Others were raucous, inspiring dances to break out, sending children to clapping in glee, and getting even the most stone-faced, grizzled old mountain men to tap their feet.

And Violet had spent her whole life in her head.

She would have been the first to say that it was safer there. She'd told that joke a thousand times. But she'd never truly understood why it felt that way until now.

It was easier to think than it was to feel. Thinking was jotting notes toward a future paper, all from an analytical distance. Feeling was looking around the Mine at all these gruff yet welcoming people who seemed happy enough to take her as she was and wishing that she had the right to stay here. And while she was at it, get out there and dance.

Thinking was composing opaque emails to a man whose face she was having trouble picturing, in the hopes of completing a mission to rescue a job that she knew she loved—even if she couldn't quite remember why, just now. While feeling was looking at Quinn, remembering that kiss, and wishing she was truly the woman of action she wished she was.

Because that woman would jump up from her seat, march through the crowd, and claim another kiss, right here. That woman would never have agreed to his silly ground rules, which so far seemed to amount to very little more than her lying awake in her pretty little guest room while her body treated her to a master class in unrequited longing.

Feeling meant only that she had heedlessly, recklessly, gone ahead and fallen in love. With this beautiful place, this remote lake covered by ice and snow, so stark and beautiful it hurt. She had come here because this piece of land in the middle of nowhere was seen as an emblem of the stark choices the people she worked with aimed to influence—conservation and preservation or corporate mining—never expecting that it would steal inside her, take her over, make her bones ache with that same deep longing.

Just like the man.

It was too easy to imagine a life here, not just a vacation. It was too easy to imagine indulging the wonder inside her, and who cared if that made her even more scandalous. Maybe it was high time she embraced the fact that she didn't want a life she'd stumbled into by default, but one she chose. No matter how hard it was.

It was all too easy to imagine making that choice. And

the ease of it felt hard and heavy inside her, like a condemnation and a caress at once, and Violet was shocked when she realized she was *this close* to brimming over into tears.

Less feeling, more thinking, she ordered herself.

But her heart had turned traitor. She dropped her gaze to her mug, as if an espresso drink that reminded her of crowded cafés in all the cities she'd ever loved might save her. When she already knew that for better or worse, she wasn't going to leave Alaska in one piece. It would claim a part of her, forever, and it was better if she accepted that now.

She would go back to the beautiful city by the bay, with its graceful red bridge, its pastel buildings, its chilly summers and blue-green winters. But all the while she would dream of ice and snow, cozy fires, bright warm light against the deepest dark. Green and ghostly auroras in the sky at night and the occasional burst of sun so bright it hurt.

So really, she thought a bit ferociously when she blinked back the moisture that threatened to spill out, gathering herself into some semblance of order, she had a decision before her.

It wasn't a question of whether or not she would leave her heart here. It was *how much* of her heart.

When she found Quinn in the crowd again, she wasn't surprised to find his eyes still on her.

But it helped. It was clarifying.

Because it was time Violet made a plan to get exactly what she wanted here. So that when she returned home, she could regret the things she'd actually done, like a truly scandalous woman might, with a life well lived.

All she needed to do was decide to start living well. With her heart, not her head.

With Quinn.

Ten

❧

Quinn usually liked market day. He liked the commotion. He liked catching up with people, those he liked and disliked in turn. Because he was the closest thing Lost Lake had to a mayor—though he knew Grand Mia liked to claim that title—and for all he liked to act like his responsibilities were a great weight upon him when he was talking to, say, the irresponsible Bowie, it was on market days that he acknowledged that he liked his position.

If only to himself.

He liked hearing opinions. He liked hearing complaints. He liked being the person who everyone took a moment to talk to and touch base with.

"I wasn't going to come all the way up from Hopeless," Bertha Tungwenuk told him, frowning severely as if he'd personally ordered her to come against her will. Then she shrugged. "But everyone wants to meet your professor."

"She's not my professor."

That made the older woman smile. "My mistake."

And Quinn found himself watching Violet more than

was wise, especially when there were so many eyes on him. He told himself he was just making sure his current pet Outsider didn't wander off into the snow and get herself killed.

But that kiss lingered, making him a liar.

"If I'd known professors were so pretty," said Nyx Saskin, a man of prodigious appetites who Quinn had considered a good friend until now, "I might've applied myself a little more to my studies."

"She's a professor," his sister Ruby said from beside him. "Meaning she's smart. So, you know. Not your type."

Which kept Quinn from having to slap down a man who spent entirely too much of his time doing hard labor on oil rigs. For fun.

All three main Old Gold families were represented here today. The pack of old ladies everyone called the Gray Foxes, because they were a set of octogenarian sisters and cousins who still lived in the little mining cottages up above. The younger members of the Fox family, like Maryam and Sylvie, who'd brought a bakery into the mix here. There were any number of assorted Barrows, from drunk Old Harry right on down to defiant eighteen-year-old Victoria with her little toddler.

There were the usual suspects up from Hopeless, like Bertha and her kin. A few folks who timed supply runs to coincide with market day, bringing news from up and down the Kuskokwim. There was food and there was drink. There was music and storytelling, warmth and light to stave off the darkness outside, and in the middle of it there was this woman in pink who had taken over everything.

The strangest part was how little he resented it.

"That's how we did it in my day," drunk Old Harry Barrow crowed at some point, when afternoon was getting swallowed up into evening and everyone who didn't plan to travel this night was getting merry. "If a live one turned up, pack her off to your cabin and call her yours. I didn't think you had it in you, Fortune."

Quinn couldn't really say he wanted to be celebrated by the likes of grizzled, disreputable Harry, who'd run off four wives and counting. The wonder wasn't that they left him. The marvel was that they came in the first place. If Quinn hadn't grown up knowing most of Harry's wives personally, he might have wondered if a spot of kidnap was the explanation after all.

"I suggested that our guest get to know the land before she told us what to do with it," Quinn told Harry, the same way he'd told everyone else. In the steady tone he'd adopted for discussing Violet with his friends and neighbors. Because it was that or give in to the wild and howling thing inside that was far more possessive of her than he intended to admit. "I would have put her up in a hotel, but you know. We don't have any."

"Last I checked, son," Harry said with a canny sort of look and a bark of laughter, "we still have a bunkhouse right here in the Mine. But I'm sure the good people of Lost Lake appreciate your sacrifice, holed up out there. All alone. With a pretty little morsel all dressed in pink."

He might have thought of Violet that way, a bright little treat, but he felt nothing short of murderous when anyone else did it. Especially this anyone else.

"Harry," Quinn said mildly. He even smiled. "If you disrespect Professor Parrish one more time, you disrespect me. She might not make you answer for that, but I will."

The old man hooted. "You seem to be confused, boy. You might represent the land, but that doesn't make you the boss of anyone. You work for us, not the other way around."

And Harry staggered off to help himself to more whis-

key on the tab he never settled, while Quinn was forced to
face the unsavory truth that despite all his big talk about
duty and responsibility, he kind of wanted to get in a fist-
fight with a man who had been old when he was born.

Not a great look.

The crowd had thinned out some when he did another
round through the gathered community and found Bowie,
Noah, and Jasper Saskin over by the big fireplace, trading
boot camp stories and cracking each other up.

"Are we going to hear from the Pink Professor?" Silver
Saskin asked. She was sitting on the couch, vibrating with
her usual tension. Next to her, her sister Amie appeared
sedate as she knitted a pair of mittens. Quinn had always
figured they did that *at* each other.

"She's a guest and she's not staying," Quinn said. For-
biddingly. "She doesn't get a nickname."

Because nicknames were how folks around here claimed
each other. He couldn't allow it—and he opted not to dig
too deep into why he couldn't let that happen.

"Call her whatever you like," Amie murmured. "But is
she going to tell us why she's here? Piper said she wants to
talk official conservation."

Quinn glared across the room in the direction of his
sister, who was standing at her stall, telling a story with her
hands. "Professor Parrish has a proposal, yes," he told
Amie. "But I told her I won't hear that proposal until and
unless she makes it through the season here."

Silver sniffed. "Maybe folks want to hear the proposal
now."

"I don't," Quinn said shortly.

She glared at him. The way she always glared at him.
"Rude."

"It's almost like Quinn was made the representative of

this community according to all the usual customs, Silver," Amie murmured, her calm gaze on her mittens. "And that you've had a chip on your shoulder about it ever since you figured out that you missed that honor by being born two weeks later."

"It's funny that the firstborn is always a boy. That's all I'm saying."

"Is it funny or is it nature?" Amie replied to her sister. "You do realize your entire argument boils down to you being mad you weren't a preemie, right?"

Quinn, who refused to engage with Silver when she leaned too far into her conspiracy theories—that Lois had fudged the date to take Quinn's position away from Silver and other such nonsense—decided that he would rather talk about the military experiences he hadn't had.

And when he grew tired of the tales of drill sergeants and lining up for too many vaccinations upon arrival, he found himself seeking Violet out. She was already under his skin, so why not wedge her in deeper?

She'd moved on from the chair where she'd spent a lot of the afternoon. He wandered in and out of the stalls and shops and finally found her deep in conversation with Rosemary, Piper, and a smattering of Barrows and Foxes by the espresso machine.

A conversation that came to a screeching halt when he appeared.

"You should smile more," his sister told him after a long pause that made him wonder what they'd been discussing. Maryam Fox couldn't look him in the eye. Elsa Barrow couldn't look away. Violet only grinned. "Looming around with a smile is charming. Engaging. Approachable. When you lurk nearby with murder all over your face, it's a little more serial killer. Just throwing that out there."

But Quinn was focused on Violet, so bright and happy-looking it made him feel . . . Well. It was like the breakup each spring, when all the ice finally melted, the rivers ran again, and the world smelled sweet and new.

Especially when she aimed that smile at him, with so much of that easy light of hers that he forgot to be horrified by his own urge toward terrible poetry.

"Are we leaving?" she asked him.

Quinn had spent the better part of the day sternly disabusing everyone who came near him of any notion that he and Violet were together. But he liked it when she said *we*. Even though he knew better. Even though he already knew how this would end.

Even though they hadn't begun in the first place, so the ending shouldn't have mattered either way.

"Later," he told her, his voice rough. "And maybe we'll stay over tonight."

He wanted to tug her out of the group. He wanted her to himself—and wasn't that something, given how much time they'd already spent together, just the two of them?

It was beginning to wear on him, the things he wanted.

And maybe it wasn't wise to head back home to his cabin in this state. With her. When he felt so . . . unsettled.

When he felt anything at all.

It was easy to cling to his principles in theory. It was harder when Violet was here. Because she smelled like apples drenched in honey, she was pink and bright in the middle of such a long winter, and it turned out he had a powerful hunger for all her cotton candy sweetness.

Maybe that was why he indulged himself in some whiskey, Old Harry–style, and decided it was better to stay put tonight.

Because here at the Mine there was always someone around. That meant opportunities for intimacy were few and far between and he would thereby do himself—and Violet—the favor of getting himself under control before they went back out to the cabin.

That was what he told himself, anyway.

And had a drink or two to cement the decision.

But market day meant folks were in no rush to end the gathering. The semiprivate bunkhouse rooms filled up quickly. As the night wore on and the merriment stopped, people hunkered down all over the big hall the way Quinn remembered doing all too often as a kid.

It was late when Quinn went to find Violet again, only to discover her curled up in a different chair. The big fire was still going and the light from the flames danced over her, the crackle and pop a kind of counterpoint to the snores he could hear from nearby. It reminded him that there was an audience.

He hated the fact that he needed reminding.

Still, he squatted down in front of the chair. Because she was awake, huddled up under her parka, her gaze just sleepy enough to make Quinn forget at least 90 percent of the reasons why he shouldn't touch her.

"How did you like your first market day?"

Her eyes lit up, almost too much gold to bear. "Are you making small talk? What terrible magic is this?"

Quinn felt something like lighthearted and he hardly knew where to put that, especially when he couldn't keep his smile at bay the way he usually did. "No magic. Research. Isn't that why you're here?" Her gaze didn't dim any. Had he wanted it to? "I thought you'd appreciate meeting the community. After all, they're the people you think you should tell how to live."

Because despite the smile he couldn't control, the whiskey had made a pretty strong case that he should make certain she knew her place here.

Or maybe that you do, too, some voice in him commented darkly.

And he would never understand, when all she did was reach out a hand, how Violet ripped his overactive heart out of his chest and threw it on the floor.

By simply sliding her palm to his face. "Before I came here I wanted to protect the land from greedy Outsiders like me, but not me," she said softly. "Now I want to preserve the land, just as it is, for you. All of you. What you have here is special, Quinn. You should never, ever consider letting it go. No matter what."

He reached up and peeled her hand from his jaw, intending to drop it.

But he didn't.

"You liked it, then." He was lost somewhere in her gaze. "The market."

She let out a breath that shuddered a little. And he realized that he was running his thumb along the back of her hand, almost absently. Almost mindlessly.

Almost.

"One of the things that fascinates me about this place is how it's free from distraction," she whispered. "Not only out there in a solitary cabin, where there's nothing for miles around. But here, too. It's like everything is stripped down to the good parts."

He thought of drunk Old Harry. "It's not all good parts."

"Even the bad parts here are good parts," she argued softly. "You take care of your own."

"We do."

He did.

Though it took him a minute to recollect that she wasn't his own. She wasn't his at all. He couldn't say he liked the reminder.

And later, when he was lying wide awake on the uncomfortable floor with his coat as a pillow, he would remember the way her eyes seemed to fill. Then shimmer, an impossible gold. The kind of gold a man would go a little crazy trying to keep.

He would remember that he'd wanted her to make a statement. To tell him that she wanted to be one of the people he took care of. To be a part of this community.

To be his.

But she didn't.

Instead, she pulled her hand away from his and retreated behind one of her bright Violet smiles.

"Thank you," was all she said, when there was so much else in her gaze. So much more in the air between them. Too much. "I hate to think I might have lived my whole life without knowing how much I love it here."

And Quinn considered himself a lifelong ambassador of all things rural Alaska. He should have been overjoyed that she felt the same.

But *overjoyed* was not what kept him awake long after everyone else in the cavernous Mine was asleep. *Overjoyed* was not what made him think, grimly, that this was going to be a very long winter.

If he survived it.

In the morning Quinn woke up out of sorts. Regretting the night before—not so much the whiskey, because he knew his limits, but the sentiment that had somehow crept into him like a wily little draft of frigid air. Until it had taken him over. When he would have said he'd insulated himself against that kind of thing years before.

He rolled up from his makeshift bed and made his way over to the diner area, where he helped himself to the coffee Grand Mia always had going. He avoided the fancy-looking espresso machine that, rumor had it, Old Harry Barrow had given his first wife as a wedding gift, then kept when she'd left him. Purely out of spite.

It wasn't that Quinn minded a cup of spiteful espresso. But he didn't want to talk to anyone just then and the machine would wake up everyone in the Mine.

He drank his coffee black and hot enough to scorch the back of his throat.

Maybe it wasn't forty-year-old spite, but it would do.

Then, making his way across the wide floor of the Mine, he picked his way through family groups sleeping in piles like puppies. He saw Noah Granger stretched out on a tabletop, hands folded like he was practicing being a dead man. Every chair and couch was occupied, though he didn't look to make sure that Violet was where he'd left her.

Somehow, he knew she wouldn't go anywhere without telling him.

He pushed his way outside into the dark of the early morning.

The cold rushed at him, filling him up.

Reminding him who he was.

He walked out, away from the old mine in the little town that clung to the hill, a marker of a time gone by. When the veins of gold that traced their way through much of the Kuskokwim valley had been assumed to make it up here, too. When the miners had come, braving the winters, the cold, the conditions of the mine itself, in the hope of better. In the hope that somehow, it could be better.

Quinn didn't have to turn back to look at the red buildings climbing up the side of the hill, lights twinkling against the dark.

He knew this place like he knew himself.

And maybe he'd needed to come out here on a morning

like this to remind himself that he was descended from miners, sure enough. He knew that.

But he also knew that his people had mostly chased down fool's gold by this lake.

He would have thought he knew better than to do the same.

Quinn could feel the wind picking up in a way that set the back of his neck to tingling, almost like it was exposed when it wasn't. There had been muttering yesterday about a nasty weather system coming in, dumping snow and maybe even working itself up into a blizzard. A day off yet, he would have thought.

But the wind suggested otherwise.

And Quinn decided he didn't have it in him to spend another day, maybe two, in the glare of this much attention.

Maybe he was just that selfish. Or just that foolish. Maybe he didn't care what he was, because that wasn't going to change what he was going to do.

He wanted Violet all to himself.

He *wanted*.

And he didn't have to act on the things he wanted, Quinn reasoned. But he would take what he could get for as long as she stuck it out here. He would take cozy evenings in front of his fire, tucked up on his couch, and the dangerous fantasy of a life like that. With a woman so bright, lighting up the dark no matter what time of day the sun set.

That was the thing about fool's gold. It was pretty in and of itself. The trouble only came when a man tried to pretend it was the real thing.

He knew better.

But Quinn stood out there in the cold until he was sure.

Back inside, he woke up Violet, nodding at other folks he could see slowly blinking and sitting up, rubbing at stiff necks from less-than-ideal bedding options and a few look-ing like they had deeper regrets about the night before than he did.

"We can eat back at the cabin," he told Violet as she sent a longing look in the direction of a plate of hash browns Grand Mia was serving up in the diner.

She sighed mightily, but didn't argue. She went off to the bathroom in the bunkhouse, then returned to gear up for the trip. And together they trooped back outside, loading up the few purchases he'd made onto the snow machine and then setting off.

The sun wasn't up yet, but there was a lightening in the sky. Quinn would have said he didn't need it, so well did he know this lake, but winter could be tricky and he was grate-ful for the extra visibility.

And he was so busy concentrating on all the things he wasn't feeling as they zipped out onto the ice and headed out into the middle of the lake that it took him too long to recognize what he *was* feeling.

That damn wind, picking up.

Picking up hard. Then the driving snow to go with it.

Quinn checked—but they were too far out on the lake now to turn back, and that was a problem.

Because it looked like that blizzard had come early.

And it was headed right for them.

Eleven

❧

It happened fast. Too fast.

First the wind, then the snow.

Within moments Violet could barely see. And when she turned to look behind her, it was as if the Mine had simply disappeared. Not only the Mine—the lake itself.

You'll be next, came a voice inside her with a horrible certainty.

She tried to shove it aside, but she didn't see how it was possible that they could make it back to the cabin. That they could make it anywhere. She heard Quinn shout something, but the wind took his voice away.

Violet held on tight and realized as she did that for all her grand protestations of having crushed the Alaskan weather, she'd only seen the faintest hint of it.

This was real. And this was not something any tiny little human could *crush*. She wasn't sure she'd ever really known what *humbled* meant before.

She tried to squint up ahead, not sure how Quinn could

keep driving the snowmobile when visibility got worse by
the moment.

But it wasn't as if she had an alternate plan.

Violet had never felt more useless in her life.

And just as she thought that surely the fact that he was
still driving the snowmobile through the near whiteout
was verging on suicidal, he stopped. Or slowed, she realized the next moment, as it was clear that they were climbing a hill again, and then he seemed to aim straight for a
wall of snow—

But before she could protest, she realized that he'd
stopped the snowmobile beneath some kind of overhang.

It was quieter here, though the wind had an edge to it
and she could hear the way it howled like it had gotten inside her head. But the snow was no longer pelting her, and
for a moment, that was enough. Then in the next moment,
she felt her heart going wild in her chest. Left over from
that humbling, flattening fear, she thought, and she knew
she wouldn't soon forget what it was like out there. So vul-
nerable, so exposed, so outrageously fragile in the face of
real weather.

She felt too shaken to do anything but sit there, but
Quinn was on the move.

"Let's go," he ordered her brusquely as he gathered
things from the snowmobile's storage compartment, and
then, in the little cocoon they found themselves in now, lit
up by the snowmobile's headlamp, he reached out and
pulled her from her seat.

That was when she realized she had kind of frozen solid
there. And not from the cold.

Quinn paused for a moment, looking down at her though
she could see almost nothing of him, between the goggles
he wore when he drove the snowmobile and his balaclava.
"You okay?"

Violet was not okay, as a matter of fact. She couldn't think of a time she'd ever felt in such total jeopardy while also so powerless to do anything to change it.

But she also knew that she had to suck that up.

"Was that . . . is that a blizzard?"

"Looks like it."

"How very Alaskan of you." She attempted a laugh, because that was so perfectly laconic. Her attempt fell a little flat, she could hear. "Where are we?"

"This is one of the summer cabins. Folks down in Hopeless come up, spend a week at the lake, maybe two. It's as good a shelter as we'll find out this way, anyway."

"Aren't we close to the Mine?" They'd hit the ice of the lake maybe five minutes before the storm had hit. Maybe ten.

"Not close enough." When she didn't react, he moved, pushing his goggles up to the top of his head so she could see the flash of his dark eyes, and more fool her that she instantly felt significantly, measurably better. But she did. "It's easy to get turned around in the storm. This cabin was the last thing I saw before the storm came in, so I gambled that I could make a straight shot from where we were on the ice to get here. I wouldn't want to turn around and try to make my way back up the hill. That's a great way to get found three days later, frozen solid. Or, you know. When things thaw."

He spoke so matter-of-factly. Violet tried to take that on board, failed, made herself smile anyway. "Yes. Well. Let's not do that."

Quinn looked almost amused for a moment and then he was moving again, so she followed him even though she felt . . . outside herself. Also, she couldn't think of anything else to do in the middle of a blizzard. And besides, she *wanted* to stay close to him.

Purely for survival reasons, she told herself. Purely because he was the one who would get them through this, if getting through it was possible. Because it had occurred to her out there in the thick fist of the storm that simply sleeping on some furs on a cabin floor really wasn't *survival*, was it? It was making herself slightly uncomfortable and mildly inconvenienced and calling it a moral victory.

She was just lucky that when an actual survival situation came about, she wasn't left to her own devices. Because for one thing, she knew she absolutely would have tried to get back to the Mine. And therefore might not have been found until spring.

Violet shuddered at the thought.

Quinn went over to a wall hidden away in the snow and began digging at it. It wasn't clear to her that he was looking for a door until he found it. Then it took several more minutes of some brute force to pull it open. When it was open he ushered her inside and let the light pour in from the snowmobile headlight.

While Violet stood there, feeling profoundly useless, Quinn moved quickly. Before she knew it, he'd started a fire in a far smaller woodstove than any of the others she'd seen, then moved back outside again. When he came in again, he was carrying a pile of snow-covered wood that he tossed in the corner—to dry out a bit, she knew that much from the shack—and he shut the door behind them to seal them in.

While outside and all around them, she could hear the storm rage on.

"What can I do to help?" she asked.

"Not a lot." He went and looked through the cupboards, pulling out some supplies. Cans. A bag of rice. Then he opened another cabinet and pulled out a pile of blankets. When he saw her looking, he made a low noise. "People usually stock basic supplies in these cabins."

"That's very thoughtful of them."

"It saves lives."

Violet looked around the cabin while he went through the cabin's supplies as well as his own from the pack he'd brought in. Then he checked the perimeter of the cabin for reasons he didn't specify. She hoped, fervently, that it was too cold for a spider situation—but she couldn't think about spiders. It was adding insult to injury. She focused on the cabin instead. Like the shack, it was one room. It had a couple of bunk beds built into the wall, the tiny woodstove, and little else. She thought maybe there were windows, but if so, they were boarded up.

"Are we going to be okay?" she asked. Cautiously.

Quinn looked up from where he squatted on the floor. "That's my plan."

"I've never seen a blizzard before," she told him. Maybe a little nervously. "I've never seen any storm quite that closely before, to be honest."

"Mother Nature doesn't mess around. When she's pissed, she's pissed."

"Have you been caught out before? Like this?"

"Being caught out would be digging a snow cave." His mouth crooked. "This is the height of luxury. Consider it part of your Alaskan adventure."

Violet no longer felt even remotely adventurous. She wanted to cry, as a matter of fact, but she made herself smile widely instead.

"You know me," she declared with great bravado. "I am *all about* adventure."

He didn't succumb to a full smile, but the curve was still there. And she thought there was some softening around his eyes.

She couldn't say that solved the anxiety kicking around inside her, but it didn't hurt any.

"It's not going to get all that warm in here," he said after a while, apparently satisfied with what he'd brought in. "We'll handle that, but you definitely don't want to sweat too much in all those layers. Strip down to where you're comfortable, but not overly warm."

Violet decided to take it as a good sign that being told to strip down by this man—even if she knew he didn't mean strip naked in any fun sense—kicked around in her like an extra log on the little fire he'd built.

"Why won't this warm up like the shack?" she asked as she shoved her hat and gloves in her parka's pocket, then unzipped it.

"This is a summer cabin," he said, as if that was self-explanatory. When Violet only gazed back at him, he made a low sound. "It's not insulated. We're lucky that the snowpack around the cabin will do some of that, but I don't know how comfortable it will be." He studied her face a moment. "Don't worry. We'll share the heat."

"Until someone comes to rescue us?" she asked.

Hopefully. Very, very hopefully.

Quinn shook his head. "No one's coming out in this. We'll lie low until it blows over, dig ourselves out, and let everyone know we made it."

"But wait . . ." She stopped in the act of hanging up her parka on the ever-present pegs by the door. "People know that we were trying to get across the lake. Does that mean they think we're . . . just out there? And they'll really wait for days to find out if we survived?"

"They'll be hunkering down and concentrating on their own survival. And assuming we're doing the same."

That did not seem like a reasonable response to Violet, but he didn't elaborate. So she took off her outer layers, then squatted down there against the wall and settled into a kind of barbed waiting.

Quinn seemed tense but not scared as he investigated the old pot sitting on the woodstove. He went outside with it briefly, then returned, and seemed no tenser as the cold he brought with him swirled inside. Violet decided to take that as a good sign.

Or anyway, as a guide, even as she shivered.

"Okay," he said. "We have food. I'll melt and boil some snow so we'll have water."

"Can we just eat it?"

"It'll make you colder. The act of eating snow burns more calories and dehydrates you more than it hydrates. Better to melt it into liquid."

He came toward her, shrugging out of his parka. He threw it on the end of the lower bunk that Violet had been ignoring. She looked at it now. There was an old camp mattress and that was it. It was narrow and uninspiring, even when Quinn spread a blanket over it, and there was absolutely no reason her heart should have started kicking at her the way it did.

And harder still when Quinn came over and took her parka from its peg and put it in the bed with his. Violet lectured herself that proximity of outerwear should not make her feel so . . . fluttery.

But it did.

"Take off your boots," Quinn told her, all gruff mountain man. Commanding and rough. "Don't get your feet wet. Then get up on the bunk."

Violet obeyed him, of course. It didn't occur to her not to. But she was overly aware of everything. Her fingers felt twice their natural size when she could see very well they were not. She took off her boots without getting her socks wet and then, gingerly, she crawled onto the mattress and hunched there. She was closer to the wall and it definitely wasn't as secure as the wall near the door. She could feel the cold, but worse, she could hear the violence of the weather outside.

It was no less humbling than before. Violet would even go so far as to call it terrifying—and it didn't help that she knew no one would come looking for them. No one was going to save them.

Her anxiety ratcheted up from a solid 11 to the neighborhood of 167 or so.

And yet she found herself focusing on the way Quinn moved to remove his own boots, then set them beneath the bunk with hers. Side by side, as if they were a matching set.

As if the boots themselves were getting intimate.

Coats and boots, she chided herself. *You are losing it.*

Then he was crawling onto the narrow little mattress with her and Violet made a little squeaking sound against her will, shrinking against the wall before she could think better of it.

"We're going to huddle together for warmth," Quinn told her, patiently. Too patiently, to her mind. "If I was making a move on you, Violet, you'd know."

"I didn't think you were making a move. I was trying to . . ." She gestured wildly with one hand as if there was extra space somewhere when his body was so *big*. "Make room for you. With a small cheer of solidarity for good measure."

His gaze lightened. "Sure you were."

He stretched out beside her, and Violet had to order herself to at least pretend that this felt perfectly normal. Run-of-the-mill. *Just another bed I'm lying in with a man, no big deal*, she told herself—but even her internal voice sounded much too intense. Because his marvel of a body was pressed to hers while she was wide awake and she could feel the difference. His arms were coming around her, then he was rolling over and hauling her on top of him.

That was also different, God help her.

He dragged the blankets up over them and as far as Violet was concerned, they'd basically flung themselves head-first into a blazing fire.

The silence in their little cabin didn't help.

She was sure that he couldn't help but hear not only the racket her pulse was making, but the way she was breathing. Too fast, too loud.

What a difference it made to be wide awake and *aware* of him.

His chest was hard and she found herself melting against him, as if her body was going out of its way to get closer. Softening, accommodating. Making itself a part of his heat and scent and—

"Relax," he murmured.

Violet refused to lift her head from his chest, because she knew that she would topple over into his gaze, and she couldn't risk it.

Slowly, surely, it began to feel slightly less overwhelming. Like she might actually be able to touch him like this *and* breathe.

He was warm, as ever. And pressed up against him, she could only marvel at how powerfully made he was, all of that muscle so gorgeously packaged, so rock solid and yet she was more comfortable than she could remember being on softer feather beds.

She settled her head against his chest, keeping her hands curled up beneath her chin and her legs rigidly straight down one of his large thighs, so she couldn't possibly be accused of any . . . lasciviousness.

"Is this how we're going to wait out the storm?" Her voice sounded funny. High-pitched and strange.

"Pretty much."

It was maddening that their situation seemed not to

bother him. Maddening and very male, she thought. He could simply lie there in a blizzard, unbothered.

While Violet kept getting *more* bothered by the moment. Once she stopped being hyperaware of him, of the heat and strength, she found herself a little too aware of herself.

The way her breasts felt, pressed tight against him. As if first they'd melted, but now they'd swelled, and it felt a little too good every time they shifted slightly. Like when he breathed. At the way the pounding of her pulse became something else, moving down to make itself a kind of ache between her legs.

The intimacy of this seemed to crash over her in waves, and she couldn't quite find her footing.

"So is this something that people just do up here?" She wasn't aware that she planned to speak until she was doing it. "In the face of too much weather, you cuddle?"

And the wonder of it was, she could feel him laugh. She could *feel* it, even though he didn't make a sound.

It felt like a revelation. It was a new heat spiraling all the way through her.

"Obviously, it's sometimes a very manly cuddle," he said, and she could hear a rich thread of laughter in his voice. "It's called sharing resources. That's the thing about Alaska. You have to be prepared and you also have to take advantage of whatever tools you find."

"Tools," Violet said dreamily. "Yes, very important."

And when it got quiet between them, she started to realize that she could actually hear his heartbeat, too. Right there beneath her head. Maybe she felt it, too.

It made her dizzy.

"What's funny," she said in that same too-bright, too-squeaky way, "is how hardy I thought I was before this."

"Why would you think that?"

Maybe if he'd sounded anything but curious, she would have taken offense. But she was too dizzy, too overwhelmed, and too aware of things like his heartbeat for her own good.

Whatever it was, any sense of self-preservation she might've had had evaporated. "I always thought that the mark of a man wasn't what he did, but what he said. How he said it, I mean. My male role models, such as they were, always *did* the right things, you understand. My father made sure he always got the full measure of the time he was permitted in his custody agreement. There was never any question that he would pay for things, or make sure that I was clothed. Fed. Educated. All the things that a father was expected to do, he made sure he did. But he didn't like to talk to me. And if he couldn't avoid it, he was always so loud. So angry. And more often than not, mean."

Quinn went still. "To you?"

"Mostly *about* me. Not even me personally, really, just the *fact* of me."

"Sounds pretty personal to me."

"It never occurs to my father to consider other people's emotions. It would never cross his mind that all his ranting about not wanting kids and how he was trapped might make the product of his entrapment feel something about his anger on the subject."

She didn't hear any response from Quinn, but once again, she felt a rumble inside his chest. This time it sounded like a growl. And anyway, she couldn't seem to stop talking, almost like she was trying to fill the cabin with her words. Her voice. With anything but the heat they were generating between them.

"Meanwhile, my mother had all these husbands," Violet said, not sure if she felt emboldened or if this was all a new kind of nervousness. Blizzard anxiety, maybe. *Or,* a dire little voice inside her said, *one last confession before the snow swallows you whole*. An unhelpful line of thought. "They were all birds of a similar feather. Loud and blustery. Always had to be the center of attention. And certainly wanted any women in their life to flutter about in a secondary capacity. I thought putting up with them all these years made me hardy, like I said. Weathered internally."

"Internal weather isn't going to help much in a blizzard."

That word. *Blizzard*. It slid down the entire length of her spine. "Well, and I also thought that was just how big, physical men acted. So naturally I wanted the opposite. Erudite intellectuals who impressed others with their wit and their thoughts, not their bank accounts or their cars or their golfing prowess. Men who were never loud or visibly angry."

She could hear his heart beneath her. She could *hear it*, and she couldn't seem to get over that.

"I'm just betting," she managed to say, "that you don't play golf."

"Yeah. No." He shifted slightly, and a different kind of heat raged through her. "And I'm guessing that your institute is filled with witty men who believe their thoughts are impressive."

"Let's say that you met a woman at a conference." She didn't know what she was doing, but she was perilously close to imploding, and it seemed like a good idea to . . . not do that. So she kept on talking. "That must happen to you."

"I've met women, if that's what you mean."

Violet frowned, glad he couldn't see her face. And glad it was dark enough that she didn't have to fiddle with her glasses to see the expression on his. Because she really didn't like thinking about Quinn with other women.

But that same bubbly, head-spinning feeling inside her kept pushing her on and she couldn't seem to stop talking.

It was better than the complicit dark. The heat. Her body against his and the terrible intimacy of this *resource sharing*. It was torture.

And there was no forgetting the blizzard.

"Let's say you meet this woman. You go out on the last day of your conference and you have a wonderful dinner. Then a single, perfect kiss before she takes a plane back home to a different country."

She could hear and feel his laugh then. "A perfect kiss? Is that a euphemism?"

"It is not."

Another little half of a laugh. "I don't like to waste materials," Quinn said, all heat and drawl. "I wouldn't waste a perfect kiss."

"A kiss can be an end in and of itself."

"Sure it can. But that doesn't make it perfect. It just makes it a kiss."

She opened her mouth to point out that they'd shared a kiss that she'd thought was pretty spectacular, but she caught herself. Because surely that was crossing a line into suggestiveness. Or crossing more of a line than lying draped over him on a narrow little bed, so close she could hear the noises he *didn't* make.

"Once you and this woman part," she pushed on, maybe a little desperately, "you begin a long-distance relationship."

"No, thanks. You're either with someone or you're not."

He sounded so definitive.

She blinked. "You're right about that. I was seduced by a lot of thoughts and flowery words, but very little action."

"Sounds like you weren't seduced at all."

"It's probably more accurate to say I desperately wanted to be seduced," Violet agreed. She warmed to the topic, scowling in the dark cabin. "Doesn't everybody want to be seduced? Isn't that human nature? Whether you're a hardy person or not?"

Quinn moved then so that he was gripping her upper arms, then holding her up and away from him. Meaning she was gazing straight down into that beautiful face and could see, much too clearly, the way his eyes were glittering.

"Why are you telling me all this?"

"I don't know. I'm just talking?"

"Why?" His voice was lower. Grittier. "Because, Violet, I'm not real interested in hearing about your boyfriend."

"The thing about Stuart," she said, from a place inside her she wasn't sure she could have named, made of shame and fury and a knowledge she'd denied for a year, "is that I don't think he ever was my boyfriend. That's how much of an idiot I am."

"Are you telling me this because you want me to convince you he's a loser?" Quinn's gaze seemed harder than it should have been. But she couldn't look away. She wasn't sure she blinked—or breathed. "Because I don't have to hear another word to know that's true."

"I don't need that," she said, though maybe she did.

"Then why?"

"The thing about Stuart is that he's a liar and a betrayer," she told Quinn, solemnly. "And if we die out here I want to make sure that somebody else knew, even if only for a little while, that yes, he fooled me. But maybe I wanted to be fooled. Maybe I was the one who did the fooling, because I liked the idea of him. Because I thought that men really were cartoon characters, like my father or esoteric poetic types like him. I had no idea there was anything else. So. Apparently, all I needed to do was come to Alaska, where men are capable of both reading books and surviving terrifying blizzards. Or at least I hope they are."

It was quiet then. Only her breath and his. The crackle from the stove. The wind outside the cabin.

But everything else was the way his dark gaze searched hers.

"Violet. Darlin'. We're not going to die, I promise."

"Prove it," she whispered.

Once the words were out, she realized it was a dare. A challenge.

A challenge that Quinn met with a rueful, edgy sort of smile.

Before he hooked a hand around the nape of her neck and pulled her mouth down to his.

Twelve

❧

Violet tasted better than he remembered.

It was that same punch, that same wild heat.

And to his mind, it just about made sheltering from a blizzard worth it.

Her sweet scent was everywhere and she was like summer in his hands, soft and warm.

She was draped over him, so that Quinn could feel her curves everywhere. Pressing into him, making him ache with a hunger he knew only she could possibly satisfy.

He pulled away, smoothing her hair back and grinning when he saw her glasses were all fogged up. He tugged them off, setting them aside and then losing himself in that sweet, unfocused gold-mine gaze that, as far as he was concerned, was only his.

And the less he heard about long-distance *intellectual* boyfriends who didn't deserve her, the better.

"I thought we agreed on no kissing," she panted.

Though she was smiling, all of that bright light, and her

eyes were warm. Almost as warm as she was, there against his chest.

"That sounds like a dumb rule."

"It was your rule, if I recall correctly. And I do."

"I think a blizzard is a Get Out of Jail Free card," Quinn said, and then he tugged her down again. "The rules don't apply."

And this time when he took her mouth, he turned, rolling her beneath him at last.

At last.

He felt like he'd been waiting a lifetime for this. Several lifetimes, maybe, for this particular pink rush of blood to his head. And elsewhere.

She was almost too beautiful to be real, so he shifted slightly, between her legs. To make her moan a little. And to make it clear that he wasn't dreaming this again—that it was real.

She was real, and she was here, and this was happening.

All while she looked at him as if he, personally, were responsible for painting the winter skies with the northern lights. Maybe just for her.

If he could, Quinn knew he would.

He stared down at her, tousled hair and dreamy eyes, her lips slightly ajar like she was still trying to taste him. He willed himself to take it slow. To enjoy himself thoroughly and make sure she did the same. To chase down each and every fantasy he'd had about her flushed, pink softness since she'd walked into the Mine a week ago.

It didn't feel like a week.

The way he wanted her ran so deep he had to check himself.

But as he gazed down at her, Violet beamed back up at him, bright and hot and welcoming. Inviting.

And sure, he wanted to eat her up. But it didn't hurt that she looked just as hungry in return.

"Ordinarily," he told her, positioning his mouth against the soft line of her neck, where she tasted of salt and smelled so sweet, "I would mark this occasion by stripping off every last thing you're wearing and then acquainting myself with all the goodness I've been imagining all this time."

Quinn could feel the way she bloomed with a new fire at his words. He could feel the way she exhaled heavily. "By all means, don't let me hold you back."

"There's a blizzard out there," he said, spacing out the words as he kissed his way down her neck. Frustrated with all the clothes she was wearing, he let his hand trail down to the waistband of the thick, pink snow pants he'd been appreciating for days. He marked that appreciation by beginning to tug them off. "It could blow a wall down at any time. It would be real foolish to get naked."

"I do hate to be foolish," she breathed.

Quinn laughed. Then he set about ridding her of select outer layers. The snow pants and the Fair Isle sweater, but left behind her base layers. Then he helped himself to a personal tour of the rest of her, even if he couldn't get his hands directly on her skin in all cases.

Eventually, having appreciated every inch of her and not sure what was better—the feel of her beneath his hands or the way she met each touch with the kind of abandon that made his head spin a little—he reversed course. Trailing his way back up from her feet, still in their thick socks, he slipped a hand beneath her waistband and began to tug her leggings and panties down, gently, until he freed one leg.

Just one leg.

And Quinn was delighted to discover that Violet flushed all over.

He kissed his way up her leg again, skirting the heat

between her thighs, and pushing her shirt up out of his way as he found her navel, then the round weight of her breasts in the wool sports bra she wore.

One, then the other, he found his way beneath the wool and tasted her as he'd longed to do for days now.

She was velvet and cream, sweet everywhere, and she responded to him like every touch was a lit match to gas.

Violet arched up against him, her artless cries wrecking him and spurring him on. She was making him crazy, taking the hunger inside him and turning it into a kind of jarring, beautiful drumbeat, deep inside.

Steady, Quinn ordered himself.

When he made his way back down her soft belly again, she surged up against him and pushed him over onto his back, pulling their blankets with her. Or he let her do it, because it was far beyond his capabilities to deny a woman—flushed with a heat he'd stoked in her—who wanted to slip and slide her way all over him. Until she got her hands beneath his shirt, then sighed as happily as if she'd found a pot of gold.

Violet traced all the ridges in his abdomen, then grinned at him.

"This situation is even better than I imagined."

"I aim to please," he drawled, and laced his fingers beneath his head because he didn't want to go slow. He didn't want to play. He wanted to drive himself inside her and make them both come apart.

But Violet was frowning down at him, fierce and solemn, applying herself to the task of feeling her way around beneath his clothes.

And Quinn, by God, was prepared to surrender himself to these explorations.

Though he had never felt like more of a martyr than he did just then.

Her hands tracked their way down to his waistband. Quinn felt his chest go tight when she lifted her gaze to his, looking . . . shy.

A word he would never have applied to this pink and fearless creature before now.

Something thumped inside him, hard.

"Go ahead," he urged her.

Then he nearly died when she pulled her lower lip between her teeth, and with great concentration, set about undoing the snaps before tugging his fly wide.

And that was nothing compared to the look of wonder on her face when she reached into his pants and eased him out.

He needed to tell her to stop, but he couldn't do it. Not when she ran her soft hands along the length of him with a reverence that made his heart thump at him, long and low. Like a sledgehammer. It was as if she was learning him by feel alone, and he suddenly found he had a whole different appreciation for his professor and the . . . singular intensity of her focus.

He wanted her to look at him like that forever.

Especially when she bent down, both her hands wrapped around him, and placed a sweet, heartbreakingly soft kiss on the head of him.

Sensation roared through him and Quinn jackknifed up, pulling her away before he disgraced himself.

"I wasn't done!" Violet protested, scowling at him.

"Yeah, you were."

"But I wanted—"

"To kill me," he gritted out. "I know."

He tipped her over again and came down with her, aware that he was already pushed to the limits of his control. Before this, before *her*, he would have said there was no limit. No boundary. Because he had made a study of control for the whole of his life and nothing could ever entice him to lose it.

But he hadn't been prepared for Violet. She was a sweet pink bomb that he was terribly afraid had already exploded, taking him apart with her.

Maybe the real issue here was that he wasn't afraid of it. He wanted it.

Because he couldn't remember ever wanting anything more than he wanted Violet.

And it was a fight to go slow, even now. To settle himself between her thighs and wait until the roar in him eased a bit, retracting the worst of its fangs. He reached between them, letting himself explore all that sweetness, all that heat, with the part of him that wanted her most before he reached into his pocket to pull out protection.

When he sheathed himself, he braced himself over her and told himself to go easy. Because he wanted her so much it scared him a little, and the last thing in the world he ever wanted to do was scare even a shred of her brightness away.

Violet braced her hands against his chest and he realized he'd rarely seen her face like this. Open and without her glasses. Warm and soft. She moistened her lips, which he felt like another blazing flame right through him.

"There's something I have to tell you," she said, very seriously.

"If it involves any exes or thoughts on golf, Violet, I'll pass."

"I'm debating telling you at all." As he watched, fascinated, those glorious eyes of hers focused in on him. That frown was quick to follow. Quinn took the opportunity to lean in and put his mouth on the soft little wrinkle between her eyes, the way he'd wanted to for what felt like much too long.

And sure enough, Violet melted into a sigh that became a smile. He could feel her quiver, everywhere.

He congratulated himself—with gritted teeth—on somehow managing to keep himself from going straight over the edge.

Quinn watched her fight her way back into frowning. Her fingers dug into his chest a little, as if she needed to grip him to remember herself.

"Virginity is just a story we tell ourselves," she told him, in a very serious voice that would not be out of place in a college lecture hall. "The cultural weight placed upon it, the patriarchal connotations, the idea that worth is in any way connected to sexuality is, at best, ridiculous."

"If you say so."

Her hands turned into fists against his chest. "It's not that *I* say so, Quinn. There are entire fields of study on the subject. Just look at the differences in how we treat male virginity versus female virginity and how we apportion shame in such a diametrically opposed manner to each. It's a pageant of commodification, a bizarre conflation of purity with property—"

"Professor. Darlin'. I have no idea what you're talking about," Quinn drawled. "And I especially don't know why you're talking about it now."

She stared up at him, flushed and solemn-eyed, her chest heaving with each breath.

She didn't speak. For one beat, then another. Then another still.

And he realized he'd never known his pink professor to be speechless.

Which was when it all clicked.

"Violet." Quinn said her name quietly. Carefully. "Is this little lecture your way of telling me that you're a virgin?"

"I actually reject the very concept of virginity," she whispered. "As personal policy."

"Have you had sex before?"

"Well. No. Not as such."

"Define *not as such*."

"I've always been very focused on my studies," she told him.

Primly.

So primly that something in him that he could only describe as primitive seemed to . . . wake up.

"I've done some studying in my day." Quinn got his hands in her hair so he could please himself by tucking it behind her ear. And please them both, he thought, when she shivered. "It never kept me from having sex when I had a mind to."

"Everyone is so obsessed with sex," Violet said in a rush. "But I was obsessed with research. There are whole worlds available to a person who sees with her head, not her heart. Or . . . other parts."

"Let me see if I got this straight."

Quinn felt a rush that wasn't as simple as affection. Or as clarifying as hunger. It was far more complex. Layered. It howled around inside him like the blizzard outside and grew stronger with every breath.

But it was impossible. Because the only thing he'd ever felt possessive of was this land.

"You're the product of what I'm guessing was a hot little affair gone wrong," he said. "They wouldn't be so pissed about it, thirty years later, if it wasn't hot."

"It's obviously horrifying to think of my parents and the word *hot* in the same sentence." Violet made a face. "But I think you're right."

"And they've spent your whole life keeping up this war of theirs."

"They have. They fight over holidays they don't actually celebrate, and that they certainly don't want to spend with me, just to score points off each other."

"And yet you, the smartest woman I've ever met, really

believe that you hiding yourself in books and research . . . is an accident?"

She scowled at him. "I don't think I expected a side helping of psychoanalysis with my deflowering, Quinn."

"There will be no flowers involved. We're in the middle of a blizzard. And I thought psychoanalysis was one of your pet hobbies. What else were you scribbling in that book?"

She sniffed, but the effect was lost because she was beneath him, warm and soft and welcoming. "I think I preferred it when you were taciturn."

"Here's what we're going to do, darlin'," he told her, letting his voice get a little bit stern again. It did just what he wanted, because he felt her sigh, then press closer to him. "You're going to stop thinking for a change."

Violet's frown deepened, but her hands relaxed against his chest. "Am I?"

"Oh yeah," he promised her. "You are."

Quinn dropped down and kissed her then. And demonstrated his version of a perfect kiss.

He kissed her, deep and hot and slow. He kissed her until she was soft and wild against him and shivering a little with it, making those greedy little noises in the back of her throat.

He kissed her until she moaned, and he kept kissing her until the moaning was his name.

"Quinn," she begged him in her sweet, hot way, "Quinn, *please.*"

Only then did he guide himself to the center of all her heat, find the barrier she considered nothing but a construct, and slide beyond it with a single, swift thrust.

And then he held her tight as she broke apart all around him.

Thirteen

❧

The sudden shattering took Violet by surprise.

She had expected pain. A sense of strange fullness, perhaps, and then the opportunity to slowly work her way past the onslaught of sensation toward something approaching pleasure, like all the books had promised—

But this was more like jumping off a cliff.

And she didn't know if she was falling or flying when the wallop of it made her shake, then quiver, then come apart at the seams. Into so many pieces she wasn't sure she was *her* any longer.

Yet somehow, it didn't feel like a loss.

The only thing she could manage to think was that she'd never known the truth of her body. What her body was for, what it could do, what it wanted.

All this time she'd imagined she was alive.

But there was no time to mourn all those things she hadn't known. All those years she'd wasted inside skin that had never been as sensitized as it was now. Limbs that hadn't moved the way they should have. Heat and hunger that had clearly been lurking within her all this time.

The confines of the clothes she still wore seemed to inflame her, because everything was too sensitive. Too much—yet not enough. Everywhere he'd touched already, everywhere he still touched now, was *alive* in a new way. And instead of floating off into the ether, gauzy and removed, she felt anchored into this. Here. Now.

Him.

Violet could feel him deep inside her. She could hear the crackle of the stove. She was aware of the cold air against the side of her bare leg and the sound their skin made against the fabric of their blankets and the mattress beneath her. But mostly she was aware of Quinn.

The glory of Quinn, big and hot and beautiful. He held himself above her, his arms so muscled and strong while his face was set and stern. Yet his eyes gleamed.

And she had found him beautiful from the start, but that was nothing in comparison to this.

Fierce, possessive, beautiful beyond measure, and deep inside of her.

Inside of her.

On some level, Violet couldn't understand how it was possible to survive this. Not intact. Not as herself. The notion made her feel lit up from the inside out, hotter than before, and almost unbearably alive. As if until this moment, right here in the middle of a storm in a rickety cabin, she hadn't known why she breathed.

When clearly it was for this.

For him.

Quinn's gaze was like magic, a marvel of heat and light that danced over her and inside her like the northern lights. Or maybe she was the aurora here, a graceful reckoning splashed wild across the night, because he smiled at her and everything changed. Got better, deeper.

Then he began to move.

And all Violet could do was hold on tight, follow his lead, and revel in every new level of sensation.

There was always more. There was always better. Deeper, hotter, this beautiful crisis she wanted to last forever. She felt it begin to build in her, deeper than before.

Quinn shifted to drop his head to the crook of her neck as his hips moved, faster and faster, slick and hot.

Perfect.

And when she burst into flame and then shattered all over again, Quinn groaned out her name. He held her tighter and closer, everything seemed to go molten, and then he followed her over that glorious cliff.

It seemed to take a lifetime for Violet's senses to make their way back to her.

First her senses. Then her position in space. Her back sank into the mattress and the solid weight of Quinn above her, pressing her down deeper.

He murmured something as he moved himself off her, and part of her wanted to track him. Watch where he went, what he did, simply because she wanted to hold on to the connection. Maybe forever.

But she couldn't bring herself to do even as little as lift her head.

Quinn came back to the bed and his gorgeous hands were on her again. He pulled her layers back into place. Then he wrapped his arms around her and pulled her close, her back to his front, before snuggling them deep beneath the blankets again.

She knew this was called *spooning*, but the word struck her as wholly unequal to the moment.

Violet reveled in how tactile it was. She could feel his breath against her hair. His blazing heat and the hardness of his chest. His arm was heavy as it wrapped around her, but she liked the weight of it. It felt like an inversion, to have his arm on her rather than her head on his arm. And somehow, that made sense, too, because everything was upside down. Inside out.

And a long, long while later, her brain finally came back online.

Violet sighed a little, because it turned out that it was perfectly all right to turn it off for a while. The world hadn't ended. She'd been transformed, yes, but she was still her.

Maybe more you than ever before, something in her suggested.

She had no idea what time it was. Whether it was day or night or how long they'd been here and, very distantly, she felt as if she ought to be more concerned about such things.

But she couldn't muster up much in the way of caring about any of it while she was wrapped in Quinn's arms. Not when their breathing took on the same rhythm. Not when she could feel his heart beat against her back until it seemed that hers and his were the same slow drumming. Like they could be one again even without him inside her.

Slowly, Violet became aware of the storm outside again, but she wasn't panicked any longer. And it was then—curled up in Quinn's arms, feeling safer in the middle of an Alaskan blizzard than she ever had at any other point in her life—that it hit her, hard.

He had been onto something when he'd talked about her reaction to her parents and how she cut herself off from sex. But it wasn't just sex. It was everything.

Now, here, she finally understood connection.

His heart. Her heart. Their breath, their bodies. Here, at last, she understood *togetherness*.

And because she understood it, because she'd soared over that cliff and had shattered as she'd flown, she could finally see how lonely her life had been all along.

The realization walloped her, too hard for her to do anything but lie there and accept it. It was that or be sucked out to sea in an undertow she feared would never let her go.

And on the heels of all that, with the taste of the ocean thick in the back of her throat, Violet knew with perfect, gutting clarity that she'd simply accepted her loneliness a long time ago. She'd tried to make it a virtue. And had always prided herself on her relentless positivity no matter the provocation. Not because she enjoyed being called Pollyanna and other, less complimentary, names. But she knew too well the consequences of swinging to the other side of the pendulum.

If she let herself go negative it meant that she would become her parents. And if she became like them, bitter and mean and always so vicious, that meant they would win.

Violet had always been determined that they could not, under any circumstances, win.

But she hadn't realized what she was missing. Suddenly, in this narrow bed in a summer cabin packed down deep in a blizzard that she wasn't sure she was going to escape, she knew better.

"I have to tell you something, Quinn." Her voice was loud in the quiet dimness of the cabin.

"Good." His voice was a low sort of growl in her ear. "Your head makes a lot of noise when you think that loud."

She frowned, but she couldn't let him distract her. "I want to thank you. I've heard a lot of stories about the way people lose their virginity, many of them horrific."

It was funny that she could feel when he smiled. She didn't have to see it. She just knew.

"I'm real glad that I could elevate the experience from horrific."

"I mean it. I'm grateful. I didn't actually realize . . . what it was like. What it meant." She turned around in a rush, still in his arms, and wasn't sure that was an improvement. Because they were face-to-face. Close enough to kiss, and that was distracting. But it was also even more intimate than before. "Don't worry, I'm not making declarations. I've read enough to know that men don't like those."

He closed his eyes briefly, as if he needed strength. "I think you're talking about your garden-variety Stuart type." The way he said *Stuart* delighted her, because he sounded so deeply unimpressed. And because Stuart was the sort of man who assumed that he was so unique that he could never be a *type*. "I'm a grown-ass man. I'm not afraid of a declaration."

"I'm told that a person remembers her first time forever," she said, because Stuart had nothing to do with this. This was about Quinn. And her. And what had happened between them that was nothing short of life-altering, no matter that all those treatises had claimed it wasn't. She'd had this man *inside her body*. How could that be anything but momentous? It made a person want to question what non-life-altering first times were like, and what the point of them was. But not now. "And assuming we live through this blizzard, I expect this will be an excellent memory. Thank you, Quinn."

He smiled at her and it was a thing of wonder. A curve in the corner of his mouth, but then it spread until it took over his face. It made his cheekbones nearly angelic, but his mouth stayed wicked. And the midnight fire of his gaze set the world to toppling end over end.

Again.

"Then we really owe it to ourselves to make sure it's the best memory it can be, Violet," he drawled. "If only for research purposes."

Violet felt buoyant, as if she might have floated up to the

ceiling if he wasn't holding her down. "You know I love my research."

And got that delicious growl of his in return.

This time, he let her play with him. He taught her how to take him in her mouth and how to make him lose control, grab her hair in his fists, and hurtle over the edge. Having him in her mouth was a wonder. It made her melt and shake, too hot and too needy, and then the rough male taste of him filled her up. He flipped her over and lay against her back, twisting her head around so he could take her mouth that way, his kisses deep and dirty and delicious.

Quinn found his way between her thighs, stroking her there until she writhed beneath him, shattering with the thrill of so many sensations.

Then she learned how easily he could build her up again, sliding her snow pants down to take her that way, the thick heat of him filling her, changing her, completing her.

Much later she woke with a start to find Quinn standing in the middle of the cabin.

"Did something happen?"

"The storm has ended," he replied.

Maybe he didn't say it the way she heard it, so filled with portent. But it echoed that way inside her anyway. And he had scrupulously dressed her after each time they'd come together, gruffly insisting that she stay warm. So she wasn't self-conscious in the least as she dutifully swung to sitting position and tried to look excited that the blizzard had moved on and left them whole.

When what it meant was that she would have to go back out there and rejoin the world.

"*Great!*" she exclaimed, with what was clearly a psychotic level of enthusiasm. Because his brows rose as he looked at her. She cleared her throat and tried to dial it back. "Do we head back outside now?"

"We don't." Quinn regarded her a little too closely, though there was that curve in the corner of his mouth. "And I'll try not to take your eagerness to leave too personally. But it's almost ten at night. No point digging our way out in the dark and potentially getting ourselves right back into trouble."

Violet tried to imagine what serene casualness would look like in a situation like this, then tried to exude it.

"No," she said, *exuding*. "We wouldn't want that."

She scrabbled around for her glasses and when she shoved them back on her nose, she could see that Quinn was laughing. It made her heart do funny things in her chest, even though she suspected he was laughing at her. Or because of her, rather, because whatever else Quinn was, he wasn't mean. She didn't think he had a mean bone in his body— and she had spent some time today investigating that body closely.

He lifted his chin in a kind of invitation. "Come over here. We should eat something."

They sat there by the stove, huddled together and saying very little. Violet sat in his lap while they ate some nuts, shared a couple of power bars, and drank melted snow.

And yet she knew that when she looked back at this, it would be a magical evening that she would carry forever, because it was a part of her now.

Just like he is, something in her insisted.

Later, they lay in the bed again and she could feel the thick length of him against her back, though he seemed strangely content to ignore it.

Violet could not ignore it. She couldn't think of anything else.

"Don't you want to . . . *do* something?" she demanded at last, feeling shy and silly.

She felt his laughter and it comforted her. "I always want

to do something, Violet," he replied, so easily. As if this was all *easy* for him. "But you've never done this before. You might want to take it easy."

Violet did not want to take it easy. Because she had to take her chances while she could. She had to gather all this up, as much as she could. No matter when she left Alaska, she would have to take what she could of this with her.

And hoard it for the rest of her life.

"I think," she whispered into the dark, to him, to Future Violet who would treasure all of this, she was sure, "that I am constitutionally incapable of taking anything easy."

"Let's put that to the test," he replied, his mouth at the nape of her neck.

So they did.

And the next time she woke, Violet knew instantly that he wasn't there.

She sat up abruptly and nearly slammed her head into the upper bunk, catching herself at the last moment. And she was glad that he'd covered her up again in the blankets, because it was infinitely colder without him, though the little woodstove was still chugging along. Keeping them from freezing to death last night despite the drafts and the wind outside. But she was happier all the same when she pulled on her thick snow pants again.

His boots were gone, so Violet stamped hers on. She wrapped herself up in all her layers before she went to the door and heaved it open.

And was blinded.

Because everything outside was *light*.

The sun was bright, bouncing off the snow all around, a dizzying kind of madness. It was nothing short of exhilarating after the blizzard and the long night she'd believed might be her last.

With Quinn there in the middle of it, gazing at her from

the other side of the snowmobile that she saw, now, he'd managed to park beneath the overhang of the cabin's roof.

It was dazzling. He was dazzling.

And it felt as if that light punched through her heart. Because she knew two things with a terrible certainty, as if she had always known them and the light was merely bringing them to the surface.

First, that somehow, she had fallen head over heels in love with this man.

And second, that if he ever knew that he—and this place, gleaming white and too bright and stunningly beautiful behind him—was little more than a trophy to her colleagues . . . and had been the same to her, to her shame, he would hate her forever.

"You okay?" he asked.

"Perfect," she managed to say.

They packed up, got on the snowmobile, and headed back to the Mine to let everyone know they'd lived through the storm.

Violet rubbed at her eyes, thinking about karma, as she and Quinn sat in the little diner. But there was no mistaking it. Grand Mia had slapped down a pile of messages in front of Quinn when he'd taken a seat.

And the one on top said, unmistakably, *Stuart Abernathy-Thomason.*

She stared at that name in horror. Her stomach chimed in, immediately beginning to hurt, while all the blood in her body drained down to her feet. Somehow, she remained upright.

Quinn flipped through the pile of messages like it was a deck of cards, shrugged, then tucked the stack of them into one of his back pockets.

Violet braced herself, waiting for a round of recriminations. Accusations.

But all he did was smile at Mia. "That's enough to put a man off his appetite."

"I told them you'd wandered off into a blizzard." Mia cackled. "There's no one to say you came back."

Quinn shifted his smile across the small table toward Violet. It made her heart stutter every time. He was that beautiful. And she couldn't stop thinking that she not only knew how he tasted, but what it felt like to have that mouth on just about every part of her body.

Too many sensations seemed to rock her at once. The shock of seeing Stuart's name on a message for Quinn, not her. The endless tumble, over and over like she was caught in the surf, that was Quinn's effect on her.

It was a wonder she didn't topple straight out the side of the little booth and spill out on the floor of the Mine.

"Do you normally get so many messages?" she asked, and detested herself for the note of studied casualness in her voice.

"One little gold mine with the rights free and clear and the vultures come circling." But Quinn's smile only deepened as he looked at her. "Not that all the vultures are bad."

Violet managed to smile. And Quinn's attention shifted to a couple of members of the Fox family, who wanted to share their stories about blizzards—the one that had just stormed through and a great many in the past. Even though it was clear Quinn already knew almost all the stories himself.

But she was glad of the distraction. Because she knew she was exactly the kind of vulture he disliked, but unlike those who'd called in from afar, she'd taken it a step further and had showed up. Then she'd gone ahead and compounded her sins by falling in love with the man.

Now Stuart had tracked her down and who knew what nasty little stories he would spin this time?

Violet had to hope that Stuart would restrict himself to calls Quinn was unlikely to return and emails he only ever answered tersely. She had to take comfort in the fact that this was a man who had claimed he couldn't take a plane from London to San Francisco. A man who, as far as she knew, seemed to deeply enjoy his creature comforts while giving a lot of lip service to greening the planet, returning to the old ways, and so on. It was, happily, impossible to imagine him following her path and showing up here.

The mere thought made her stomach twist.

"You doing all right, professor?" Quinn asked, snapping her back to the present.

Violet wondered how long he'd been watching her. And worse, what secrets might have been visible on her face. And she hated, suddenly, that they were in this public place. She wanted to reach out and touch him, to assure herself that he was real. That last night had happened. That she hadn't simply dreamed the whole thing, no matter that she was a little tender today.

"I," she declared, pulling herself together and beaming at him, "am absolutely *fantastic*."

Because this was what she did and who she was. Maybe she'd had a few too many painful epiphanies of late, but it didn't matter. Violet made lemonade from lemons, wherever lemons appeared, and there was no need to change that now.

Just like she couldn't control her parents, she couldn't control Stuart, either. All she could control was herself. She was exactly where she was supposed to be. And she decided, then and there, that Stuart didn't get to disrupt this life, too. Because Violet just couldn't bring herself to end what was happening with Quinn sooner than necessary.

She couldn't.

And she was delighted to find later, after they made it all the way back across the lake to his cabin this time, that it was still happening.

They went inside, stripped off their outerwear, and Quinn hauled her up into his arms. Then carried her back to the master bedroom, where he took his time stripping her naked, like she was a feast. But he only sampled her before he carried her into his shower.

"You don't have to carry me everywhere," she told him, frowning.

"I do what I want, Violet," he replied, with a growly certainty that made her shudder.

They stood there in the spray, and Violet didn't know what was better. The way that Quinn took his time soaping up and then rinsing every single part of her body, or the fact that while he did these things, she got to do the same in return. She got to not only touch all the marvelous parts of his body, she got to study them, imprinting every square inch of his marvelous body into her head.

Hoarding it, an inner voice whispered, *as always.* For what came after.

"Do you often have groups in the shower?" Her voice hardly sounded like hers as he knelt down before her, grinning up the length of her body. "It's so . . . big."

"I'm a big guy. I built it to make sure I'd never feel cramped. But this is better."

Then he drew one of her legs over his wide shoulder, grinned wider as she leaned back against the slick wall for support, and then licked his way between her legs.

That night, they slept together in Quinn's wide bed. Violet assumed that because the bed was so much bigger and wider it would be like sleeping alone, but Quinn hauled her to him, holding her close, as if they were still in the narrow little cot.

The next morning, while Quinn was out in his shop—a large garage sort of area filled with equipment and tools and a variety of other alarming-looking devices like *saws* that she wouldn't have the slightest idea what to do with—Violet pulled out her phone, connected to the internet, and held her breath as she waited for her messages to download.

She saw Irving's name. And then, sure enough, Stuart's.

Violet was frozen into place on Quinn's big couch. She knew she ought to open the messages. She'd never been the kind of person who let an inbox fill up, like dirty dishes in a sink. She liked to read everything, sort what needed sorting, and start each day fresh.

But no matter how she stared down at the phone in her hand, she didn't click on her messages.

"Bad news?" came Quinn's voice, making her jump.

Looking up at him made her breath catch in her throat, the way it always did.

And she knew they had a sell-by date, and there was nothing she could do to change that, even if she made it through the winter. The prize was a chance to make her case, not him.

No matter how much she wished it could be him.

Maybe if she'd believed that this was something more than temporary, she would have made a confession. About the way she and her colleagues jostled the idea of this place around between them like a shiny bauble. How unspoiled little pieces of wilderness like this lake had become celebrated causes for people in her line of work who liked to argue that it was communities, not corporations, who truly mattered—and who would spearhead systemic change. *Starting small is the only way to start,* she had been known to say with great seriousness in meetings. *And starting is what matters if we ever hope to finish.*

But this wasn't going to last.

And that meant she wanted to savor every last moment she had.

"No bad news," she replied as lightly as she could. "Nothing but spam."

When she shut off her phone again, she resolved to leave it that way. Because there would be time enough to answer messages when this was done.

And in the meantime, there was that smile on Quinn's beautiful face. There was that flash of heat in his dark gaze as he walked toward her, then came down before her so he could pull her off the couch into his arms, then tumble her down to the floor in front of the fire.

In the meantime, there was joy.

There was Quinn.

And there were all the ways Violet intended to love him, while she could.

Fourteen

❧

The blizzard had changed everything, even though they were common around here. Quinn had lived through too many to count.

But this one had taken his world, shaken it up like the silly snow globes that Mia claimed *just showed up* in the Mine, and never quite settled into place again.

Quinn knew that he was being careless. That for some reason, when it came to Violet, he couldn't quite bring himself to lay down all the laws he usually trotted out far ahead of any potential complications. He always wanted to make sure that no one got any ideas about what he did and didn't have to offer.

He knew he needed to do it now, with Violet. He knew he needed to get out ahead of any expectations—

But then, maybe that was the trouble. She wasn't a local. Sure, the way their relationship had shifted complicated things, but she wasn't going to stay.

That was the truth of things no matter how good it felt to wake up with her in his bed. To hear her moving around his cabin, muttering to herself the way she did, so cute and bright it made his bones ache and his heart squeeze tight in his chest.

All of that was fine, he assured himself. He could let himself appreciate her because she was only temporary. He'd known that the first time he'd laid eyes on her.

She might claim she could last the season, but he doubted it. And even if she did, he knew she'd be gone with the thaw. Brainy professor types who spent their lives wrapped up tight in their ivory towers preferred central heat, accessible shopping, and a whole lot of infrastructure. Once the novelty of off-grid Alaska faded into the grind of familiarity, she'd head back to the easier life.

Sometimes he had to remind himself. A lot. Otherwise he'd find himself slipping into too many what-ifs. And that way lay nothing but madness.

Meanwhile, January wore on. For the first time in years, Quinn didn't go all the way down the river to Aniak to join the Kuskokwim 300 Campout. Because he could see dog races any year, he reasoned, and join in the social camping aspect where the weekend race turned around. But this was likely the only year he would have Violet.

Not likely, he would correct himself. *It's a certainty. Outsiders don't stay.*

That made everything simple. Though as the days passed, a truth he didn't particularly feel like facing was that it didn't feel simple. Every time they had dinner with his family, they treated her less like a stranger and more like she belonged. Quinn should have objected, but he was pretty sure that it was coming from him.

"So you're just living together now?" Piper asked on one of those occasions, entirely too much speculation on her face.

"She doesn't live here," he said, which was true—and likely didn't require that much force behind the words.

And yet when he looked past Piper to find Violet standing there, looking both crushed and like she was trying not to look crushed, he felt guilty.

As if he'd betrayed her when he was only speaking the truth.

That night when they got back to the cabin he figured they'd have it out, this thing that had been brewing between them all this time. But when they arrived, the aurora was out, putting on a show. They stood outside as long as they could, soaking it in.

And once inside, it seemed that the northern lights were still licking through them, because they didn't make it to the bedroom. They seemed to be equally desperate, tearing off each other's clothes in the living room in a wild rush to get closer. To stay close.

Quinn didn't want to acknowledge that his hunger for her was only growing. It was laced through with the awareness that she would leave him, and that made it deeper. Hotter.

Worse and better all at once.

He gathered her in his arms when they'd finished, after they'd lain on the floor where they'd ended up, panting together. He carried her into the bedroom and curled around her body in his bed as if it was second nature—she fit against him so well he'd almost forgotten that there had ever been a time when he didn't fall asleep like this, breathing her in.

Quinn reached for her again and again that night. And in the morning he waited in the kitchen, with the coffee made, for her to come shuffling out, her eyes behind her glasses cloudy with sleep.

"We need to talk," he said at once, because he didn't want to say it at all. But he liked to think that no matter what else he was—including, with her, a Grade A fool—he wasn't a coward.

"How funny." She gripped her mug with both hands and delivered a baleful sort of look his way. "You read about that phrase all the time, don't you? Or watch it on TV. It turns out it sounds as ominous as promised."

"Things between us have gotten complicated," Quinn said, sounding rougher than he needed to. "I think you and I need to discuss how to simplify them."

He figured she would react immediately and loudly. Instead, she held on to her mug and frowned at him. Not like she was going to have an emotional reaction. More like she was studying him.

When he realized that pissed him off, he caught himself. Did he really *want* her to have a big reaction? He shouldn't. He knew enough about women to know that could leave marks. But there was no denying he'd expected more fireworks.

"Which complications do you mean?" she asked in a scholarly tone. As if they were discussing an esoteric bit of theory. "Pretend I've never had a conversation like this before."

"I'm guessing you haven't."

"It shouldn't be a stretch, then."

Her chin tilted up as she said that and Quinn was struck by the contradictions in her. Her bravery threaded through with vulnerability, and it made him feel scraped raw. He wanted to gather her in his arms and make it better.

But he couldn't, not now, because he had to make certain they were on the same page.

He told himself that she would thank him later.

"I want to make sure that we're both crystal clear about what this is," he said gruffly. His sister's question was still kicking around inside his head, and worse, his reaction. Not what he'd said. But what he'd wanted. Because images of what it would be like if Violet really was living with him had cascaded through him, and he'd liked it. Quinn gritted his teeth and pushed on. "I don't have a lot of experience with virgins."

Violet looked startled. "How is virginity the issue?"

"You've never done this before. And sex can change things." It cost Quinn something to sound so patient when really, who was he to talk? He felt a whole lot more changed than he intended to admit. "If you don't know better, it can make you imagine that things are more serious than they are. That's all."

He thought she had a death grip on that coffee mug, but her expression was bland.

Maybe a little too deliberately bland.

"You caught me," she said after a moment, deadpan. "I've been plotting our wedding this whole time. I hope you share my passion for Stargazer lilies woven into head-dresses. And tulle."

"Sex can confuse the issue." Quinn made himself go on in the same even tone, despite threats of tulle. "Especially in a situation like this. You were already staying here. The blizzard made everything high stakes. And now we're act-ing like there's no end in sight when you and I both know differently."

"Last time I checked, it's still winter outside. Unless summer occurred in the last two hours, I was under the impression that I was still adhering to our agreement. An agreement that I graciously agreed to extend even though I obviously already met your initial terms. Twice. I showed up at your favorite bar to buy you a beer *and* clearly lasted longer than a week."

"You're never going to make it through the winter, Violet." He sounded too harsh, but she needed to hear him. "It's not going to happen."

But the only thing that happened in the wake of his matter-of-fact statement was a faint narrowing of her eyes.

"Is it not going to happen or is it that you don't want it to happen?" she asked after a moment.

"Doesn't matter."

Violet sighed. And if he wasn't mistaken, rolled her eyes as she took a long sip of her coffee. "I can't tell the difference between the ordinary masculine panic that I might *get ideas* because we're sleeping together and your whole *this is Alaska and no one from California can survive here* thing. You're going to have to be more clear, Quinn. Sorry."

She did not look even remotely sorry. And his teeth seemed to be grinding together of their own accord, so he made a point to unclench his jaw.

And to get his drawl on. "It's easy for things to feel heightened, darlin'. I want to make sure that no one's confusing this situation for something that has longevity."

Violet set down her coffee mug with a decisive click. "Remind me, please, when exactly you found me clinging to your pant leg, begging you for . . . What did you call it? *Longevity?*"

"You're getting emotional," he told her, when that wasn't exactly true. The word he should have used was *scathing.* But maybe that was the same thing. "I'm not trying to upset you, Violet. I only want things to be clear."

"I think that actually you're the one getting emotional, *darling,*" she said with a sniff.

Then she waved her hand in the air, so languidly it was just this side of insulting, and it was almost enough to keep him from noticing how that *darling* landed. Like a lick of her tongue down the length of him.

But Violet was still talking, languid hand in the air as if

he was the one who needed letting down easy here. "You clearly have an emotional connection to my virginity that I don't have. You've extrapolated from that that I must feel a host of different emotions, but that's coming from you. Not me. Has it ever occurred to you, Quinn, that I'm using this situation as an opportunity to explore a sexual relationship in a convenient package? It's basically one-stop shopping and has the added benefit of taking place in almost total isolation. Maybe you're the one who needs to check your emotions at the door."

He might have bought into it if her gaze wasn't glittering with all the emotions she claimed she wasn't having. And he would have argued the point except—what was it he wanted, again? To convince her she was emotional when she claimed she wasn't? How would that help . . . anything?

"If you say so, professor," he said, matching her lazy arrogance with his drawl. "I'm just trying to look out for you here. I want you to remember that."

Violet let out a long-suffering sigh that would have put his teeth on edge if he wasn't already clenching his jaw again. "I understand. Never let it be said that you weren't bound and determined to do your duty, no matter what."

"What's that supposed to mean?"

The look she trained on him then made him feel as if she'd stuck him under a magnifying glass. "I think you know."

"What I know is that a lot of people around here have a lot of opinions about how I handle my responsibilities. But I'm not clear why you share those opinions, having been here five whole seconds."

That seemed to clear the smoke some. Or maybe she saw straight through him. Either way, he had to fight to keep his hand from rising to rub at his chest.

"There are a thousand ways to climb up on a cross,

Quinn," Violet said quietly. "What's a lot harder is climbing back down."

"What would you know about it?" He looked down to find that his hand had moved of its own accord and dropped it to his side. "What sacrifices are you called on to make locked up in your fancy little ivory tower, far away from the real world?"

And he realized how much he wanted her to rise to the bait when she didn't. When instead, she gazed at him. As if he made her sad.

A notion that made Quinn want to break things.

"Has it ever occurred to you that you hide behind the duty you feel to Lost Lake?" She smiled, but it wasn't her usual smile. "I'm not attacking you. I'm looking out for you."

"No," he bit out. But something inside him resonated unpleasantly. "It's funny to me you would come to find me, talking protection and conservation, but then question my commitment to both of those things. It's not like you haven't been around, Violet. You know there aren't a lot of places like this one. I'm not going to apologize for believing that the people who live here deserve to decide what to do with this land. By ourselves."

"I'm sure they appreciate what you do. But have any of the people here ever actually *asked* you to sacrifice yourself on their behalf, Quinn?"

It was like she'd struck a tuning fork deep inside him. It hummed. A long, lone note he couldn't ignore.

He hated it.

Quinn was profoundly sorry he'd brought any of this up at all. He moved toward her, solving the issue with his mouth on hers, hauling her up against him until her legs moved around his waist.

It was only later, when they were both wrecked and

panting and trying not to fall into a heap on the kitchen floor, that it occurred to him to question if maybe, just maybe, he was a little more emotional here than he wanted to admit. He spent the rest of the day buried in the sober, serious, wholly unemotional mechanics of the job he kept thundering on and on about, just to prove it couldn't be true.

He'd been ignoring his inbox as well as that stack of messages Mia had given him after the blizzard, and it was high time he stopped playing games. He sat down with his laptop, ignored Violet when she curled up on the far side of the couch with a prim look on her face and a novel in her lap, and began to systematically go through everything he'd been ignoring.

When he looked up again, a solid couple of hours had passed. He had a crick in his neck, his eyes were tired, and he was feeling the kind of cranky he always felt when faced with all the disingenuous salesman types who clearly believed he was a dumb Alaskan hick who couldn't possibly understand the ways they tried to maneuver around him. The good news was that they were easy enough to deal with, especially with a terse email. The bad news was that they not only never learned their lesson, there were always more.

Like mosquitoes, the unofficial Alaska state birds, which descended in hordes every spring.

Quinn moved and set his laptop aside, then stood up and stretched. He could feel Violet's eyes on him but when he glanced over at her, her attention was on her book. In a saintly fashion that, despite himself, tugged at him.

The real trouble with Violet wasn't that he couldn't keep his hands off her. The real trouble was that he genuinely liked her.

That warning note sounded in him again.

And he was sizing up his next move—because merely

looking at her always gave him a hankering for another taste of her, but he really needed to get back to that still-overflowing inbox—but he was saved from having to make that critical decision by the ringing of his phone.

It was Abel Lincoln, which never boded well. Since he usually called up from Hopeless only when there was trouble of one stripe or another. Last time it had been Violet.

"What now?" Quinn asked by way of greeting as he walked into the kitchen, leaving Violet in peace with her book.

Abel laughed. "There's another Outsider here. But not as cute as the first one."

Quinn congratulated himself on not reacting to Abel calling Violet cute. She was cute, obviously. But she wasn't his. He had no right to object if other men appreciated her.

Though he did, in fact, object.

"I hope that means your sister isn't making like a taxi service this time," he said instead of noting his objections.

"Here's the thing about that," Abel said, and he sounded . . . wary. Quinn braced himself. "Normally Rosemary would be halfway to the Mine by now, thrilled to be able to provide folks with a little bit of entertainment on such a cold day. But she's taken against this one."

"I'm not getting why I'm the one on the other end of this call. I thought I made my feelings pretty clear about the Lost Lake gossip chain. About ten thousand times already."

"Thing is, he's asking for you by name." Abel sounded almost apologetic. "Says he's come all the way from London to rescue you."

Quinn laughed. "Rescue *me*? From what?"

Able made a strange sort of sound. "Violet. He's come to rescue you from Violet, Quinn. He called her . . . Well, he called her a con artist."

And Quinn made as if to laugh, but stopped. Abel's

words settled into him and as they did, it sparked a memory. The stack of messages Mia had given him after the blizzard. The name on top and, more important, the way Violet had gone pale at their table in the diner. At the time he'd figured she was simply reacting to what had happened. Hiding out from a blizzard. Losing the virginity she might have called a *story*, but it was a story she'd held on to an awfully long time. Maybe a combination of the two. It had seemed reasonable enough to him.

So reasonable that he'd done little more than glance at the messages and put them away, but he should have remembered that name. Stuart.

How many Stuarts were there likely to be, all of a sudden? It wasn't the 1950s.

He ended his call with Abel and turned back toward the doorway that led into his living room. To look at Violet, dressed in pink, as usual. Her legs were curled up beneath her. Her hair was piled on top of her head so that little curls fell down around her face. Her glasses were always sliding down her nose. She was playing with her lower lip, pulling it between her fingers as she read her book.

And all of it was a lie.

Maybe it wasn't such a shock after all that she'd reacted the way she had to their earlier conversation.

Maybe she'd never been the one getting ideas.

Maybe there had only ever been one dumbass here, and it was him.

That tuning fork hummed louder, filling him up until he thought he might bust wide open. He'd never wanted to feel like this again. He'd never imagined he would.

And this time it was a whole lot worse, because he'd known better. The worst part was, he knew he had no one to blame for this but himself.

Quinn felt something like sick. She had eaten dinner

with his family. She'd been accepted, at his home and at the Mine. People liked her.

He liked her.

And he had no one to blame but himself, because she'd told him, hadn't she? She'd been up-front from the first moment. He knew that she was here for the land.

Quinn had known all along that he should never have let himself get caught up in anything personal with an Outsider. And especially not one who wanted to tell the locals what to do with land that would never be hers.

She must have felt his gaze on her because she looked up, and his chest hitched when she smiled automatically. And then again when that smile faded.

"Is something wrong?" she asked.

And the worst thing yet was that Quinn didn't want to do what had to be done now. He wanted to pretend. Just for a little while longer. Just until he could make sense of this somehow.

His own weakness felt like a kick to the gut.

"You need to pack," he told her.

Violet blinked. "What?"

"Your ex has showed up down in Hopeless, looking to save me from a con artist," he said, still too soft-spoken. Too dark. *Broken*, something in him whispered, not that it mattered now. "But I don't need to be saved. I'll do everyone a favor and deliver you straight to him. And then, Violet, the pair of you can go away, straight to hell, for all I care, and never come back here."

Fifteen

❧

O nce again, her life had turned itself inside out in the space of a moment. Except this time, she could only blame herself.

And she did.

Violet felt numb, and for once that wasn't because of the weather outside.

She had no doubt that Stuart had found his way to Alaska, just as she'd fervently hoped he wouldn't, but she'd let the situation with Quinn get more involved when she'd known that was a distinct possibility. She'd seen that message. And she might not have lied, exactly, but she hadn't been as forthcoming as she could have been. More, she knew that had been a deliberate choice.

She'd been waiting ever since then for the other shoe to fall, and it had.

Serves you right that it's landed directly on your head, she told herself.

Violet was used to riding on snowmobiles now, but it

was different this time. The force of Quinn's fury was like
a living thing, chasing them all the way across the lake and
then down that rutted path to Hopeless that she remembered only in little snippets from before.

It had been so dark that night and she had been so taken
aback by the cold. The stars. She'd had no idea what she
was getting into.

Now she wanted to sob out all the things she knew, all
that she'd learned, but she didn't dare indulge herself. Not
only did she not want to risk Quinn's reaction, but surely
tears in subzero temperatures was just asking for unpleasant consequences.

And everything was already unpleasant enough.

As Quinn rode them into Hopeless, the small frontier
town seemed like a booming metropolis to Violet after
weeks by the lake. She could remember feeling the opposite weeks ago, but maybe that was because she'd seen it
only in the dark. The sun was still up today, barely. She
could see more of the town. The houses clustered together,
the quirky little shops with their peculiarly Alaskan mix of
practical and whimsical. She remembered thinking they
were squat and ugly before, but now she liked the look of
them. Sturdy and slyly welcoming, if you knew where to
look. She wanted to explore each one of them.

But Quinn was pulling up before the general store and
this wasn't a shopping trip. He was off the snowmobile in a
flash, unloading her hastily packed bag and setting it down
in the hardpacked snow out front.

That he did it with great precision, even gentleness, only
made her stomach knot. Harder.

"Quinn—" she began.

He held up a hand. "I don't want to hear it."

"I want to explain—"

"There's nothing to explain," he said, and this bit of precision was like a hail of bullets. Each one hit its mark. "Have a nice life, Violet."

Then he climbed back on his snowmobile and drove away.

Violet couldn't believe it.

Long after the sound had faded away, she was still standing there, her heart a sickening beat in her chest, her stomach nothing but an ache, and a heaviness everywhere else that made her want to lie down and never get up again.

Because she couldn't bring herself to believe that it could end like this. That he could drive away without hesitation. Without looking back. And yet the weight of her present circumstances felt inevitable, irrevocable, as if there'd been no other way this could go from the start.

She hadn't even mounted an argument. She'd gone cold at the look on his face, and she'd packed quickly. Too easily.

And later, maybe, she would wonder if she might have fought more if she hadn't felt so guilty.

But it was too cold out here to stand around wondering.

Violet grabbed her pack from the ground and wheeled around, stamping her way into the general store because apparently, everything about her Alaskan adventure was going to be bookended like this. She was going to go out the way she came in. Complete with the urge to cause Stuart bodily harm.

Though she could have done without the hollow feeling inside her that threatened to take her to her knees.

Inside, the store was precisely as she remembered it, but now it was overlaid with everything else she'd experienced since she'd come here. She saw Abel at the counter talking in a low voice with a local she recognized from market day. And she looked past him to where Rosemary was standing, arms folded, while she glared at someone sitting at the food counter.

Knowing exactly who she would find sitting there, Violet marched grimly in his direction.

She remembered thinking that the store was stocked bizarrely, but now she understood it. Everything here had to hold folks over between bigger deliveries or, for some, stand in for the supermarkets that didn't exist out this way. More than that, she understood now the benefit of these gathering places. When isolation smarted a bit, a person could come in, have a chat, and spend some time with other people before going back out into the deep embrace of the relentless wilderness.

The truth was, she wanted to go back out into the wilderness herself.

Violet gritted her teeth and walked up to the counter, looking at Rosemary over the unpleasantly familiar head before her. The other woman caught her eye and shook her head like an indictment. It felt that harsh—but then, Violet had earned it. And she couldn't think about the losses piled on top of losses now.

Not while Stuart, who for some reason fancied himself her nemesis, was right here.

He swiveled around on his stool and then . . . there he was. He looked exactly as she remembered him, if a bit more tired and rumpled—likely a testament to how he'd traveled into the interior. How had she never noticed his face wasn't erudite, but petulant? She'd thought he was tall and academic-looking, but he was shorter than Quinn, narrow everywhere, and his mouth was set in a mulish, ugly little line.

She had the unwelcome memory of him involved in naked calisthenics and her stomach rebelled.

But then he turned away, circling back toward Rosemary with no sign of recognition, and she almost laughed.

"Why am I not surprised that you don't even recognize me, Stuart?" she asked. "It really says it all."

He wheeled back toward her, comically shocked. Violet peeled off multiple layers to reveal her face. She watched his expression change, and felt . . . strangely detached.

"My God, Violet," he breathed.

It could have been someone else entirely who had fought with him through her laptop on Christmas Eve. Someone else who had listened to him say those cruel things to her. And still someone else who had felt so awash with fury. Enough that she'd stormed out of the Institute and taken herself off to the ends of the earth to prove . . . something. She hardly remembered now.

When all she could think or feel was Quinn.

"Darling," Stuart said, in the voice that had once washed over her like a warm hug. Or what she'd imagined a warm hug from a man would feel like, anyway. Now it scraped over her and made her stomach tight. And it certainly wasn't Quinn's *darlin'* that made everything in her dance like fire. "I've been looking everywhere for you."

When she didn't say anything, he stood up, reached over, and took her hands.

And it was a lucky thing she was wearing her thick gloves, because she thought that the touch of Stuart's skin to hers might make her vomit. She stared down at their hands and couldn't get past the wrongness of it. Stuart had long, slender fingers that even Violet could tell were surpassingly soft.

If he was left to keep them safe from a blizzard, they would be dead.

And she would still be a virgin.

No thank you, she thought.

"There seems to have been a terrible misunderstanding," Stuart was saying in the voice she remembered him using for most of the past year. His fake voice, in other words. And a glance at Rosemary's scowl made it clear he'd used a different approach on her, too. "I worry that somehow, I gave you the wrong impression."

When she looked again, she saw that Stuart had arranged his face to look appropriately mournful. Beseeching, even.

And that was the good thing about being numb straight through. All Violet could do was laugh.

She yanked her hands out of his, stepped back, and kept laughing. So hard that Abel and his customer stopped what they were doing to watch. So loud that Rosemary joined in, as if she couldn't help herself.

"I've no idea what's so amusing," Stuart said, and there was a flash of who he really was then. The Stuart she'd seen for the first time on Christmas Eve. The one who'd had no trouble whatsoever being cruel. Just as she could see how he struggled to maintain that concerned mask, threaded through with a hint of bashfulness. "I've traveled a bloody long way to see you, Violet."

"Sorry," Violet said with a smile that made it clear she was apologizing without apologizing. "I'm astonished that I ever wanted to sleep with you. And grateful, Stuart. Deeply, *deeply* grateful that I never did."

He jerked as if she'd hit him. Making Violet realize that actually, she would have liked very much to hit him.

But she had survived weeks in the Alaskan bush and he was . . . well, him. It wouldn't be a fair fight. She would crush him like a bug.

Though it was appealing, she refrained.

"What I don't understand is why you chose me to mess with," she said when her laughter faded. "I would very much like to be removed from whatever this equation is.

You've already stolen my paper. Isn't that enough? Why are you tracking me down in *Alaska* when you couldn't make it to San Francisco? Surely you have enough to do, what with swanning around at conferences, telling lies about me, and taking credit for the Institute's work?"

"You're not fooling anyone," Stuart sneered, dropping the mask completely. "You think that if you come back having finally put your stamp on this godforsaken place you'll make me look bad by default. I know how your mind works, Violet. And I'm not about to let that happen."

"Aren't you?" She laughed again. "What do you think you're going to do? If Quinn Fortune wanted to see you, he would have come inside just now. He didn't. He's not interested in anything you have to say."

Stuart let out a jeering sort of laugh. "You can't possibly imagine that you're more persuasive than I am, darling. Don't be silly. You'll only embarrass yourself."

And suddenly, in a flash, it occurred to Violet that being a scandalous woman and a floozy of the highest order was a power, not a detriment. Why hadn't she realized that before?

"Oh, Stuart," she said pityingly. "I don't think you're his type."

It was remarkably satisfying to watch his face turn purple.

Nothing he said was particularly coherent after that. And when it got much louder and more insulting, Abel came over, stone-faced, and told Stuart that he could cool off in the shower or outside, his choice, but he needed to take a break from the conversation.

When he was gone, slamming the door to the shower room behind him, Violet looked at these people she'd actually considered friends, meeting their gazes as evenly as she could. She owed them that much.

"I'm going to need to find a way back to McGrath," she said. Quietly. "Or wherever I can catch a plane to Anchorage."

Abel only stared back at her, as impassive as she recalled from the first time she'd met him. Rosemary folded her arms and shook her head again. "That's it, then? You're leaving?"

Violet refused to react the way everything in her wanted to. She shrugged. "Isn't that what Outsiders do?"

"I had a feeling about you," Rosemary said, too sharply to be sorrowful. "Or I wouldn't have taken you up to the Mine. But I guess you're not different after all."

And Violet wanted to fight, but what was the point? It wasn't really Rosemary she wanted to have words with. Or not only Rosemary.

She smiled, because a smile was better than a scream. And anything was better than sobbing, so she would stay positive. No matter what.

"Do I need to go around knocking on doors to see if there are any stray pilots about?" she asked.

"I have a better idea," came a voice from closer to the door.

When she glanced over, her heart jumped—but in the next moment, she understood. It wasn't Quinn. It was Bowie.

It was only Bowie. Tall with chiseled cheekbones, but still not Quinn.

"You'll fly me to McGrath?" she asked, and told herself there was no reason her heart should be carrying on like that. Just like she cautioned herself against reading too much into the considering gaze Bowie shot her way. She stood straighter. "I don't want to put you to any trouble. I made my own way here, I can make my own way back."

"No wonder Quinn likes you," Bowie drawled. "Same martyr, different day."

And that was how Violet found herself on Bowie's terrifyingly small little plane, which he flew like he really was trying to kill himself, or her, all the way to Anchorage.

Where she bought the first flight she could to San Francisco, by way of Seattle, and then, just like that, she was home.

She sat in the taxi from the airport, a splurge because she thought attempting to take public transportation was beyond her just then. Too overwhelming. And as they inched up into the city in the usual Bay Area traffic, even this late at night, she reminded herself that San Francisco was truly one of the prettiest cities in the world.

All she saw was how crowded it was. Cars. Buildings. Concrete. And the people, everywhere.

The taxi let her out in front of her building and the noise on the street shocked her—when she knew, rationally, that it was a quiet night in her neighborhood. But all the rationalizations in the world couldn't keep her from feeling as if she were wearing someone else's skin. And that it didn't fit.

She marched inside and up the stairs and then she let herself into her apartment. Into someone else's life.

Violet dropped her pack on the floor and then stood there for a moment, swaying slightly. Then she followed it down.

And right there in the entryway of an apartment that felt wrong, still wearing too many layers as if the Arctic might have followed her home, she finally gave in and let herself cry.

And cry. And cry.

But the next morning, Violet was done catering to emotion.

She woke up early and took her time getting ready. It was almost as if she'd forgotten how, especially with her eyes swollen red from all the tears. And everything was strange and loud, even inside her apartment, but she supposed that was to be expected after weeks away in so much isolation. She would adapt.

Because I always adapt, she told herself firmly.

She took the long way to work, walking down to the marina and then along Crissy Field, with its views of Alcatraz out in the bay and the towering Golden Gate Bridge leading her along until she cut up toward the Presidio. It was a typical San Francisco morning, fog clinging to the edges of things, and she could remember the exhilaration she'd felt the first time she'd taken this same walk. How she'd charged up the steep hill toward the Institute, electrified by the prospect of the life she intended to build here.

Maybe Quinn was right and it had been nothing more than hiding herself away from anything real.

Violet walked into the Institute and had a moment of pause, remembering too clearly the last time she'd been here and the humiliating confessions she'd made to her colleagues. The veiled and not-so-veiled innuendos she'd gotten in return. Her stomach tied itself in a painful knot.

But then she remembered. She was the new, improved Violet Parrish. This version had been prepared to spray a bear. And was not afraid of being called a floozy.

Because this version knew the truth. First, that she had not slept with Stuart, praise be. But second, and more important, that she *had* slept with Quinn. A lifetime of reading academic takedowns of the very notion of virginity didn't change the fact that losing hers to Quinn made her feel empowered in a way she hadn't before. She felt like she could do anything—because being with Quinn felt like flying.

She couldn't pretend she didn't know what wings felt like, simply because others had never taken their feet from the earth.

Violet marched into her old life with her head high.

And when she presented herself in Irving's office moments later, she did not cringe in embarrassment or start off with apologies. *Wings*, she reminded herself.

"I haven't had the best internet on my trip," she announced as he stared at her as if she were an apparition. "I'm not sure I'm up to date on everything that's happening here. Can you explain to me why Stuart Abernathy-Thomason trekked into the Alaskan wilderness to find me? Apparently to make snide remarks?"

"I don't know, Violet," Irving said, and he was not, for a change, tomato red. "Perhaps he finds you irresistible."

His voice was so dry that had he been anyone else, Violet might have thought he was being droll. But this was Irving.

"I've always been irresistible, Irving," she replied, in much the same tone. "And yet, as I believe I mentioned to our mutual embarrassment the last time I saw you, he did not previously seem to find that quite the lure."

Irving smiled. "After you hung up on me last time," he said, and only lifted a brow when she attempted to deny that she'd done exactly that. Violet tried to look contrite. "After I recovered from the incivility, I decided to review our options. And I decided that Stuart's disgraceful behavior and rumormongering do not deserve to be rewarded."

"I couldn't agree more," Violet said quietly.

Irving made a harrumphing sort of sound. He stood, jerking the cuffs of his exquisitely tailored suit. "Stuart is not the only person in our field who can have a quiet word in the right ears, and accordingly, I did not retract the Institute's presentation from the conference. My feeling is if Stuart Abernathy-Thomason wishes to pit himself against the collective might of the Institute, he's most welcome. I think he'll find that the reputation of this organization far exceeds his own."

"I knew he had to be desperate," Violet said, as Irving's words rang through the office. "Why else would he come all the way to Alaska?" She shook her head. "But I do wish I understood why he picked me as a target."

Irving straightened to his full height, which did not exceed Violet's. And as she watched, the tomato again began to bloom red.

"I'm not one to comment on the personal lives of my colleagues," he said.

"Perish the thought."

The gaze Irving trained on her then was steady. "He underestimated you, Violet. He thought, as I regret to say too many do, that because you are bubbly and optimistic, you're a fool. It's a sad truth of human nature that we believe a dark sort of grimness, a self-indulgent jadedness, is more serious somehow. More meaningful. When cynicism is nothing if not the refuge of the shallow. It is far more difficult to maintain enthusiasm for a world that does not share it. A world that we know, furthermore, is in great peril."

Violet choked up, but knew that if she let her emotions show, Irving might actually keel over and die. She blinked back her tears and made herself smile.

Even though it hurt.

"Thank you," she said, and meant it, deeply. "I've loved working here. You're a good man and I'm lucky that I've had you as my mentor all these years."

"Anything that was said in the heat of the moment before you went to Alaska was said in undue haste," Irving said, frowning at her. "Your position here is secure, Violet. I hope you know that."

And maybe she had known that she would do this back

in Alaska when she'd stopped reading her email. Maybe she'd understood even then that whatever happened next, she couldn't return to her tiny little life.

Last night, when she finished crying on the floor, she'd gotten up, turned on the lights, and really soaked in the life she'd built here. The life she'd left much too easily and, truth be told, hadn't thought much about since.

She'd walked around her apartment like a tourist, looking at the art on her walls, the books on her shelves. Stanley's hutch, her collection of adorable teapots though she drank coffee, and her lonely bed she'd piled high with pillows and bright colors as if that would disguise the fact that she'd always been so alone.

Violet had always maintained that her solitary state didn't bother her, but she couldn't now. She knew what it was like to be close to another person. She knew what it was like to have him inside her body, to sleep tangled up in him, to know him with her eyes closed. What it was like to share her days and nights with another person, meals and conversation, silence and showers.

She couldn't unknow any of it.

Not only that, she couldn't fit herself back into this small space now that she knew what it was like to stand free beneath a sky so big she hadn't felt lost in it at all, only elevated. Only *more*.

Be careful out there, Bowie had said when they landed in Anchorage.

There are no bears in San Francisco, Violet had replied, because all the other things she wanted to say were inappropriate. She didn't need a lifetime of romantic experiences to know that a grown woman didn't ask the brother of a man who'd ended things with her to pass on messages. No matter how tempting it was to ask. *None who are likely to feast on me, anyway.*

It's not the bears in the forest you need to fear, Bowie had told her, and for once he hadn't been grinning. He'd tapped his finger against his forehead, his midnight eyes so like his brother's watchful gaze. *It's the ones up here. Not enough bear spray in the world to save you from them, if you're not careful.*

That was the thing about learning how to fly, Violet had discovered. It made a person far less worried about things like bears.

"I'm going to offer you my resignation again, Irving," she said quietly now, and this time, she let her emotions show a little. Because she wasn't sure she could hide them. "And this time, I'm going to need you to take it."

Sixteen

❧

After Quinn left Violet down in Hopeless and assured himself it was a good-riddance situation, he grudgingly accepted the fact that it was clearly going to be harder to get back to normal than he'd anticipated.

His temper fueled his ride back up to the Mine that day, where he stopped for a beer before heading back to his cabin. And yeah, maybe he'd stopped for that beer to make the point that he was alone again. Because this was Lost Lake. He didn't need to make announcements. Her absence would do it for him.

That and the gossip Abel was sure to keep spreading.

Quinn reminded himself he was better off now. He believed that, truly. He did.

But everything seemed off.

His bed was too big. The cabin was too empty. He woke up the next morning and hated that she wasn't beside him, then went ahead and made her coffee before he caught himself.

"Pathetic," he muttered to himself.

Like that might change things back to the way they were. They didn't.

He poured out the coffee Violet wasn't there to drink and wished he could pour her out of his head as easily.

Quinn could track exactly how long it took for word of what happened in Hopeless to spread across the lake. Because sure enough, his mother turned up exactly one week later with a tray of his favorite lasagna.

"Why are you bringing me comfort food?" he asked when she handed it off in his entryway and then sauntered in. "Did someone die?"

"Good to see nothing's changed with you since you were ten years old," Lois replied. She disappeared into the kitchen, leaving Quinn no choice but to follow her. When he did, he found her rummaging in his fridge to make room. She straightened and motioned, impatiently, for the heavy tray she'd brought. "The more hurt you get, the more you react to it like an animal with its foot in a trap."

"Thanks for the lasagna, Mom. Maybe next time you can deliver it without the commentary."

Wishful thinking on his part. His mother didn't bother to respond. She Tetris-ed the lasagna into place and then stood, facing him with a look that didn't bode well for Quinn.

He braced himself.

"So whose fault is it this time?" Lois asked.

Quinn stiffened. It was as good as proclaiming she'd hit the target head-on, damn her. "What do you mean by *this time*? Do I want to know?"

Lois shrugged. "I think you need to remember that your Carrie liked the idea of her Alaskan heritage at school in Seattle where it made her special. The only one surprised she didn't want to stick it out here was you. I see her aunt every time I go down to Bethel and she's only surprised, all these years later, that Carrie ever pretended she wanted to live out this way."

"Why are we talking about ancient history?"

"Violet, on the other hand, came here because she wanted to come," Lois pointed out. "And stayed longer than she needed to stay to get her point across. It's not the same thing as chasing up the vague idea of a family legacy with a cute young man you meet in law school, is it?"

"I don't know why you're drawing comparisons. I'm not."

"Aren't you?"

He knew the look she trained on him then too well. It was her *save me from suffering these fools* look, most commonly employed at her dinner table, but also put to great use in all expeditions to the Mine.

Quinn's jaw tightened. "No."

"You've been beating yourself up with the same ghost for much too long," Lois told him. "Sooner or later, you're going to become a ghost yourself. And then what?"

"I don't want to talk about ghosts, Mom," Quinn gritted out. "The only thing that haunts me is the fact that I brought a slick operator, who was after our land and our mine for her own purposes, to family dinner. More than once. I should have known better."

Lois only shook her head. Then lifted her hand when he tried to keep talking and let herself out, leaving him to his brooding.

After she left, Quinn dedicated himself and the better part of an evening to a rousing defense of his position. To himself and his empty cabin. With lasagna. It left him full up on cheese and pasta and forced to sit in a living room that seemed not just empty, but desolate.

Eventually, and grudgingly, Quinn faced up to some facts.

He might not have liked his mother's delivery, but like it

or not, what she'd come to tell him was true. He'd made his past happen all over again.

The difference was, this time, he didn't see how he was going to live through it.

Not that you've been living with the first round all that well, a voice inside him countered. *It would be hard to do worse.*

Ouch.

Quinn didn't want to think of himself as a martyr. And yet all he could think about now was the look on Violet's face when he'd ordered her to pack. He'd been all fired up with a sense of betrayal, fueled with an underlying righteousness that, looking back, felt familiar.

Welcome, almost. Like he'd been waiting for her to prove she was wrong. Wrong for the lake. Wrong for Alaska. Wrong for him.

Funny thing was, the farther he got away from that moment, the more it seemed that he'd been the one who'd betrayed her.

Maybe she'd come and figured she could operate some kind of honeypot operation to get that beer with him . . . But he couldn't work up a full head of steam down that road, because he always came up hard against the fact she'd been innocent.

She'd been beautifully, incandescently innocent, and more than that, she'd been Violet.

And Violet was a lot of things. Too smart for her own good. Too rashly, undeservedly confident when she shouldn't have been at all. She was funny. She was tender. She lit up the Alaskan night without even trying and her absence from his life was like a missing limb.

Quinn didn't know how to function without her anymore.

And yet, as much as he wanted to deny it, there was a

part of him—a larger part of him than he liked—that had taken a kind of grim satisfaction in history repeating itself.

Except Lois's words were now clattering around in his head, and he had to wonder about his own history. Carrie hadn't reached out to him after she'd left, but it wasn't like he had tried to track her down, either. He'd taken her absence as a declaration and that had been that. Once enough time had passed to suggest she wasn't returning, he'd shipped what she'd left behind to the only address he knew for her.

Then he'd thrown himself into his job here like he was taking a swan dive onto a funeral pyre, burning himself up like the patron saint of Lost Lake . . . that no one around these parts had ever wanted him to be.

And now it occurred to him—sitting alone in the vast solitude that he'd always thought he wanted, but couldn't seem to settle into any longer—that if he was going to spend his life haunted he had better make sure that the rattling chains he heard upon occasion were from the right ghost.

"Thanks, Mom," he muttered into the quiet surrounding him. "Thanks a lot."

He figured that up at her head of the lake, Lois was smiling. Because she always knew.

And in the end, it was so easy to find Carrie that he had to ask himself why he hadn't done it before. A quick message on social media, his number tossed out like a Hail Mary, and then an hour later his phone rang.

"I don't believe it," came that voice from his past. "I never thought I'd talk to you again, Quinn. And I've wanted to apologize for years."

He and Carrie talked for the better part of an hour and when he hung up, Quinn found he'd let go of a whole lot of bottled-up crap. It turned out that he liked knowing that the girl he'd thought he'd marry so long ago was happy. She lived down in Oregon with her husband and kids, was a local district attorney, and couldn't imagine how or why she'd ever wanted another life.

"I wish we'd had this conversation years ago," he'd told her. "Because I'm happy for you, Carrie. I mean that."

"I don't think we could have had this conversation years ago," she'd replied with a laugh. "But I'm glad we've had it now. I hope you know I never wanted you anything but happy, either, Quinn."

But then, with one ghost vanquished, Quinn was left with the far more troubling specter of himself, like it or not—and he didn't like it at all.

It wasn't lost on him that he'd been using the ghost of Carrie as the bad guy all this time. If Carrie hadn't left. If Carrie hadn't betrayed him. A whole lot of ifs wrapped up in the actions of a woman who clearly wasn't right for him or she wouldn't have run away, and he'd used that as a reason to out-hermit folks in a place where there were more people with an eye toward the isolated life than not.

Carrie had done him a favor. In more ways than one. Because Quinn didn't like to change his mind when it was made up, so he wouldn't have. And that would have been a shame, because he doubted he could have made her happy—and it was clear she could never have been happy here.

But understanding all that now meant that he was forced to face the real villain in all this.

Himself.

This is never supposed to be just a job, his father had told him, time and again.

But Quinn had always been so certain that he knew better than anyone else. That what was required of him was a terrible sacrifice. Because look at what he'd sacrificed already. He'd been sent away to school. He'd been expected to take things too seriously, too soon, because of the honor conferred on him. He'd had to suffer Silver Saskin and her jibes for their entire lives. While Bowie and the other kids their age were building ice hockey rinks, performing death-defying stunts with their four-wheelers, and taking off on a whim to go fishing for weeks, Quinn had been forced to sit in on the quarterly vote meetings, learn how to talk to each and every member of this community whether he wanted to or not, and hear about *responsibility* day and night.

His reward for putting up with all of that was that he'd lost his woman.

And oh, how he'd milked that ever since.

Because it was far easier to throw himself prostrate before a place, a community, than it was to face the fact that deep down, some part of him resented the fact that he didn't get to choose this place like everyone else did.

Quinn found himself staring around his own living room as if he'd never seen it before. As if he hadn't built it with his own two hands and had somehow missed that so much of it was put together on a foundation of resentment.

He was used to his matter-of-fact acceptance of the lake. Of this world. Of this place they'd all grown up in, the stories they all told and retold, and everyone's place in their own families and the community as a whole. He was used to seeing what he'd always seen—a tangled mess of duty, personality, and history, everywhere he looked. The same people doing the same thing in the same places, with the spectacular scenery all around.

And, apparently, a bone-deep grudge against his own good fortune.

But now he'd spent most of January seeing his world through Violet's eyes, not his own. And she'd come in hot, a fizzy rush of pink delight, and washed away everything except what she saw here.

Beauty. Light. Wonder.

She made notes. She immersed herself completely. Her focus was so total, so complete, that before the night of the blizzard, he'd spent entirely too much time wondering what it would be like to have all of that aimed his way. And now he knew.

Why pink? he'd asked her the night of the blizzard, tucked together in that narrow bed.

He hadn't seen her roll her eyes, but he could tell she had. *Why not pink? I wear pink all the time.*

It's silly, isn't it? And your profession is not about silliness. Presumably.

At a certain point, Quinn, we all have to ask ourselves why we're afraid of being happy, Violet had said with her usual brisk cheer. *And then do something about the answer.*

Which in your case meant . . . pink.

No, I just like pink. Violet had shifted around to look at him, grinning. *I think maybe you need to work on the happiness thing, though. Because pink is just a color, but misery is forever.*

Once she'd kissed him, he'd stopped the train of thought about pink and happiness, but now he understood. She was a force no less powerful than the weather here. She'd roared in, uprooted everything, and left him forever changed.

If there were any ghosts left knocking around inside of him, Quinn knew they were his. And his alone.

And he was more than ready to be rid of them.

He made his decision swiftly, the way he always did when it was time to make a call—but he had to laugh at himself when he realized that despite himself, he was going to have to wait.

Because the quarterly vote was in two days, which meant he didn't have time to go chasing after gold mines like every last miner who'd come before him. Not just yet.

He would take care of his people. He would take care of this place. He would do the job that was, truly, his honor, and for once he would try to do it without climbing up on that cross Violet had mentioned.

Without taking out the resentments of the child he'd been on people who needed him to be the grown man he liked to claim he was. He made it a vow, right then and there. He would handle himself like a man who knew how lucky he was, for a change.

And when the meeting was done and the vote was in, Quinn intended to find himself some gold.

The real stuff, this time.

When voting day arrived, Quinn got up early and handled all the usual chores around his house. It was almost February, and he was beginning to see the light on either end of the day. Just that little bit more—enough to remind him that somewhere out there, spring was on its way.

When he got his snow machine out onto the lake, he wasn't surprised to find a procession of Fortunes out there already, all of them heading off together. Bowie pulling stunts. Piper following suit. His parents alternating between leading the pack and acting as foolish as their kids. This time, Quinn joined in on the antics.

As they zipped across the ice on a sunny, *warm for Alaska this time of year* morning, he couldn't seem to remember where his old resentments had come from. He knew full well that folks in the Lower 48 didn't get the beauty of this life. His whole family racing on snow machines across the frozen lake. Waving at the neighbors as they made it up to the Mine, then trooped inside. Where there were music and lights, food and laughter, and familiar faces all around.

For voting days, Mia arranged the tables down the center space—or, to be more precise, ordered her grandsons to arrange them that way, a section for each of the four main families—so everyone could feel like the proper governing body they were, up here around a lake that was almost as lost as its name. Because no one stumbled across this old mining town by accident. They had to come looking. They had to like what they found. And most important, they had to want to stay put and make a life here.

The truth of it rang in him a bit differently today.

You didn't think you had a choice, but you did. You could have gone off to college, then law school, and never come back, like so many others. You could have stayed gone. You didn't.

He didn't. He wouldn't.

It was a regular old voting day in January, but to Quinn, it would always be the beginning. Of the life he chose here. Of the life he planned to live here, from now on, with intention, not regret.

Starting right now, he thought.

"It's my honor to present to you all, His Highness, Quinn freaking Fortune," Bowie called out as they all walked toward the gathering together. "Ready to preside over another quarterly meeting whether we like it or not."

And this time, the half-mocking applause that would have outraged him normally made him grin. Because he'd learned a few things about brightness this winter, and he liked it better than the dark. He even dropped a mock bow.

"I'd like to revisit the idea of reopening the old jail cells here," he drawled as he stood at the head of all the tables. "And I'd furthermore like to volunteer my brother, Bowie, as the first prisoner."

"You can't lock me up, big brother." Bowie smirked. "Though you can try."

"I'm all for the jails," Old Harry belted out. "Next time Beatrice runs around without her skivvies and scares off the wildlife, in she goes. Who's with me?"

Then there was nothing but the usual commotion for a while. The Fox family attempted to keep Beatrice from stripping down there and then. The Barrows did their best to contain Harry's taunts and, when that failed, drown them out.

And he'd turned a corner, Quinn knew, because he found the whole thing entertaining. He wished a certain professor type he knew was here, because he'd bet she'd fill up a whole new book with all her scribbling.

When everyone settled down again, he waited for quiet. It was long in coming, but eventually everyone got there—except Silver Saskin, who preferred to mutter about how she'd been robbed of her birthright, as ever. She kept it up until Amie stabbed her in the ribs with a knitting needle. And once the squawking and threats of murder subsided, thanks to an assist from Grand Mia, Quinn finally opened his mouth to begin the meeting.

But he was stopped by a flash of pink on the other side of the Mine, over by the entrance. When everyone was already here.

And none of them wore pink.

It was like déjà vu—except this time, Quinn knew he had to be dreaming. Because he had this dream pretty much every night since she'd left.

But this time, it was a little too real.

A little too bright. A little too loud as she marched across the floor, pink-cheeked and steel-eyed.

It was Violet, dressed like a strawberry and bristling with determination.

That part, he dreamed a lot.

But what made Quinn suspect that it was really, truly happening this time, as she marched toward him with her eyes bright and golden, was the fact that he would never dream up what looked like at least ten pounds of a ridiculous bunny—complete with droopy ears and twitching whiskers—that she held draped in her arms.

Seventeen

❧

The new configuration of tables threw Violet for a loop as she approached, so she drifted to a stop on the far side of them, clutching Stanley to her chest like he was a security blanket. A security blanket who might express himself via his bodily functions at any moment.

Maybe, despite the trek north once again and all the time it had given her to tell herself she was prepared for this moment, Violet still wasn't ready.

When it came to Quinn, she might never be fully ready for this.

Her lenses cleared slowly, but she could already see too much. He was standing there on the other side of the clumped-together tables, and he looked spectacular.

It reminded her of the first night she'd arrived and had been half-drunk on the cold, the dark, the burst of light and warmth in the Mine, and then him. He was wearing another T-shirt that was really more of a taunt, highlighting his glorious form that she remembered entirely too well. Pants that made it difficult to drag her gaze away from his attributes. But she did, because his eyes were like midnight, and he was looking straight at her.

And she couldn't read him.

She still couldn't read him, though her heart was going so wild in her chest that she thought it must have been drumming directly into Stanley. She was surprised he wasn't grunting his displeasure, a prelude to a nip.

"Is that a rabbit?" was how Quinn chose to greet her.

All the people at the tables swiveled to look at Quinn when he spoke. Then back to Violet as if this was the day's entertainment and they were prepared to settle in and enjoy it.

Terrific.

"No," Violet replied. "It's an albatross. Named Ferdinand." She let out a sigh that was more nerves than exasperation, shifting Stanley in her arms. To keep him from being attacked by her heartbeat. And because he was soft and warm and didn't hate her. "Obviously he's a rabbit."

"Named Ferdinand?"

Violet scowled at him. "Of course he's not named Ferdinand. Ferdinand is what you call a bull. His name is Stanley."

"Stanley," Quinn repeated. "My bad."

She saw that hint of a curve in the corner of his mouth, though. Violet stared, blinking to make sure she wasn't seeing things. But it was still there.

And for the first time since she'd left San Francisco— having agreed to remain a consultant with the Institute, packed everything she owned into a shipping container, said her surprisingly emotional good-byes to Kaye and Irving and her other friends and colleagues, and struck out like a pioneer woman to *face the frontier*—something in her settled.

As if this might all end up okay.

But at the moment, everyone was staring at her. With varying degrees of interest, speculation, and wariness. Violet looked around, a bit wildly, and then thrust Stanley toward the nearest person. Noah looked faintly traumatized to find himself holding an oversize lop-eared rabbit, but she assumed his military training would kick in and prevent him from dropping Stanley on the floor. Or she hoped it would.

Then she stood up straighter, practically at attention, and cleared her throat.

"I understand you all have your vote today," she said to the whole group. "I originally came here to make a proposal. I'd like to do that now, if I could."

She meant to address the whole group, she really did. But it was Quinn's reaction she was waiting for. And the crazy thing was that he was across the room, with maybe all twenty people who lived around here between them, but every time their eyes caught it was like they were alone.

"It's not up to me," he drawled after a moment. Then he nodded at the crowd. "Well? Now's the time to share those opinions you've been bludgeoning me with all month."

"I'll show you a bludgeon," Old Harry shouted.

Then Violet, who had expected an orderly exchange of ideas because that was the way they did things at the Institute, stood blinking in astonishment as the room . . . erupted.

There were instant factions. Some grouped by family, some apparently linked by nothing more than noise. Silver Saskin shouted something about a stolen birthright. One of the Barrows seemed to feel unduly passionate about the fishing industry in the Bering Sea, which, as far as Violet could tell, had nothing to do with the matter at hand. If only because the Bering Sea was hundreds of miles west.

On and on they went, until she found herself looking

over their heads to locate Quinn. He was watching the commotion, his gaze bright with amusement.

So bright that she could feel it like a glow inside.

Wow, she mouthed. Ostensibly about the crowd. The
glow she would keep to herself.

Quinn's nod seemed to say that this was how it always
was. Only to be expected. *Welcome to Lost Lake*, his expression said.

And maybe Violet was fooling herself, the way it seemed
she particularly liked to do where he was concerned, but she
could have sworn that Quinn seemed less . . . forbidding
than when she'd left.

No more wishful thinking, she told herself sternly. That
he was used to her betrayal of him by now didn't mean he
was okay with it.

"Let's vote, then," Quinn said when the chaos died down
a decibel or two, managing to make his voice big enough to
fill the Mine without having to shout. "Those against Violet
addressing the community directly, raise your hands."

Two people raised their hands. Old Harry, looking mu-
tinous. And a doddery older woman sitting next to him,
who didn't look as if she knew quite where she was. Violet
figured that Harry Barrow had the look of a man who was
against everything, on principle. She knew the type.

"And those for letting the professor speak?" Quinn
asked.

This time, almost every hand in the Mine went up, along
with a small roar. It took Violet a moment to realize it
wasn't a negative sort of roar, necessarily. The Fortune
table was not *quite* cheering, but they did all look intrigued.

"I'm reserving judgment," Piper shouted to Violet over
the din.

"Fair enough." She figured they probably all were.

As the noise wound down again, Quinn sighed, looking

toward a group of gray-haired ladies sitting clustered together near the front. "Yes, Mary Louise?"

One of the ladies stood. "I abstain," she declared proudly.

"Try having an opinion for once, Mary Louise," said another old woman from beside her. "I think you'll find they're free."

"You know what else is free, Mary Joseph Fox?" shot back Mary Louise. "Keeping your mouth shut."

From the laughter, and what appeared to be reasonably good-natured ribbing, Violet understood that the two wrinkled old women had been fighting, possibly exactly the same way, for nigh on forever.

"You have the floor," Quinn told Violet, inclining his head very slightly in her direction. "Propose away."

And now that the moment had finally arrived, Violet was amazed to find herself . . . ever so slightly nervous.

Maybe more than slightly.

She'd never been put off by public speaking. Not when she greatly enjoyed sharing her opinion, and she did. She'd always liked a presentation and, theoretically, this should be no different.

But everything having to do with Lost Lake, Old Gold, the Mine, and even Hopeless was different. Because everything here was different—to her.

This place, these people, weren't *theoretical* to Violet. She knew their names. She knew their stories. She'd made friends here that she hoped she hadn't lost. She'd bought their crafts, drunk their coffee, eaten their food. She'd given her heart away—and not only to Quinn.

Focus, Violet.

And finally, she began. "Lost Lake popped up on my radar following a geological survey on mineral resources five years ago that I was following because of the keen interest most environmentalists have in places like Alaska, where old ways and new ideas clash in real time. You will know the one, I'm sure."

"There's oil in them thar hills," one of the Saskins cried.

"But never our hills," Levi Fortune replied.

"I can't imagine if we had oil," one of the ancient Barrows said. "It's bad enough fending off the gold prospectors every time gold prices go up."

There was a spate of cross talk that covered the history of mining in this region, the cost of both gold and oil, more commentary on the fishing industry because maybe it was a tic, and then a lot of expectant faces turned Violet's way again. Including Stanley's on Noah's lap, where he was looking perfectly at home. Noah looked less comfortable.

But she couldn't deal with that just now.

"I don't need to tell you all about the mining industry in Alaska, the debate over wildlife refuges, or the competing schools of thought about what to do with the kind of mineral rights you're all sitting on." Violet smiled as a current of muttering moved through the crowd. "For one thing, you're all certainly better versed in such topics than I am. The institute where I work has spent a lot of its time trying to work out initiatives within corporations to address the impact of destructive large-scale mining practices. That's always been a critical part of our mission."

She waited for another current of commentary to rise and fall. "While we do that, we—along with many of our colleagues and competitors—also spend time identifying smaller concerns. Places where the presence of historic gold might mean that more could be found with today's technology. We know that if we're looking, so are the large corporations. We like places like this because groups like mine want to use them as opportunities to communicate our vision of what the pristine wilderness ought to be. We consider these communities jewels in our crown."

Old Harry Fox offered his caustic thoughts about Outsiders and what they could do with their visions. And their jewels. Violet adjusted her glasses, smiled wider, and opted to ignore him.

"There are a number of places in Alaska that meet our criteria," she continued. "Most of them are represented by people who are only too happy to sit down and weigh offers and proposals. Not just from us, but from the big companies, too. But there's always been one standout, and that's Quinn."

Violet was unduly proud of herself that she didn't choke up while saying his name. But she also didn't dare look over at him, because bravado wasn't the same thing as bravery. And because she wasn't sure what she'd do if he was looking at her the way he had that last night in the cabin.

She repressed a shudder and kept going. "Quinn is famous in these particular circles for refusing to sit down at the table, no matter who does the asking." That got a cheer. "Because of this, the land he represents has come to be seen as a kind of gold trophy, no pun intended." That got another, longer cheer, mixed in with a wolf whistle from Bowie. Violet swallowed hard and got into the parts they might not like as much. "When your job is to convince people that they should work against their own interest to preserve the earth for future generations—to plant a tree they'll never sit under, if you will—managing to talk around someone as infamously hardheaded as Quinn Fortune would make you a superstar."

And she couldn't resist looking his way, while the community laughed and called back and forth to each other, mostly with some posturing about who, exactly, had the hardest head in these parts. But she didn't find the fury and condemnation she'd expected on Quinn's face. If anything, he looked . . . considering.

It made her stomach flip over, so she faced the group again and carried on. "Having suffered a setback professionally, I decided that instead of trying to claw my way back into the good graces of the people I worked for, I'd come up and go for the gold instead. Literally and figuratively."

"Am I the only one uncomfortable with the notion that Quinn is a prize?" Bowie asked, to no one in particular.

"You are not," Piper replied.

"Definitely not," Jasper Saskin threw in from his table.

Quinn shrugged, his T-shirt making the gesture into a small pageant. "I'm fine with it."

"And I'll tell you that my initial proposal still makes sense," Violet continued, before she lost her train of thought somewhere on Quinn's muscly arms. Though she did have to cough. Delicately. "Create an easement. Preserve the land here. Apply to list the mine itself as a piece of national history. Pledge not to rip it apart in the name of a gold mine that will contaminate this area in too many ways to count. But I know that's not taking into account a whole lot of things that are easy to hand-wave away from down in California, or so I'm told." She was gratified when she heard Lois laugh. "It is my firm belief that we can never overprotect our natural resources. That we, and I mean that as a person who lives on this planet, should unite in keeping our beautiful spaces beautiful."

"I expect a representative from a mining company would have a different take on things," Quinn countered.

"I can tell you what their take is," Violet said, nodding. "It would be to minimize the inevitable environmental impact and talk infrastructure. Jobs. Prosperity. And before I came here, I would have rolled my eyes and thought it was just talk. Just a little salesman patter." She took a breath. "I'm grateful that I got the chance to come and see what's

actually here. It made me think about a lot of things differently."

Against her will, her gaze was drawn back to Quinn
again, who seemed to be regarding her steadily from over
his crossed arms.

"I can see the allure of bringing in a big company and
everything that goes along with it." Was she speaking to the
whole gathering? Or to him alone? "It's easy to theorize
from afar about the effect of infrastructure on the beauty of
a place. Without understanding the challenges of living in
all of this unspoiled splendor, from outhouses to how
shockingly expensive basic necessities are. A thousand pictures of the beautiful starkness could never really show
what it's like. I know that now."

"Is that your proposal?" Quinn asked quietly.

Violet smiled. At him, but also at her audience at all
the tables. "All of you welcomed me here. You didn't have
to do that, but you did. And because of you all, I'm not the
same person I was when I showed up in Hopeless with absolutely no idea what I was walking into. Or snowmobiling
into."

There was some laughter. "We call it a snow machine in
Alaska," Lois said. "Your Outsider is showing."

Violet accepted that with a nod. "I'm sure you must receive a thousand proposals from people on either side of the
argument, but none of them have spent any time here. I
doubt any of them will."

And then, because she couldn't help herself, Violet
found her gaze tracking back over the crowd to Quinn.

"I don't have a stake in this any longer," she told him.
And everyone. But mostly him. "I've quit my job and broken the lease on my apartment. Because I've decided to rent
a dry cabin, right here on the lakeside."

She could hear the crowd murmuring in reaction, but

she couldn't drag her eyes away from Quinn. Her heart seemed to fill up not just her chest, it was taking over her body until every breath made her ache.

And it ached more when she jerked her gaze from his. She noticed Piper giving her a little thumbs-up. Beside her, Lois and Levi were grinning at each other. Across the table, Bowie tapped his finger to his forehead and mouthed *bears*. Then smiled.

"So I'm going to tell you this as a new resident, not a complete Outsider," Violet said to the crowd, her heart in her throat as she looked at them, then past them. To the gleaming lights strung from the ceiling, the rustic wood and artfully arranged stalls, almost inviting and never cluttered. The coats and boots carefully placed inside the door. The hand-lettered wooden signs leading to the bunkhouse, the antlers hung with pride and decorated with new accessories every time she saw them. And the people. Most of all these people. "It takes a particular kind of person to thrive here, and you do. I don't know whether it's Alaska, or this old mine, or the peculiar alchemy of the families who've built all this. But it's not just beautiful, it's special. I don't think there could ever be another place quite like it. This place, you people, are magic."

And she knew that she was standing there, in public. She knew that all those eyes were on her.

But once again, all she could see was Quinn.

"Save the magic," she urged him. *Them*, she corrected herself, though she didn't look away from him. "Save it for love, not money."

Violet felt like she'd run up the side of a mountain. Or had found herself leaping out of a plane like the one she'd chartered from Anchorage to bring her straight on to the lake, piloted by a lunatic who had scared her silly—and still had in no way been as terrifying as Bowie.

She nodded to herself, because she'd finally said what she wanted to say. No beer, as promised—but a lot more magic and meaning. On her part, anyway.

The swell of voices rose up around her again, but still, all she could see was Quinn. All she could hear was Quinn.

All she wanted was Quinn.

But Violet had decided to move to Alaska, not to him. She had to assume that Quinn would want nothing to do with her, ever again. And if that was the case, she needed to know that she was prepared to live in a place where she would see him, always, and be okay with that. Seeing him would be only one of the hardships she was taking on out here in the middle of the Last Frontier.

And if the answer was no, she wasn't okay with it at all.

But she still wanted to live here.

That was why she'd come back, so she tore her gaze away from Quinn as some of the garrulous older women converged upon him. Noah was still holding Stanley, looking frozen but fine.

"Are you okay with him for another minute?" she asked.

Noah blinked. "I don't know how to answer that."

Violet smiled as apologetically as she could and left him to it. She marched over to the Saskin set of tables and stood in front of the older woman until Mia deigned to look her way.

"Pretty little speech," Mia said.

"I can't tell if that was a compliment or not," Violet replied. "But thank you."

"Can't say I know myself." Mia huffed out a laugh. "But to my way of thinking, infrastructure is everywhere. You can order it with your cappuccinos and your coffeehouses down where all the people are. And I've never been much for foam or foolishness, no matter if everyone else is doing it."

Violet was surprised to find that she was touched. She hadn't let herself think about who would or wouldn't vote her way. But she liked the fact that it seemed she had Mia's vote all the same.

"I need to stock up on supplies," she said, returning to the task at hand. "The rental agency in Fairbanks said the door to the cabin is unlocked, but I'll need to bring my own firewood and—"

But Mia was smiling. "I don't think you'll need firewood."

Violet had no idea what she was talking about, since it was the dead of winter, until the older woman's gaze shifted to a spot behind her.

She wheeled around and found Quinn standing behind her.

"You're not renting here," he said.

Though it took her a moment to hear him over the clatter of her heart.

"I've thought a lot about it," Violet said, as if she was giving another speech. "And this is where I want to be. I know you said once that Alaska won't necessarily love me back and I'm prepared for that. And I understand that you're the unofficial mayor, or whatever you like to call yourself, but you don't get to decide if I rent here or not."

Or anyway, she didn't think he did.

"Well, Violet, I sure am glad you thought about it," Quinn drawled. "You know how I feel about those thoughts of yours."

He probably meant it as an insult, she knew, but she just wanted to bask in him, standing there before her. Close to her. Talking to her. It hadn't been entirely clear that any of those things would ever happen again.

"It's a big lake," she said, though it came out a whisper. "You won't even know I'm here."

"Oh, darlin'." And Quinn's dark eyes seemed particularly midnight blue then. "You're wrong about that."

270   M. M. CRANE

Then he bent, put his shoulder to her midsection, and lifted her into the air. And wasted no time carrying her across the floor of the Mine.

To the sound of the loudest cheers yet.

"I've got your bunny!" Piper shouted above all that hollering.

Quinn put her down by the door. And Violet was so startled—and a bit overcome at getting to feel him and smell him and feel his *hand* on her as he'd walked like she weighed as much as a box of air—that she did nothing but stare while he pulled on his cold-weather gear. Or while he set about putting her feet into her boots, lacing them up, and then tugging her parka into place, too.

"Better zip up," he told her sternly. "I know it's a summery eleven degrees out there today, but you'll want protection on the lake."

"Quinn," she began again, trying to gather her scattered thoughts when all she could think about was how *wide* his shoulder was as he'd carried her and how she'd missed the opportunity to investigate his astonishingly beautiful back from that inverted angle and— She took a breath. "You can take me back down to Hopeless again, but I'm just going to come back. I'm sorry, but I like it here."

"Okay," he said in an amiable way she did not trust at all.

He stuck her hat on her head himself. And while she was shoving it off her glasses so she could see, he picked her up again.

This time he carried her outside and proceeded to strap her onto the snowmobile. Snow *machine*, she corrected herself.

"This is beginning to seem a little bit like a kidnapping," she pointed out. Helpfully.

He looked over his shoulder at her as he swung into place on his snowmobile.

"Oh, it is," he agreed.

She tried feeling appropriately outraged and appalled as he drove them down the hill and out onto the ice.

But it was an act, and Violet had given up lying, even by omission.

What she really felt was exhilaration.

And for the first time since Quinn had dropped her off outside the general store in Hopeless without looking back . . . hope.

Eighteen

✤

Quinn didn't take her to his cabin.

Because this called for extreme measures and where Violet was concerned, that could only mean the shack. It was the place where he'd first realized what a problem she was going to be. He figured it was the place to solve it.

This time, he didn't mess around with the forced hike up the hill. He drove the snowmobile straight up into the clearing where the shack sat, then pulled up in front.

"You really can't go around kidnapping people," Violet said as she clambered off, sounding remarkably upbeat. "It's rude. And also illegal. This isn't the Wild West."

"As the duly selected, never-elected representative of this unincorporated community, I'd be happy to listen to your concerns, ma'am." Quinn threw open the shack's front door and beckoned her inside. "After you."

Violet sailed in with her head held high. But once she'd cleared the doorway, she didn't stand there the way she had the first time. This time around, his bright pink Outsider-turned-local knew what to do. Quinn watched with pride as she marched over to the stove to get the fire going, then picked up the pot on the stove to march right past him to get some snow that she could set to melting.

When she'd done all that she came back over to the door, shrugged out of her coat and tossed it near his, then turned to face him with her hands on her hips.

And for a minute it seemed like both of them got a little caught up in just . . . looking at each other.

"Violet," he began.

"I meant what I said back at the Mine," she hurried to say, with a frown reappearing between her brows. "I think Lost Lake is magical. And maybe it's weird for you that I want to move here, but I'm hoping we can be adults about it. Because that cabin is for rent and there's no Quinn clause in the fine print."

"Settle down, professor."

They were facing off across the floor of the shack. She was within reach. He'd already tossed her over his shoulder. And yet Quinn still had the feeling that if he took his eyes off her she would disappear, possibly in a puff of pink smoke.

"I understand that you're furious with me," she said, almost primly. And she stood a little straighter, a lot like she was trying to conceal how fragile she was. A notion that made everything in him seize up tight, a lot like it had done when she'd walked through the door of the Mine. "I don't blame you. You can say that, you know. That you're furious. You don't have to be patronizing."

Next the familiar pink flush he liked to think of as his washed over her face.

And it undid him.

The simple truth was that life without her was a torment. Happy as Quinn was that he'd put his past to rest at last, he knew full well that hadn't been the case when Carrie had left him. If he'd been even remotely tormented by her loss, he would have gone after her. The way he'd been planning to go after Violet.

The way he would have, if she hadn't showed up here today.

"Why?" he asked, folding his arms.

She scowled at him, which was an improvement on *fragile*, especially when she jabbed her glasses back up her nose. "Why shouldn't you be patronizing? I can think of a thousand reasons, but let's start with the fact that men are always telling women to relax while never relaxing themselves. I feel like there's a word to describe that phenomenon. It rhymes with . . . hate-riarchy."

" 'Hate-riarchy' is not a word. What with all your fancy degrees, I'd think you'd know that."

Violet sniffed, but her cheeks got pinker. "Language evolves with usage, *Quinn*."

"And anyway, that's not the why I'm after." He shook his head at the mulish set to her mouth. "Why are you here? Why did you come back?"

She blinked a few times, but she didn't look away. Not Violet. She held his gaze, her own darkening. "I wanted to speak to everyone. I wanted to make my case."

"Your case for your proposal? Or do you mean your case for moving here? Because the way I figure it, if we'd voted to start mining for gold today, you might have wanted to rethink your dramatic relocation."

"Did the vote actually happen? How did I miss it?"

"You didn't miss it. This is Lost Lake, Violet. Amie Saskin said she wanted to carry the vote to the next quarter so we could see if you looked like you might make it through the winter before we took to heart any talk of magic. My mother seconded it. And a majority agreed right then and there."

"How did that happen without me even noticing?"

"You were talking to Noah. Then Mia." Not that he'd been paying close attention or anything. "I hope you're ready for every single person you saw in the Mine today to tell you that you're going to have to personally convince them before the next meeting."

Violet let out a laugh and then beamed at him. "I'm irresistible, actually. A woman of action who is also a little bit of a floozy, and I fully own these things. I'm not afraid of being disliked. In fact, I thrive under those conditions. As it turns out, Quinn, I'm good at winning people over."

It was typical Violet. Brash and puffed up with bravado, and he wanted nothing more than to draw her close—and lose himself in all of her light, her confidence, and that surefire optimism that made him want to laugh out loud.

But he needed to clarify a few things.

"There are a lot of beautiful spaces in Alaska," he pointed out. "The state is full of them. You didn't have to pick this one."

"I'm renting a cabin," she retorted grandly. "Not marrying myself to the land for all time, like some people I could mention. I said I would finish out the winter and that's what I intend to do."

"So, to clarify, this has nothing to do with me. You made a rash promise and you intend to keep it. In your very own dry cabin."

"You don't have to concern yourself, Quinn," she said loftily. "I have a hardy pioneer spirit, thank you very much, and will be perfectly happy boiling my own drinking water and marching myself to and from my outhouse, all without any input from the Fortune family peanut gallery. Though I think I will upgrade to a custom-made Styrofoam seat. Because there's no reason I can't be Alaska-fancy."

"Will it be pink?"

Her eyes narrowed. "It will be now."

"Trouble is, I don't know when you're going to order it," he said, conversationally enough. "Because I have no intention of letting you out of the shack."

And he knew that she was in no way alarmed by that declaration when all she did was scoff at him.

"Are you *jailing* me?" she demanded. "That seems extreme, even for you. I thought you might demand some apologies, but I have to say, kidnapping and *imprisonment* didn't occur to me."

"Violet."

But she was gazing at him, looking as determined as she did emotional, and no longer brimming with mischief and grand gestures. "I'm sorry, Quinn. You should know that. I'm sorry I didn't tell you everything I should have about why I was here. I'm sorry that my being here brought Stuart down upon the town of Hopeless. You both deserve better. But most of all, I'm sorry that I hurt you. I could have lived my whole life without seeing that look on your face." Her gaze searched his, and all he saw was sincerity. "I'm sorry."

Quinn wondered when he would accept that when it came to this woman, any expectations were pointless. She was simply Violet. And whatever it was he thought she might do, she lit up and did the opposite.

"Violet," he said again, because even her name was beautiful. It sounded like an incantation. Like the spell she'd cast on him the moment she'd appeared.

"I didn't intend to come back here without apologizing to you," she told him, her eyes wide, as if he'd accused her of something. "To be honest, I thought it was going to take a while before you spoke to me again." She looked around the shack as if she'd never seen it before. "Though I suppose marooning me in a shack for the rest of the winter is a pretty eloquent—"

"Violet. Shut up."

Her eyes flew to his, wide again, but outraged this time. "Kidnapping is one thing, Quinn, but there's no need to be *rude*."

"I'm in love with you, for God's sake," he thundered at her.

She stopped whatever she'd been about to say, frozen in mid-outrage. And as he watched, her gold-mine eyes filled up, then sparkled. "You are?"

"I am," he said, like he was making his vows. "And I'm real glad you fell in love with Alaska, Violet. And even happier that you came back. I like that you're a woman of action. But I really am hoping that beneath all those speeches, you came back for me."

Her lips parted, though for once, no sound came out. The flush on her cheeks deepened, and then she was staring at him with the exact same look he'd seen when she'd first glimpsed the aurora.

Sheer wonder.

He crossed the length of the shack in a step. And then carefully, like his life depended on it, he gathered her in his arms.

"Because I bought a ticket down to San Francisco," he told her. "And I don't like cities, but I was prepared to do my time in one until I could convince you to give me another chance."

And this time, while her eyes got wetter, he could feel her melt against him. "You were?"

"I love you," Quinn said, and this part was easy. "I love everything about you. You're brave. You're bright. You showed up with a rabbit and somehow I know he's not for dinner, because that's not who you are."

"Certainly not." But she was smiling. Then smiled wider when he took the opportunity to slide her glasses back into place. "Stanley is family, not stew."

"When you left you took all the light with you," he said gruffly. "And I can't live like that, darlin'. I want the pink. I want your mind. I want lazy, quiet days, when the only music is the way you talk to yourself. Or the sound of you singing in the shower."

"I have a Mariah Carey problem," she whispered, her head tipped back as she looked up at him. "Most of the problem is that I'm not Mariah Carey."

"I figure you can think right here, with me, as well as you can think anywhere else."

"Maybe even better," she agreed. "But—"

Quinn wasn't finished. "I'm done with the past. I'm done climbing up on crosses that no one else even knows are there. I want a future, Violet. I want all the messy stuff. I want a wedding but I want the marriage even more. I want kids and grandkids. I want everything. As long as it's with you."

There were tears on her cheeks then, but she didn't pull away. "A person could argue that I'm a bad bet," she said quietly. "Sins of the parents, and all that. All those things you want are things I want, too, but at least you've seen people doing them."

"I can't hate them, because they made you," Quinn told her. A corner of his mouth crooked up. "And we can use them as a guide. What not to do."

"I've been doing that for years and mostly it's been an excellent guiding light. Except . . ." And to his delight, she turned an even brighter shade of red. "I had no idea how lonely I was. Until you."

Neither did he. "And yet you came all the way up to the loneliest place on earth to lock yourself away in a rental cabin for the rest of the winter?"

It wasn't really a question. He smoothed her hair back from her face.

And waited.

Sure enough, when her smile broke, it was like sunrise. It lit them both up. It warmed up the cabin.

And changed the world again.

"If all I wanted was the Alaskan dream, I could've gotten that in Juneau," Violet said, brighter with every word. "Between you and me, it's possible that I moved to the Last Frontier for a boy."

"That sounds foolish." But Quinn was grinning. "And I'm no boy."

"You certainly are not." She wrapped her arms around him and gazed up at him. There was all that Violet confidence, like she was the one claiming him. Like she was the one who'd known all along where they were headed. "I love you, Quinn. On or off your cross."

"I love you, too," he replied. "The first time I laid eyes on you, I knew. Nothing was ever going to be the same."

"That sounds like a promise," she whispered. "And you still owe me that beer."

"You can have all the beer you want, darlin'," he told her as he swung her up in his arms.

And then he honored the promises they'd made in the best way he knew how, right on the floor of the shack where they'd begun.

Much later that afternoon, they made their way back to his cabin, where he made her laugh while he carried her over the threshold in all their outerwear that made them puffed-up versions of themselves. And then, once they'd shed all their layers, spun her around and around in his arms again.

A lot like he was chasing out the last of his ghosts.

"Does this mean that I get to be the Lady of Lost Lake?" she asked, much later, when she was wearing one of his henleys and sitting astride him on the couch.

"I guess." He kissed her. A perfect kiss—because it built on all the kisses that had come before. And it was a herald of all that would come after. Too many kisses to count, stretched out into forever. All theirs. "Why?"

Violet reared back and looked down at him, shaking her head in mock despair—though she couldn't seem to keep her gold-mine eyes from sparkling. Like every miner's dream come true.

Like his future.

Like forever.

"Because I am going to be *amazing* at that," Violet told him, as if confiding a great secret. She beamed, big and wide, letting all the light in. Letting it shine between them the way Quinn knew it always would, bright and beautiful, and entirely theirs. "Just watch."

Don't miss the second
Fortunes of Lost Lake romance,
Reckless Fortune, *coming from M. M. Crane in*
September 2022!

Bowie Fortune has always liked a risky proposition. As a bush pilot out in the Last Frontier, flying in and out of places that give most pilots nightmares is what he lives for. That and his off-the-grid home out by Lost Lake, where his family has been living up close with the elements for generations. When his sister dares him to put in for the local version of a mail-order bride contest, he's not interested—but Bowie doesn't back down from a challenge. Even when the challenge turns out to be a woman who makes him want every last thing he knows he shouldn't.

Entering a summer-long publicity stunt of a contest in far-off Alaska might seem extreme, but Autumn McCall has always had an indomitable spirit. She took care of her sisters and father after her mother died, and this is more of the same. Since she intends to win. Immersing herself in the pioneer lifestyle is one thing, but what she isn't expecting is brooding, sharp-eyed Bowie with his wicked smile. As the sparks fly between them, will they burn each other alive—or learn how to simmer their way to a much bigger prize . . . together?

Ready to find
your next great read?

Let us help.

Visit prh.com/nextread

Penguin
Random
House